The spar
fire in her...

"Find anything?"

Trista froze at the sound of Morgan's voice. "I warned you not to expect too much."

"Believe me, where you're concerned, I've learned never to expect too much."

Trista struggled to keep her emotions in check. She couldn't let herself care. She looked down at the files she'd been going through. "I'm sorry."

Morgan leaned over the desk, his face a mere six inches away. She could see the dark stubble on his chin, the blue fire of his eyes. She turned away, scorched by the contact. But his next words made her heart jump.

"I've got bad news for you, lady. You're going to have to continue dealing with me. Until I solve this case, or we both go crazy with the effort."

Dear Harlequin Intrigue Reader,

Harlequin Intrigue has just celebrated its fifteenth anniversary and we're proud to continue to bring to you thrilling romantic suspense that leaves you breathless!—plus your favorite ongoing miniseries—into the new millennium.

To start the New Year off right, Kelsey Roberts launches into the second installment of her new series, THE LANDRY BROTHERS, with *Landry's Law* (#545). Over the next year you can expect more exciting Landry stories. Don't miss any!

We're also continuing our amnesia promotion A MEMORY AWAY... This month a woman wakes up with no memory and morning sickness, but she can't remember who's the father in *The Baby Secret* (#546) by Joyce Sullivan. And if you love a good twins story you must not miss *Twice Tempted* (#547) by Harper Allen. Finally, Harlequin Intrigue newcomer C.J. Carmichael explores the life of a devoted man of the law and the woman for whom he'll break all the rules in *Same Place, Same Time* (#548).

It's romance. It's suspense. It's Harlequin Intrigue.

Enjoy, and Happy New Year!

Sincerely,

Denise O'Sullivan
Associate Senior Editor
Harlequin Intrigue

P.S. Starting next month, Harlequin Intrigue has a new look! Watch for us at your favorite retail outlet.

Same Place, Same Time
C.J. Carmichael

HARLEQUIN®

TORONTO • NEW YORK • LONDON
AMSTERDAM • PARIS • SYDNEY • HAMBURG
STOCKHOLM • ATHENS • TOKYO • MILAN • MADRID
PRAGUE • WARSAW • BUDAPEST • AUCKLAND

For my husband, Michael, with thanks and love.

ISBN 0-373-22548-2

SAME PLACE, SAME TIME

This edition: Copyright © 1999 by Carla Daum

First published in 1999 as a serialization entitled
"The Detective's Woman" in the *Toronto Star*.

This edition published by arrangement with Harlequin Books S.A.

® and TM are trademarks of the publisher. Trademarks indicated with ® are registered in the United States Patent and Trademark Office, the Canadian Trade Marks Office and in other countries.

Visit us at www.romance.net

Printed in U.S.A.

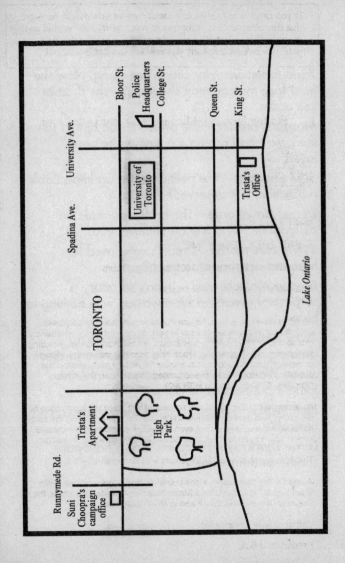

TORONTO

Lake Ontario

Runnymede Rd.

Suni
Choopra's
campaign
office

Trista's
Apartment

High Park

Spadina Ave.

University Ave.

University of
Toronto

Bloor St.

Police
Headquarters

College St.

Queen St.

King St.

Trista's
Office

CAST OF CHARACTERS

Trista Emerson —Her clients are dying. Now she must face the one man she thought she'd never see again.

Morgan Forester —The pressure's on him to solve the case—and protect the woman he once loved....

Suni Choopra —The politician has an impeccable reputation. Is it deserved?

Daniel Hawthorne —The professor made an assignation—and met an untimely end....

Sylvia Hawthorne —Daniel's wife loved her husband—perhaps too much?

Brenda Malachowski —Trista's secretary is surprisingly secretive for a woman with nothing to hide.

Jerry Walker —The king of hardware was cheating on his wife. But did he deserve to die?

Jason Walker —Is he as reluctant to inherit his father's business as he claims?

Nan Walker —Does this timid widow have a core of steel?

Lorne Thackray —He covets Jerry's hardware chain—and his wife?

Prologue

"Excuse me," she called to the desk clerk. He'd watched her walk in the motel entrance, but hadn't stirred from his chair by the television screen. "My husband's locked us out of our room. Number 14."

The clerk had colorless hair and skin, and a long lean body that looked as though it might snap in half if he moved too quickly. There seemed to be no danger, however, of that happening. He unfolded himself and stepped slowly to the counter, his pigment-free eyes fixed on the buttons of her trench coat.

"Your *husband,* hey?"

He was leering, the pervert. Would he think it was so funny if he knew what she had in her pocket? Wouldn't it be fun to show him... But she had to play this cool.

"That's right. My husband. John Doe." She forced herself to smile, then held out a gloved hand. Was it her imagination or did he pause before dropping the large brass key into the cup of her leather-clad palm?

Perhaps he thought it strange that she was wearing gloves in May. But the air was cool today, reminiscent of the cold winter Toronto had endured this year. She felt his gaze between her shoulder blades as she turned to leave, and it was a relief when the door finally closed behind her.

There. That had gone well enough. Now she felt a calm sense of inevitability. The pangs of nervousness and anxiety she'd suffered last night were gone. She dug her right hand into the pocket of her coat and gripped her gun reassuringly. Mentally, she reviewed the remaining steps of her plan. The worst was almost over.

Room 14 was located conveniently at the end of the motel, down a long concrete walkway and as far from the office as possible. Traffic on the Gardiner Expressway was loud and constant. The perfect backdrop for murder.

At the door, she paused. There was no one else around. No sounds other than engines and the incessant rumbling of wheels over concrete and asphalt.

The key slid easily into the doorknob. As she twisted, a tantalizing cooking odor seeped out the crack around the door. What in the world...?

She held her ear to the small space between door and frame and thought she heard singing. A man's voice, attempting opera. Clearly the song was coming from another room.

With her gloved hand she pushed on the knob and slipped into the room, closing the door behind her. She walked around the king-size bed, where a red rose lay on one of the white pillows. Such a romantic touch.

The sleeping quarters were separated from a kitchenette by a ceiling-hung set of cupboards and a long, waist-high counter. Between the two, she could see the midsection of a man. His clear, tenor voice worked its way to the climax of "The Music of the Night" from *The Phantom of the Opera*.

She stepped forward cautiously. Her gun was ready and so was she.

A creaking hollow in the linoleum gave her away as she stepped off the carpet into the kitchenette. The man turned, obviously expecting someone, but his smile of welcome slipped down from the corners of his mouth as he stared at the barrel of the gun pointed at his chest. He stiffened and stepped backward, pressing against the metal edge of the stove where the contents of a large iron pot boiled. It was tomato sauce, she saw now.

"What are you doing with that gun? What do you want?"

Dispassionately, she watched the bobbing of his Adam's apple as he swallowed once, then again.

Calmly she uttered five carefully chosen words.

His eyes widened. Good. It was important that he understand why this was happening. She pulled the trigger.

He jerked backward with the impact of the bullet, knocking the pot of tomato sauce over on its side. Then his body slowly slid down and forward, until he collapsed on the floor. Sauce from the overturned pot poured unchecked off the stove, landing precisely on the small balding area at the back of his head. There was no reaction from him as the scalding hot sauce hit his bare skin.

She allowed herself a slight smile. It had gone according to plan.

Jerry Walker was dead.

Chapter One

"Sometimes I feel like taking that gun out of his night table and shooting the television! Right in the middle of *Star Trek!*"

Chartered psychologist Trista Emerson pressed the stop button on the tape recorder, cutting off Nan Walker's explosion of rage toward her husband, Jerry. It marked the first time Nan had been anything but meek and agreeable, and Trista had taken it as a very good step forward. But now Jerry and Nan had missed their four o'clock appointment and Trista didn't know what to think.

The Walkers were relatively new clients, part of a recent trend that she'd been trying to avoid.

Marriage counseling.

Trista preferred individual therapy, but often it was impossible to separate the two. A client might come to her initially because of personal problems. If that client was married, however, often the problems spilled out into the relationship.

When that happened, she was honest about her own history.

"I have training and counseling experience in this area. But you should know that my own marriage ended in divorce."

For some reason that knowledge turned very few of them away.

"Your own trauma has made you wiser, more sympathetic," a trusted colleague had told her—a man she'd gone to for therapy following the breakup of her marriage.

Certainly the results she'd seen in her practice gave testimony to his opinion.

But sometimes, she wondered. Was she the best person to advise these people? Like Nan and Jerry Walker. She'd been seeing them for a couple of weeks now, and she was determined to do her utmost to help them in the one-month trial period they'd all agreed upon. But it wasn't a good sign that they'd missed this session.

Trista put the Walkers' file in her out basket for her secretary, Brenda, to file later. She might as well go home—theirs had been her last appointment of the day. But she didn't want to leave her office. She never did.

For three years now, since her separation and divorce, she'd been alone, and she still couldn't get used to facing an empty apartment at the end of each day. Not that it had been any better than the last year of her marriage. Neither counseling nor time seemed to lessen the pain of her losses, the memories hanging like dark storm clouds on the horizon of her mind. The past. Her present. The eternity of a future that stretched unendingly before her.

When she concentrated on the problems of others, her malaise lifted. Her work, in this way, had become her salvation.

After work—that was the problem.

Expelling a breath, Trista stood up from behind her desk and walked over to the window. Her office building was located just south of King Street, and her suite on the south side of the top floor had a nice view of Lake

Ontario. Usually the sky was hazy, and the lake broody and gray.

But today the spring sun shone, and the water sparkled, blue and inviting. A deceptive appearance, for in fact Lake Ontario was so polluted that swimming was considered dangerous.

"GOOD GOD." Detective Morgan Forester considered himself a hardened cop, but he wasn't prepared for the sight that met his eyes as he stepped inside the motel room at five-thirty Tuesday afternoon.

The deceased, a large man in his late forties, sat on the kitchen floor by the front of the stove. Thick lumps of meat and tomato sauce covered his head, and had dripped down over his shirt, merging with the dark red stain marking the bullet wound in his chest. The sauce and the clotting blood had congealed into a thick red pool around the body.

Adding to the scene's repugnance was the smell. Although the body had only been there for about twenty-four hours, the scent of death in the room was unmistakable. That, combined with the cloying odor of the day-old tomato sauce, was lethal. Morgan shook his head, feeling damn weary of his job.

"Any fingerprints?" He turned away from the body and walked over to the table where Kendal, one of the I-dent officers, was finishing up his work.

"Some. But they're probably the maid's and the deceased's. I wouldn't get my hopes up."

Morgan raised his eyebrows. "I never get my hopes up. I suppose you guys have already talked to the desk clerk who was on duty?"

"We have. A Mr. Kyle Litherman. He says that at about twenty past one yesterday afternoon, a woman wearing a tan trench coat, leather gloves, hat and sunglasses walked into his office. He didn't notice a car, figures she probably took a cab. They usually do. Who wants to risk having their vehicle identified in a motel parking lot in the middle of the day?

"Anyway, the woman told him she and her husband were locked out of room 14. He gave her the key and says he didn't notice anything unusual after that. Which isn't surprising, given how far this room is from the office and the proximity of the expressway."

He rolled his eyes, indicating the traffic noise which was clearly audible even with the exterior door closed.

"You questioned the other motel occupants?"

"Yup. No one heard a thing."

"Of course not." Even if they had, Morgan doubted they'd be willing to cooperate, on the same principle Kendal had just stated. Who'd want to admit to being in this motel on a weekday afternoon? "So, are you guys finished here?"

"Just about. We've taken the photos. We just need to bag the rest of this stuff and send off the body, but we knew you'd want to see everything first."

Morgan gave a short nod of approval. "What about time of death? Does the coroner's estimate coincide with the timing of the woman asking for the room key?"

"Yes."

"She sounds like the one we want, all right. Now tell me about the deceased."

The officer flipped open a notepad and began reading from his notes. "The guy's name was Jerry Walker, although he booked into the room as John Doe. He runs a chain of five hardware stores, with a main office on Queen Street. We talked to his wife this morning."

Morgan shook his head. Arriving late on the scene like

this—it was far from ideal. He'd received the call from Inspector Zarowin around eleven, but he'd been out of town tying up loose ends from a previous case. Fortunately the crew on the Identification Unit knew what they were doing.

"Who found the body?" He stretched his shoulders, fighting the ache from his six-hour drive. No sense thinking about how tired he was. The day that had begun at six that morning would doubtlessly be continuing far into the night as well.

"The maid. She was doing her rounds and reached this room at about 10:00 a.m."

"And how did Mrs. Walker take the news?"

"She broke down. We couldn't get much out of her, but she did say her husband wasn't in the habit of spending nights away from home, and she'd been worried sick."

Morgan looked around the motel room as he listened, rubbing his hand over the stubble on his chin, wishing he'd had time to shave that morning. As he scanned the room, he took in details without conscious effort.

The table was set with flowers and candles. A bottle of red wine sat open beside two clean wineglasses. He picked up one of the white plates from the table and fingered a chip, barely visible to the human eye.

"The dishes are from the kitchenette," the I-dent officer told him. "Walker must have brought the candles, flowers and wineglasses himself."

Morgan's eyes settled on a rose that had been placed on the untouched bed. "He went to a lot of trouble here. What did you find in his pockets?"

"Wallet, with a hundred and sixty dollars, and identification. Some matches, a couple of condoms—pretty optimistic for an older guy.'' He pointed to the items, already packed away in a plastic bag on the table.

Morgan ignored the attempt at humor. He wondered about the woman this guy had been waiting for. She must have been something special to warrant all this effort.

''Well, pack it up. I've seen enough.'' He nodded to the other officers, then turned on his heel and left the room. Back outdoors, he took a deep, reviving breath of fresh air. He hadn't eaten in over eight hours, but he no longer felt hungry. And it would be a long time before he'd be able to face a dish of spaghetti again.

TRISTA'S FINGERS paused over her computer keyboard, the phrase she'd been about to write slipping out of her mind.

She'd heard something. Hadn't she? She listened for several seconds, but all was silent. Her gaze slid to the clock on the edge of her desk and she was surprised to see that it was already past nine.

The building was probably all but deserted by now. Maybe she'd heard the security guard making his rounds.

She finished her sentence then saved the document. That was enough for one day. If she went home now she'd have just enough time to eat dinner and watch a program on television before going to bed.

Scooping up the day's tapes from her desk, she headed for the reception area out front where she dumped them into Brenda's in box to be transcribed tomorrow. She was about to return to her office for her jacket and briefcase when she heard something that sounded like a chair leg scraping against the floor. The sound had come from the direction of the file room.

Trista stared at the closed door. Was someone in there? The idea of an intruder was ludicrous—the only money in the place was a fifty-dollar petty cash fund that Brenda kept locked in her top drawer—but she was reluctant to open the door and check.

If someone was there, the last thing she wanted to do was surprise him. Trista backtracked to her office and shut the door with a loud bang, and locked it behind her.

She could have sworn she heard the sound of another door opening, then footsteps. Picking up the phone, she called building security. Joe Wilkins answered immediately.

"I think someone may have broken into my suite, Joe. I just heard some strange noises in the file room, and Brenda went home hours ago."

"Don't worry, Ms. Emerson. I'll be right up to check it out. We had a squirrel in the offices above you last week. Could be the same rascal."

"I'm not sure, Joe. It sounded like footsteps to me."

"I'll be right there. Are you in your office?"

"Yes. And the door's locked." Trista set down the receiver, and waited. A few minutes later, the sound of voices in the hall made her adrenaline surge. Joe worked alone downstairs. Who could he be talking to?

Unless it wasn't Joe coming at all, but somebody else. The same somebody she'd heard earlier in the file room? She looked around her office for something, anything, that might serve as a weapon. A pair of scissors lay conveniently on the corner of her desk. She grabbed them, then hid behind a bookshelf on the wall next to the door.

Trista grasped the scissors handle so that the metal dug into her skin. The voices drew nearer. She could tell that both were men. The one who was doing the most talking could have been Joe, but the other voice was deeper, and something about the cadence of the speech made her stomach clench into a hard knot. He spoke only a few words—she couldn't make out—then the first man spoke again, and now they were close enough that she knew for sure it was Joe.

With a relieved sigh, she let the scissors drop from her hand. Crossing the carpeted floor, she opened the door.

"Joe! Thank goodness, it's you. My imagination must be working overtime. I thought…" The words froze on her tongue when her gaze fell on Joe's companion.

The man's eyes were the exact shade of dark blue-gray as the storm clouds that built over Lake Ontario during the hot, humid summers. And they were fixed on her with a ruthlessness that made her feel like an insect about to be squashed.

Trista wanted to turn and run, but there was nowhere to go, and Joe would surely think she was crazy.

"Here you are, Ms. Emerson." Joe sounded cheerful. "Detective Forester walked in the front door just after I got your call, so he decided to come with me to check out those noises."

"How convenient." She was amazed at how cool her voice sounded.

"Pretty good timing all right. And they say you can never find a cop when you need one!" Joe chuckled, not noticing that the other two people in the room were definitely not amused.

Although she'd been looking at Joe as they spoke, Trista felt her gaze being pulled back to the detective. Neither of them had acknowledged that they knew one another, but he hadn't taken his eyes off her for a second. He was still watching her, his expression grim and unyielding.

"Let's check out that file room," he said.

The deep rasp of his voice shocked her. Only vaguely did it resemble the voice she remembered, in the way a young red wine compares to a rich port. Both from grapes, yet... "It's out this way," she said, striving for the same cool tone she'd used earlier. She walked around Joe and led them past reception.

Trista paused in front of the door to the file room. "This door is ajar. Just before I called you, Joe, it was closed."

"Are you sure?" Joe asked.

Was she? She thought so, but now she wondered if she'd merely assumed it was closed. Frowning, she led the way inside.

Initially, all appeared as normal. The photocopier stood against the far wall. To its right were the file cabinets, the table with the coffee machine on it and a row of ceramic mugs. Then she noticed that one of the file drawers was partially open. That wasn't like Brenda.

"Looks okay," Joe said cheerfully, walking into the room and examining the ventilation screens carefully. "I can't see any signs of squirrels, though."

"I'm sorry, Joe. I really thought I heard something."

"No problem. Best to be safe about these things. Well, I'd better get back to my post. Coming, Detective?"

"I was actually hoping to have a moment with, um, Ms. Emerson."

Trista's heart sank. She should have known she wouldn't get rid of him that easily.

"Okay, then." The sound of Joe's whistling traveled down the hall, fading out once he'd closed the main door behind him.

Trista stared at a picture on the wall, knowing full well that those stormy eyes were on her again, seeing far more than she wanted him to see. She'd thought of Morgan often over the years—more often than she wished—and always with the hope that he'd put the past behind him and gone on to live the full and happy life that he deserved.

With the lines of anger and bitterness that outlined his mouth and creased his forehead, however, she could see that her wishes had been in vain. And now she couldn't find the strength to face the bleakness that she saw staring out of his eyes. What had brought him here, tonight of all nights? What could he possibly have to talk to her about?

"There was something about this room that bothered you when you first walked in, wasn't there?" His voice, although quiet, reverberated through the space like ice cracking on a frozen pond.

Trista frowned. She wasn't surprised that he'd noticed. He'd always had a sixth sense about things like that. "Yes. It was that drawer." She pointed at the open cabinet. "My secretary, Brenda, locks those every night. I've never seen her forget."

He walked across the room and stopped where she had pointed. "This one?"

She nodded, then watched as he flipped through the files. It was a relief to have his attention elsewhere. Now she could examine him more closely. His hair was still dark, no signs of gray. And he still wore it so short you couldn't tell it was naturally curly. He'd kept in shape, his body had the sinewy leanness that comes from a life of physical activity. As he bent over the drawer, the black leather of his jacket stretched tautly across his shoulders.

"Are these your notes on client sessions?" he asked.

"Yes, they are."

He looked at the label on the outside of the drawer. "I suppose this is where your file on the Walkers would be kept?"

"Yes." Trista caught her breath. "How did you know the Walkers—"

"The file's missing."

"I know the file's missing. But you haven't answered my question. How did you know the Walkers are my clients?"

"What do you mean, you know the file's missing?"

They were speaking at cross-purposes, and Trista had to summon her patience to keep calm. "I'll answer your question, Morgan, once you answer mine." She bit her lip. It was the first time she'd said his name, and it was clear that he'd noticed.

He stood tall and stared. They were several feet apart but she could read the condemnation in his eyes, and she had to look away. Several seconds passed before he spoke again.

"I don't want to shock you, but Jerry Walker is dead."

"Dead?" She felt behind her for the solid support of the wall.

"Yes. He was murdered. In a motel room. Probably sometime yesterday afternoon."

Morgan seemed to get satisfaction from each one of the facts he hurled at her. Trista clutched at the door handle, trying to hide her sudden dizziness. Jerry Walker dead? Murdered? "Are you sure?"

"Let me see. Bullet hole in chest. No pulse, no breathing, eyes staring forward, never blinking. Yeah, I think I can say that I'm sure."

Trista caught her breath at the beginning of a sob, knowing he'd meant to be cruel, and refusing to let him see he'd hit his mark. "Right. Dumb question." She thought for a few minutes. "It happened in a motel room?"

He nodded, leaning back on the cabinet behind him.

"Seems he had a romantic afternoon planned. And I don't think it was with his wife."

Poor Nan. She would have to deal with death and infidelity, all in the same blow. Not to mention murder...

"And I suppose you've been assigned to the case?"

He rubbed a hand over his chin, his gaze confirming her suspicion. "Can we sit down? I have some questions for you."

Questions? Trista didn't like the sound of that. Back in her office she sank into one of two armchairs, while Morgan perched across from her, on the edge of the sofa. She knew from past experience that his eagle eyes were recording every detail about her appearance: the stylish new haircut, the fact that she'd lost weight since he'd last seen her, even the new, tiny wrinkles that had developed around the corners of her eyes. Nothing would escape him. She sat still, resisting the urge to squirm, to turn away from his open staring. Eventually he spoke and the tension in her shoulders eased slightly in response.

"What time did you hear the intruder?"

"Just after nine." Trista glanced at her watch. It was quarter to ten now. She watched him reach inside the breast pocket of his jacket and pull out a notepad.

"You said Jerry was shot?" she asked.

Morgan nodded. "Died instantly."

At least there'd been no suffering. "Was the gun found at the scene?"

A half smile twisted Morgan's mouth. "No."

She shrugged. "Not that I would have suspected suicide."

"Nice to have that thought confirmed." Morgan's eyes gleamed for a moment and she knew she'd been indiscreet.

''So what brought you here, just at the precise moment I called security?''

''The timing was fortunate. The reason I'm here…'' He broke off for a moment, his eyes drawn to the dark night outside the window. ''We were looking through Walker's financial papers and saw a canceled check made out to you. It seemed a point worth checking to me. Married man is killed while waiting for his lover to show up. The same married man is going to marriage counseling with his wife. Interesting paradox, don't you think?''

What had he thought when he'd recognized her name on that check? What had he felt? He gave no indication now that he cared one way or the other. But Trista knew it must have been a shock.

''Rather despicable if you ask me. But how did you know to find me here? You couldn't have known I'd be working late.''

''Why not? You usually do.''

Trista put a hand to her throat. There was such familiarity in those words. Had he been checking up on her over the years?

''I did try calling you at home first,'' Morgan conceded.

Trista fingered her key chain nervously. Morgan had her unlisted home number? Of course, the police would have access to that sort of information. Still, it was kind of unsettling.

''Where did it happen?'' she asked. ''The murder.''

''The Night's End.''

''The motel with the flashing neon palm tree along the expressway in Etobicoke?'' It was hardly one of the area's finer establishments.

''Yes. I think Jerry had been meeting this woman there for a few weeks now. They seemed to have a routine going. Now you've got your questions answered, so how about answering mine? Why did you know that the Walkers' file would be missing?''

"Because I had an appointment with them today. Which they did not show up for, obviously. The file is sitting in the out basket on my desk.''

"Lucky for that or it would be missing right now.''

"You think the intruder was after the Walkers' file?''

Morgan didn't deign to answer. "Who has access to your office? The outside door is in perfect condition. Whoever got in here had to have had a key.''

Trista noticed that he wasn't doubting that there'd been an intruder, the way Joe had. "Only security and my secretary have keys. And mine's still here.'' She held up the chain she'd been playing with earlier.

"You're sure there's no other?''

"Well, there is a spare. We keep it in the petty-cash box. I think there's an extra one for the file cabinets, too. Just a minute. I'll get them for you.'' She walked back into the reception area and unlocked the top drawer of Brenda's desk. Inside was a small metal box. She opened the lid and pulled out two twenties and a five. A few dollars' worth of change remained on the bottom. "That's odd.''

"What is it?'' Morgan had followed her. Now he held her gaze with his own, and she saw that tension had stretched his mouth thin.

"Our keys.'' Trista looked back at the box. "They're missing.''

Chapter Two

Morgan looked over Trista's shoulder into the metal box. "Are you sure your secretary kept the key here?"

"Of course I am."

"Does anyone else have access to it?" Morgan asked, undaunted.

"This is a small practice. There's only Brenda and me."

"Well, what about when Brenda goes for lunch or to the washroom—does she lock the drawer?"

Trista felt her patience snap. "We keep a fifty-dollar petty-cash supply in there, Morgan. Hardly a fortune."

He ignored her flare-up. "So any one of your clients might have had the opportunity to take that key?"

Trista bristled further at his assumption. "Why does it have to be one of my clients? Perhaps it was a delivery-person, or a courier. Why, even the young man who comes in every week to water our plants could have found that key as easily as any of my clients."

"That's a good point. Why don't you make a list of all the deliverypeople, etcetera, that you've had through the office in the past few weeks?"

Trista sighed. She was sorry now that she'd ever mentioned anything about the noises she thought she'd heard.

"Isn't this a lot of fuss for a simple office break-in? Especially when nothing has been stolen?"

"You know darn well I wouldn't go to these lengths for a simple break and enter." Morgan's eyes flashed dangerously.

Trista was silent for a moment before asking, "You really think someone was after the Walkers' file? That there's a connection with the murder?"

"I do."

His blunt answer shook her as much as anything else had that night. She didn't need these problems in her life.

"Well, *I* don't."

"Really? You don't find it suspicious that someone has been nosing around in your files just one day after your client was murdered?"

"Ever heard of coincidences?"

"Heard of them, but I don't believe in them. And if you thought about it, I think you'd agree with me. You're just so anxious to get me out of your office you can't think straight."

Trista looked away. Yes, he was right. She did want to get him out of her office. Their past was an emotional minefield capable of blowing them both to bits. "This is doing neither of us any good."

"I agree. But unfortunately, I have a job to do. Now, would you please check your office and make sure the Walker file is still there."

Biting back a sarcastic comment on the virtual immobility of a manila folder, Trista left the reception area and went back to her office, scooping the slender file with the Walker label from the out basket on her desk. While she was at it, she slipped the cassettes from the Walkers' two most recent sessions into the file. When she returned, she saw Morgan's attention focus on the file and realized that he was interested in more than making sure the file was here. He held out his hand expectantly, but she ignored it.

"This is confidential information, Morgan. You know that."

"Goddammit, Trista! This isn't some stupid university-ethics course."

Trista's memory provided her with an instant flashback. It was early spring, just about this time of year. They were in university and Morgan was sitting against the trunk of a large maple tree, quizzing her on professional-ethics scenarios from one of her psychology courses. The air had smelt rich and sweet with the spring's new growth and Morgan's smile had made it very hard to concentrate on finals, even though they'd only been days away.

As quickly as the memory came, it was gone, leaving her with a dull aching sensation of sadness and loss. They'd been such kids back then, with no idea of the trials ahead of them.

"This is a murderer we're dealing with, Trista. And that murderer could have been the person who was in your office tonight. Doesn't that worry you?"

Trista swallowed. She hadn't thought of it quite that way. "That doesn't excuse me from releasing confidential information. Especially when you have no evidence that the information in these files could be useful."

"Who says I don't? You know as well as I do that's an issue for the courts to decide. Anyway, Jerry Walker is dead. What does his confidentiality mean to him now?"

"He may be dead, but his wife isn't." Trista spoke defiantly, but she recognized the determined look in Morgan's eyes. If he wanted to be stubborn about this, she knew he could apply to the courts for access to her files. Whether it would be permitted or not was another question. If possible, the whole situation was one she'd rather avoid.

"Look, I'll go over the file tonight. If I see anything that might be pertinent, and if it's something that can be revealed without compromising my clients, I'll tell you." She offered the concession, hoping Morgan would be satisfied.

But he just shook his head. "I don't mean to question your intelligence, but what makes you think you're in a position to judge what might or might not be pertinent to this case? Come on, Trista. If you won't let me take the file, at least let me look through it here. You can watch, if you like."

"You know I can't do that! Why are you being so stubborn? I'm trying to cooperate. If you insist, I'll review the file right now."

Morgan looked at her bleakly. He knew she was acting in accordance with her legal responsibilities. Which put him in a pretty weak bargaining position. "Oh, damn it to hell, Trista. I guess if that's the way you want to play it…"

"It is."

"Okay then. But we'll do it tomorrow, after you've had some rest."

The understanding in his words was not reflected in his expression, which was full of the anger and bitterness she'd seen when he first walked in the door. As for leaving this for tomorrow—Trista knew it was wise, but the idea of unfinished business, of having to face him again…

"I'd rather get it over with tonight."

"No. It's too late." Morgan turned from her. She

could see the stiff set of his shoulders, feel the anger radiating from him.

She bit down on her lower lip. This was as hard on him as it was on her. She shouldn't forget that part of it. After gathering her briefcase and jacket, she walked over to the master control and began switching off the lights.

Morgan met her in the hall, watching as she locked the main door behind her. "Tomorrow you should have your secretary check more thoroughly to make sure nothing's missing. And have the locks changed."

She nodded. They rode the elevator together, and paused at the outside door.

"See you tomorrow then," she said, waiting for him to walk away from her.

But he didn't budge from her side. "I'd like to drive you home."

"Really, Morgan. This is getting to be a little much. You know how safe the Toronto subway system is."

Stubbornly he stood beside her. "I'd feel better if I saw you safely to your door."

What about her? She definitely *wouldn't* feel better with him beside her. "Do you really think it's necessary to be so cautious?"

He turned to face her, his eyes bleak. "When you're dealing with a murderer, it never hurts to be cautious."

"THIS IS IT." Trista pointed out a low-rise brick apartment building with bay windows and small, square balconies with white wooden railings. Across the street, the newly budding trees that bordered the northern boundary of High Park stretched long, twisting branches into the blue-black sky. The park, which covered several hundred acres, represented sanctuary to Trista. The man sitting beside her represented quite the opposite.

"I know," Morgan said as they pulled into a rare parking spot in front of the building.

The moment he stopped, Trista had her hand on the door handle. Quickly she turned to say goodbye, only to be faced with the back of his leather jacket as he stepped out of the car.

He was at her door and helping her out of the passenger seat before she was able to say, "I'm fine, really. There's no need to fuss."

His hand on her arm was familiar, and oddly enticing. Trista's reaction frightened her and she pulled away, earning a look of pure scorn. He made no attempt to touch her again, however, as she led the way up the sidewalk and unlocked the security door to her building. When he held the door open for her, she once again prepared to say goodbye, only to find him following behind her.

"Really, Morgan. I should be just fine from here."

The ground beneath them trembled as a train passed through the underground subway that ran along Bloor Street. In the pale light of the apartment lobby, Trista could see Morgan's mouth form a determined line.

"I'm not doing this for the fun of it. You obviously prefer to risk facing a murderer in your apartment than five more minutes of my company. Or perhaps it hadn't occurred to you that if someone was desperate enough to search your office, they might also be desperate enough to search your home? That they might actually be in there right now?"

Trista drew a quick breath. He was just trying to frighten her. Wasn't he? Still, she didn't protest as he followed her up the stairs to her apartment. Nor did she question that he knew exactly which door was hers. She handed over her key to his waiting hand and watched as he first listened at the door, then turned the key in the lock.

"Wait here for a minute while I look things over."

It was as dramatic as the movies, but she complied, staying in the hallway while he conducted a search of her apartment. It was a full five minutes before he reappeared at the door.

"It looks okay."

She could hear the relief in his voice. "Of course it's okay," she said matter-of-factly, trying to keep her own fear out of her voice. They traded positions. Now he stood in the hall, and she in the apartment, her hand on the door, eager to close it and to wipe the image of him from both her eyes and her mind.

"I'll come by your office tomorrow afternoon," he said. "Around four."

She nodded. "Fine." She tried to close the door, but his hand forestalled her.

"What about the file?" he asked, his eyes on the briefcase in her hand.

She didn't understand what he was getting at. "It's in here," she said, lifting her black leather bag.

Impatience creased his forehead. "I realize that. But do you have a safe?"

"No, I don't. But I really don't think—"

"Then let me take it. I do. If someone broke into your office today to get their hands on the file, then it's much too important to leave lying around."

Trista shook her head in a slow, exaggerated motion. "Definitely not."

He leaned against the wooden door frame. "Why? Don't you trust me? Afraid I'll read the file when you're not looking?"

"I just don't think a safe is necessary."

"Since when did *you* become the expert on crime?"

Okay, he had a point. Trista opened her briefcase and took out everything but the Walker file. Closing the metal clasp, she spun the combination wheel, knowing the small lock would hardly keep Morgan out if he decided he wanted in. But he wouldn't do that. At least, the man she remembered wouldn't. She was beginning to realize there was a big difference between the two. The knowledge that part of that was her fault flooded her with guilt.

"Take it," she said, suddenly not caring if he did decide to break in. What were professional ethics compared to what she owed this man?

He eased the handle out of her hands, gently. "I won't open it, Trista." His voice was suddenly, heartbreakingly, soft. "You can trust me."

Reaching her other hand to an itch on her cheek, Trista felt the dampness of a tear. Ashamed, embarrassed of her own weakness, she closed the door between them without another word. After turning the dead bolt firmly into place, she leaned against the cold steel of the door and listened to the sound of his footsteps fading as he walked down the hall. She could feel her throat tighten and she swallowed hard, willing the tears to stop before they had a chance to get out of control.

She needed something to calm her down. She went to the kitchen and picked up the kettle. Hand shaking, she tried to hold it steady under the stream of water from the faucet. Water sprayed over the stainless-steel sides, spotting the sink and surrounding counter area. The cold metal hissed when she placed it on the burner.

Why did this have to happen? Why? Why? The quiet refrain pounded in her head as she waited for the water to boil. Why would someone murder Jerry Walker? Could it have been the woman he was having an affair with? Had Nan known he was having an affair? She must have suspected, yet neither one of them had mentioned anything in their sessions. Was it possible Morgan was right and there was a connection between the murder and what had happened in her office tonight? If so, what was it?

Trista frowned, thinking of the professional dilemma she was facing. As the Walkers' counselor, she was bound to keep her clients' information confidential. If there truly was information in her files that could help bring Walker's murderer to justice, however, morally she would feel bound to reveal it.

Trista thought back over the past sessions she'd held with the Walkers. She couldn't think of a single fact that might help Morgan in his investigation. Of course, she'd have to review her notes to make certain. With any luck she'd find nothing and then she wouldn't have to worry about the issue of confidentiality. Assuming Morgan believed her, that was.

Morgan. Trust him to insist on keeping the file at his place. Always playing the role of the protector. She felt her stomach twist into knots at the thought. Not that she didn't trust him with the file, because she did. It was knowing that she would be talking to him and seeing him again that made her so anxious. He'd been right in what he'd said to her tonight. She would almost prefer taking her chances with the murderer to facing Morgan again.

As the kettle began to whistle, claiming her attention, she found that same refrain repeating itself in her head. *Why? Why?* Only this time she pondered not Walker's death, but the great misfortune that, of all the detectives in the Toronto police force, Morgan Forester had been the one assigned to this case.

MORGAN LAY NAKED between his cool, white cotton sheets, unable to sleep despite his state of near exhaustion. God, how he hated her! And he hadn't even realized it until he'd seen her standing there at her office door, still so beautiful, elegant and slim, with fiery hair that contradicted her frosty demeanor. Her ivory skin had whitened at the sight of him, her eyes had looked more green than brown as she stared at him in shocked dismay. Not that he'd expected her to welcome him…but did she have to look at him as if he was a serial killer or something? Talk about adding insult to injury. It had taken all of his self-control to mask his fury, to resist the urge to grab her by those frail shoulders and shake some sense into her.

As for her, she was obviously far from pleased at having him suddenly drop back into her life, but that was her problem. How did she think he felt about it? Did she imagine he wanted to have to work with her? Anger rose like bile in his throat, and he clenched his fists beneath the light covers. There was nothing to be gained by letting the situation get to him. It wasn't her fault her client had been murdered, any more than it was his fault he'd been assigned to the case. There was nothing either one of them could do about the circumstances, so they'd just have to make the best of it.

He thought about the break-in at her office and wondered if the Walker file had been the motive behind it. Trista didn't want to think so, but he was convinced there was a connection. And since the intruder hadn't managed to find the file, it was certainly possible he might try Trista's home next. He felt his gut twist at the thought. Ironic that as much as he hated her, he still felt this need to protect her.

Protect her. What a laugh. He'd noticed that she hadn't

liked that he knew things about her. Like her phone number and address, where she worked, the hours she kept. She probably thought he'd found all that out tonight, when he'd learned of her involvement in the case.

But he'd always known. Whether she liked it or not, he had kept tabs on her, and would continue to do so. Despite everything else, he still felt it was his duty.

The file, locked in his safe, called to him. He longed to read it. Not only to check whether there was any information pertinent to the case, but because of its link to Trista. He found himself hungry for the sight of her strong, slanted script. For comments and thoughts she might have written that could shed some light on her own thoughts and opinions. Was she happy? Did she ever think of him? Were there regrets…?

Morgan turned, pulling the top sheet with him over to the other side of the bed. He wouldn't look at the file—and it wasn't the locked briefcase that was stopping him—so why was he torturing himself thinking about it? And more important, why was it that after three years, just the sight of her had his emotions tied up in knots? This was a case like any other. And she was just another witness. As long as he remembered to keep things in their proper perspective, he'd be okay. He had to believe that, or he'd go crazy.

"I SUPPOSE WE WERE as happy as the average couple." Nan Walker crossed and then uncrossed her legs, obviously uncomfortable with Morgan's questions about her marriage.

They were sitting in her living room, she in a tall wingback chair, Morgan across from her on an overstuffed love seat. In her early forties, Nan looked the part of a mourning widow in a black wool dress, dark stockings and black high-heeled shoes.

Nan Walker was attractive, with even features, and expensively styled hair. But all that black made her look washed-out and dull—an impression furthered by her body language and voice. An aura of uncertainty and self-consciousness surrounded the woman. As she spoke she wrung her hands, and Morgan noted her fingernails were bitten to the quick.

She must have noticed him looking. She said quickly, as if ashamed, "It's a bad habit I've had since I was a girl."

Bit of a mouse. Morgan jotted his notes in the steno pad he usually carried in his breast pocket. He'd begun a new page, starting up after the notes he'd written at Trista's office last night. Trista. Now *he* shifted uncomfortably in his chair, remembering his sleepless night and the look of her dark, empty windows when he'd driven past her apartment that morning on his way to work.

He'd been going to offer her a ride to her office, but she'd already left. He guessed she took the subway to Spadina, then caught the streetcar to King. With the hours she kept, he wondered why she bothered with a home address. She might as well set up a cot in the corner by her desk.

Across from him, Nan squirmed distressfully. He remained silent, knowing that eventually she'd feel compelled to fill the awkward silence.

"We have—I mean had—" she stumbled over the tense as people in these situations often did "—the business, and of course our son, Jason. We'd built a life together."

"Jason's in university, is that right?"

Nan sat a little higher in her chair. "Yes. He's taking

summer courses at Queen's University, in Kingston. He's studying business administration even though he swore to his father that he wasn't interested in taking over the family business.'' Nan's smile faded a little at this.

Family dispute over son taking over the business. ''And how do you feel about your son getting involved with the hardware stores?''

''Oh, I'd like it, of course. It would keep him here, close to home. I'd certainly see him more. But he has to do what makes him happy.''

Right. The answer was a little too pat. Morgan briefly wondered exactly what family problems she was attempting to smooth over before he went on to his next question. ''He's coming home?''

''Tonight.'' Her face brightened at the thought. ''He may withdraw from his courses so he can help me sort out the estate.''

Adores her son. ''Perhaps you could ask him to contact me when he gets in.''

A frown creased Nan's forehead. ''Is that necessary?''

''Routine questioning. Nothing to worry about.'' They'd already confirmed that Jason Walker had been in class at the approximate time of his father's death. And Kingston was several hours by car from Toronto.

Likewise, Nan Walker had an alibi. She'd been at work in the hardware store on Queen Street all day, except for a half-hour lunch break. As the motel was a good twenty minutes from the store, it seemed unlikely that Nan could have done her husband in rather than order a tuna on whole wheat as she'd claimed to do. Further solidifying her alibi was that the clerk from the diner remembered preparing the sandwich—apparently, requesting mustard on tuna was a little unusual.

''How's the business doing?'' Morgan continued in a

conversational tone. Their investigation had already turned up tax returns for the past four years that showed a very healthy profit in each year. But he wanted to hear what Nan had to say on the topic.

"Fine. Excellent, as a matter of fact."

"I understand you do the accounting?"

Her expression brightened. "Yes. All five stores. The accounting is centralized at our main store on Queen Street."

Proud of her work. "Was there anything unusual about your husband's behavior recently? Any changes in his habits, new people that he was seeing?"

Nan colored at his words. "If you're referring to the fact that they found him in a motel room, the answer is that I have no idea what he was doing there. I suppose you think he was having an affair or something."

"Is that what you think, Mrs. Walker?"

Nan's gaze dropped from his. "I don't know," she said softly. "I've sometimes suspected him of being unfaithful over the years, but we'd just started marriage counseling. I guess I hoped he was sincere when he told me he was willing to work on some of our problems."

Lying about husband's affair.

Nan looked back at him, her expression earnest now. "It's been difficult with Jason away from home. Our counselor says it's not uncommon for couples to go through a period of adjustment after their children are gone. To be honest, it was me that found it particularly hard. When Jason was at home his friends were always over, involved in one activity or another. And I volunteered at his school and drove for all his hockey games."

Morgan nodded sympathetically. "So when Jason left, life seemed pretty empty?"

"Oh, I still had my work. But evenings could be

lonely. Jerry never felt like doing much when he got home—he was happy to sit around watching television. Quite honestly, I have a hard time imagining him having the energy to have an affair.'' The underlying bitterness of her last comment had obviously been unplanned. Her mouth tightened the second the words left her lips and her eyes became fixed on a point somewhere to the left of Morgan's head.

''Do you know the contents of your husband's will?''

''Yes.'' Her gray eyes flashed at him, objecting silently to the question, but she answered. ''I get the house, both cars and retirement fund. The business will go to Jason, of course.''

''Entirely to Jason?'' Morgan feigned surprise.

Nan lifted her chin. ''Of course. He's our son.''

Morgan shrugged. The value of Nan's inheritance was not insubstantial, but it paled in comparison with the worth of the business. ''Sure. But your husband could have left you with a life bequest, with the shares to revert to Jason on your death. I mean, in a divorce, you would have been entitled to half of his assets. It just seems odd, that's all...'' Morgan's voice tapered off, and he pretended to look uncomfortable, all the while watching Nan's face closely for any signs of resentment. He saw none.

''Our retirement fund is not insubstantial. I'll be well provided for. And of course I draw my own salary out of the business. And I'll receive a pension when I retire.''

''Of course,'' Morgan was silent for a moment, as if thinking something over. ''But what will your son do with the business? You said earlier he wasn't interested in working there.''

''Perhaps he'll change his mind. Or he could always

hire someone to run it for him,'' Nan pointed out reasonably.

"You perhaps?"

"Me? Good heavens, no. Lorne Thackray would be the most likely choice, I'd say."

Lorne Thackray. Morgan wrote the name down on his pad and circled it twice. "Does he work there?"

"He's the manager at the Queen Street location. Jerry was talking about increasing Lorne's responsibilities by adding another store. I imagine he could handle all five if he had to."

Nan was sitting straighter in her chair now, and her voice was firmer. Morgan found the changes very interesting, but he sensed this was not the time to dig deeper. "That's all for now, Mrs. Walker. If you think of anything that might help us out, please give us a call."

Once the initial shock wore off, people's memories tended to loosen up. Knowing this, Morgan tried not to feel discouraged by the lack of information Nan had provided.

In a homicide of this type, the spouse was an obvious suspect. The marriage had been in trouble and Morgan was almost certain Nan had known her husband was having an affair. And while Nan certainly seemed anxious and distraught, Morgan had a feeling it was more because of his questions than the loss of her husband.

On Nan's side, of course, was her alibi. And the fact that she didn't exactly come away with a fortune in the will certainly stood in her favor. On the other hand, alibis could be discredited, and money wasn't the only motive for murder.

Morgan shook his head, momentarily clearing his mind of the conflicting facts and motives. If he went on gut feel, he'd have to say he didn't think she'd done it. And why?

Maybe it all boiled down to this: he didn't think Nan Walker had the balls to cold-bloodedly plan and carry out the murder of her own husband.

Chapter Three

It was noon. Trista sat and stared at her hands, folded motionless on the top of her desk. Usually she worked through lunch, eating a sandwich as she read files, or making notes on her morning appointments. Today, however, she wasn't hungry. And her thoughts were uncharacteristically scattered.

Maybe the problem was lack of sleep. But whenever she tried to close her eyes to catch a quick nap, she saw Morgan's face—the way it was now, not the way she remembered it from before—and she was stricken with guilt.

She'd ruined his life. She still felt that way, despite the months of therapy she'd undergone in an attempt to make peace with her past. He was angry and bitter, and worst of all, she couldn't blame him, nor could she criticize him for not having moved on with his life. How could he, when she hadn't either? Weak and foolish she might be, but she wasn't about to add hypocritical to the list.

How had he survived these past few years? Same as her, she suspected—by throwing himself into his work. At least now he would have Jerry Walker's case to keep him busy. He wouldn't be in her position, sitting in an empty room with nothing but her own thoughts to drive her crazy. His job demanded action. Gathering evidence, interviewing suspects—he wouldn't have time to sit and stew.

Trista separated her hands and tapped her long nails against the wooden surface of the desk. She still found it difficult to believe that Jerry had been murdered, although the basic facts had been confirmed in the morning paper.

But why? And who could have done it? His wife, Nan? It seemed impossible for such a quiet, self-effacing woman. Did her mild exterior conceal the rage it would take to commit murder? Certainly there were negative feelings, repressed hostility. But murder?

Once Nan was ruled out, though, who did that leave? The woman Jerry had been having an affair with? But why would she kill him? Because he wouldn't leave his wife, perhaps? For some reason, that scenario didn't sit right with Trista either. Who was this woman he had been seeing? Were there any clues in her session notes?

Trista was relieved when a knock interrupted her fruitless speculations.

"Yes?"

The door opened and a large woman with jet-black hair and piercing dark eyes strode into Trista's office.

"Sylvia," Trista said, surprised. Sylvia and her husband, Daniel Hawthorne, were former clients. They'd come to her after Sylvia had found out her husband was having an affair, and stayed in therapy for about two months. Trista had been sorry to see them quit the sessions. It was obvious there were still issues that needed to be resolved.

"Sorry to barge in." Sylvia spoke in her customary

booming voice and didn't sound sorry at all. "That secretary of yours wasn't at her desk."

"Brenda's on her lunch break." Trista invited Sylvia to sit down. "Can I get you a coffee?"

"I'm fine," Sylvia said as she lowered herself into one of the wingback chairs.

Inwardly Trista scrambled for the particulars of the Hawthornes' situation, wishing Sylvia had given her notice so she could have reviewed her files. She remembered that Daniel had been a sweet, intelligent man. In their conversations, he'd often been dominated by his overpowering wife.

"He's at it again," Sylvia said in quiet fury. "I asked him to take me out to lunch today—Wednesday is when he used to meet his girlfriend, remember?—and at the last minute, he canceled."

Trista assumed she was talking about her husband. "Did he say why?"

Sylvia flounced her hair with one hand. "He said they were having a faculty meeting. So, of course, I phoned the university after he left to check—"

Trista made mental note of that *of course*. Did Sylvia routinely check up on everything Daniel said?

"—and they said there was no meeting and that Daniel had even canceled his afternoon class!"

Trista remembered that Sylvia had a strong jealous streak, predating Daniel's affair. Whether those feelings were justified in this case, Trista had no idea. "Before you jump to any conclusions, I think you should talk to Daniel. Perhaps the meeting was rescheduled. Perhaps he wasn't feeling well. There could be many reasons why he had to cancel his class."

Sylvia shook her head. "No. If he wasn't well, he'd have come home or at least phoned me."

"You won't know for sure until you talk to him."

"But I don't even know where he is! How can I talk to him?"

"I guess you'll have to wait until he gets home."

"But that could be hours!"

"I'm sorry. Sometimes we have no choice but to wait. Once you've had a chance to discuss this with your husband, I'd be happy to talk to both of you, or you alone, if you'd prefer. Just phone Brenda and make an appointment."

They sat quietly for several moments before Sylvia finally gave a reluctant nod of agreement. Despite the woman's abrasive nature, Trista felt sorry for her. Waiting was never easy, especially for a woman of Sylvia's impatient nature. As Trista ushered the distraught woman out of her office, she saw that Brenda was back from lunch.

"Could we talk a minute, Brenda?"

"Sure." Brenda waited until Sylvia had walked out the main doors before standing and smoothing the skirt of her navy suit. She was about the same age as Trista, 32, but appeared older, probably because of the premature gray streaks in her hair, and a naturally sallow complexion. Trista had often thought that some hair color and a little makeup would make a world of difference, but those sorts of personal indulgences simply were not Brenda's style.

Closing the door behind them, Trista got right down to business. "I meant to tell you this earlier, Brenda. I think someone broke into our office last night."

"What?" Brenda looked disbelieving. "How did they get in?"

"With a key, apparently. The spare in your desk is missing. Wait—" She held out a hand to stop Brenda as

she went to check. "I want you to be aware that a detective may be calling with some questions." She looked
out the window before continuing, "His name is Morgan
Forester. I think he'll probably want to know the last time
you saw the key, and whether you remember anyone suspicious hanging around your desk, that sort of thing."

"The key was there Monday morning, when I needed
money to buy cream," Brenda said slowly. "What was
stolen?"

"Nothing that we know of, but maybe you could check
the files to make sure. I'm going to call security and have
the locks on our door changed."

Brenda went to leave, then paused at the door. "Work
must be slow if they're sending detectives to investigate
office break-ins these days."

The remark caught Trista off guard. Brenda didn't offer her own opinions very often. Obviously she was expecting more of an explanation. When Trista didn't say
anything, Brenda continued, "Does Detective Forester
think our break-in had something to do with Jerry Walker's murder?"

Trista sighed. Jerry's murder was something else she
should have discussed with Brenda, and she felt like a
coward for having avoided it. "I suppose you read about
it in the papers?"

Brenda nodded.

"I'm sorry. I should have told you before my ten
o'clock appointment."

"*Is* there a connection between the break-in and the
murder?"

That was the question, wasn't it? Trista thought about
the Walker file and Morgan's expectations that she review it. The prospect both exhausted and frightened her.
It was a big mistake for her and Morgan to spend time

together. If only this could be one of those rare cases, the kind that got solved quickly and simply.

Brenda was still waiting, her expression cool but expectant. Trista raised her hands helplessly. "I don't know. It's possible, I guess. But I sure hope not."

MORGAN WAS LATE for his appointment with Trista. As he rushed off the elevator and through the main door, he was disappointed to see the receptionist's chair empty, her desk cleared of the day's work. He'd asked Brenda a few questions over the phone about an hour ago, and had hoped to catch her before his meeting with Trista.

Behind the reception area, Trista's office door stood slightly ajar. Morgan walked up to the threshold, somehow reluctant to announce his presence. The silence was unsettling. With a slight push of his hand the door swung open.

Trista was on the sofa, asleep. Her body was curled in an S shape, with her auburn hair spilling loosely over the arm she had tucked under her head. She'd kicked off her shoes, and her long, narrow feet, encased in sheer hose, were resting on a pile of books on the far cushion.

As Morgan stepped closer, he was able to see more. Her face was pale, her eyelids almost translucent, her lips pulled down at the corners as if even her naps were haunted by sad dreams. Her narrow skirt had ridden to almost the top of her thighs, and his breath drew in at the sight of her long, slender legs. As far as he could see, they were as flawless as when he'd first known her, and he felt a thumping in his chest in response to awakened memories.

White-hot anger suddenly replaced the stirrings of desire. Teeth together, he sucked in his cheeks, took a deep breath and tried to fight off the vicious pull of emotions.

Turning his back to her, he picked up the phone to make a quick call. He spoke quietly, but soon heard the rustle of her suit against the stiff fabric of the sofa, and the soft intake of her breath, signaling that she was waking. He didn't turn around. The next time he looked at her, he wanted her to be back together, without so much as a hair out of place.

When he hung up, she asked, "What time is it?" in a voice husky from sleep.

"Five-thirty." He spread his hands, gripping the edge of her desk, surveying the spartan neatness of the work top and trying to erase the picture of her long, almost bare legs from his memory. This was all about business. He'd be okay if he just kept reminding himself of that fact. "Sorry if I kept you waiting."

In the background he heard sounds of smoothing and pulling, and he imagined her tidying her hair, reorganizing her clothes. Her arm must have fallen asleep, it would be tingling now. Would she guess that he'd taken a moment to stop and study her while she was asleep?

"No problem. I guess I needed the rest."

Her words were cool, composed, and suddenly he knew that it wouldn't have occurred to her that he might have been watching her. And even if she'd known, she couldn't have cared less. He felt the rage building in him again. How could she be so distant and impersonal? Even caught off guard taking a nap, she didn't give an inch. From her reaction, he might as well be the night janitor, asking if he could empty the trash from her office.

He tightened his hold on the edge of the table and bowed his head. *Get a grip,* he told himself. *You can do this.*

"Can I have the file?" she said, stepping behind her desk into his range of vision. As he'd suspected, her hair was smooth and her suit was impeccable once more, barely a trace of a wrinkle in her brown linen skirt and jacket.

He pushed the locked briefcase across the desk surface, noticing as she reached for it how smooth and even-colored the skin on the back of her hands was. They in no way betrayed the pain and unhappiness of the past. Unlike the circles under her eyes and the gauntness of her frame.

Her long nails were tapered, with a flawless covering of polish. A different color than yesterday, he noticed. God, he was falling apart and she was coordinating her nail color with her change in clothing.

Before she could open the file, he stopped her with one quick touch to those picture-perfect hands. "I think I should fill you in on the latest developments before you start."

Her nostrils pinched in as she drew a deep breath. Because of his touch, or the suggestion? Did she think he was prolonging their encounter for the fun of it?

"The more background information you have, the more likely you'll be able to pull any relevant information from your notes," he explained.

She nodded tightly in response. "Let's sit down then."

Carefully avoiding the sofa—he imagined he could still see the imprint of her body on the soft cushions—he sat in one of the chairs, pulling out his notepad and resting it on one knee.

"Obviously my main interest is in identifying the woman Jerry was having an affair with," he began, trying to pretend this was just another briefing. "Beyond that, let's start with Nan Walker. Both she and her son have motives, but they have alibis as well. Nan claims to have been at the store Monday afternoon, while Jason was at school in Kingston.''

Trista nodded, and he continued, ''She claims she didn't know Jerry was having an affair. I got the impression she was lying. What do you think?''

Trista uncrossed her legs and leaned forward on her lap. ''I can't dispute what she told you. The topic of an affair never came up in our sessions, and I never pursue those avenues unless it seems necessary.''

Morgan checked his impatience with her carefully worded reply. God, talking to Trista was like dealing with a lawyer. ''Well, it's pretty clear he *was* having an affair. Nan found a note among his personal effects today.''

That shocked her at least, he observed with satisfaction.

''A note?''

Morgan nodded. On his way here, he'd stopped at the Walkers' to pick it up, which was why he'd been late. ''Nan found it this afternoon when she was sorting through Jerry's papers. It's typed on a piece of stationery with flowers across the top. It says—'' he lowered his eyes to his notepad to read the exact words ''—*Let's make it Monday this week. Same place, same time.*''

The room was silent as Trista absorbed the information. ''Poor Nan,'' she said finally, taking a deep breath with the words. ''Having to cope with this on top of everything else.''

''Women have murdered for less.'' He saw Trista cringe at the harshness in his tone.

''Who else have you talked to?'' she asked. ''Besides Nan.'' Her voice was low, quietly encouraging. He imagined her using that same tone to inspire the confidence of her clients, and he felt the anger surge inside him again.

"The cleaner at the Night's End. She said Jerry had been coming to the motel for several weeks now, never staying more than three or four hours at a time. She'd pretty much figured out what was going on in that room and she wasn't impressed."

"Did she ever see the woman he was meeting?"

"Only from a distance. She said the woman looked like a spy from the movies. Big trench coat. Hat. Sunglasses. Arrived in a taxi, left in a taxi. Ring any bells?" he asked sarcastically. As a description it didn't have one thing to commend itself. The cleaner hadn't even been willing to guess as to weight or height.

Trista shook her head, as if sharing in his disappointment.

"The desk clerk wasn't any better," Morgan continued. "According to him, Jerry always picked up the room key. Except this last time the woman came to the desk saying her husband had locked them out and she needed another key."

"That's strange."

"Isn't it, though? Something else that ties in with the note Nan Walker found—the clerk said they normally booked their room for Wednesdays. This was the first time they'd met on a Monday."

"That has to mean something."

"I agree. But what?"

"I wish I knew." Trista held her hands out helplessly.

"Tell me about your secretary. Brenda."

Trista looked surprised at the question. "Brenda Malachowski? She's been working for me since I first opened my practice."

"Is she married?"

"No. She lives alone in a condominium on King and Bathurst."

"Does she date anyone in particular?"

"Not that I know of, although she goes out a lot." She frowned. "Is this really relevant? I don't like talking about people behind their backs."

Morgan felt his patience snapping. "Answering questions in a homicide investigation isn't exactly gossiping. But maybe you should take a look at that file now."

Once Trista was settled at her desk, Morgan turned to the forms he'd brought with him. Unlike a lot of cops he knew, Morgan enjoyed doing the paperwork on a job. It was a chance to sit and think, to pull the strands of an investigation together.

Still, it was easier to do when you'd had some sleep in the past forty-eight hours, and he'd had precious little. Slouching down in his chair, he put his feet up on the coffee table. Trista looked exhausted as well, despite the catnap he'd interrupted. Had she, too, found it impossible to fall asleep last night?

He tried to concentrate on his papers, but it wasn't long before the lines in front of him blurred then went double. He slouched down farther in his chair. The hand holding his pen went slack and the pen slipped down, soundlessly, onto the plush carpeted floor.

"YOU WANT TO KNOW what I think? You won't like it, I'll guarantee you that. I don't think there's anything wrong with our marriage. She just needs to broaden her own interests a little. Ever since Jason left for university she's been moping around the house and acting miserable. Who feels like talking to a person like that?"

Jerry's voice came loudly over the earphones Trista was wearing. She adjusted the volume slightly downward.

"What do you have to say to your husband's comments, Nan?"

There was so much that a tape recording left out. Trista could remember the hostility in Nan's eyes, the way her lips had compressed into a tight, thin line. But then, in a matter of seconds, her anger seemed to have disappeared, and she replied in a typically unassertive manner.

"I know I haven't been very good company lately, but I do have other interests. I work, after all. Maybe we need to go out more. Do things together, as a couple—"

"We do go out. We went to the Easter Seals thing just a few months ago. And before that there was the political fund-raiser…"

"The one for Suni Choopra. But those aren't the sort of things I was talking about."

That was where Trista had met the Walkers. She'd been at the fund-raiser as both a friend and supporter of Suni's. Federal elections were being held in six weeks, and Suni looked like a shoe-in as the incumbent member of Parliament for Toronto West.

"No kidding! You stood by yourself, in a corner of the room, for most of the evening. It was damn embarrassing, let me tell you! You'd think a woman over forty would have learned a few social skills already!"

"They were your friends. And you didn't introduce me to any of them."

At this point, with their time almost over, Trista had felt obliged to break in.

"Are you talking about more intimate activities, Nan? Just you and Jerry? Maybe going out for dinner or to a movie?"

"Exactly."

The sound of light snoring caught Trista's attention. She stopped the tape and looked at Morgan. He was slouched down in his chair with his head tipped back, fast asleep. Papers were strewn over his lap and on the floor beside him. She couldn't help but smile. Morgan had always survived on a series of power naps rather than a decent night's sleep, and it seemed he hadn't changed the habit.

After a moment she forced herself to look away. There was something so intimate about seeing another person asleep. They were so vulnerable... She wondered what Morgan had thought when he'd walked into her office to find *her* napping on the couch. Had he felt, like her, that he was getting a stolen glimpse of something he had no right to see?

Remembering her state of disarray, how high her skirt had risen, she felt her face go hot. But then reason prevailed. Morgan had probably spared her only the briefest glance before making his phone call. After all, he'd so resolutely kept his back to her while she'd tidied herself up.

Morgan had looked at her with desire once, but he would do so no more. And that was exactly the way she wanted it. A slight pain nagged at her forehead as she turned her attention back to the papers on her desk.

She listened until the end of the tape, then clicked the machine off. Sighing, she lifted the earphones over her head, and rubbed the tired muscles at the back of her neck reflexively.

"Find anything?"

Her hands froze at the sound of his voice breaking the almost eerie after-hours silence in the office. Now she remembered his uncanny ability to wake, fully alert, from the deepest sleep. Another thing about the man that hadn't changed.

"I warned you not to expect too much."

"Believe me, where you're concerned, I've learned never to expect too much."

Trista cringed at the bitterness of his words. There was a temptation to lash out, to defend herself, but that was short-lived. If she was honest, she knew his anger was justifiable, but more to the point, it didn't matter anymore. She couldn't let herself care, not now.

"There's nothing in this file about any affair. You can believe me or not, but that's the truth." She looked down at her hands for a second before adding, "I'm sorry."

"You're sorry." Morgan's words came out hard and bitter. "Why don't I believe you? I guess you'd say anything to get me out of your life again, wouldn't you?" He stood and walked toward the desk. Unlike hers, his dark hair never looked mussed. It was too short. And his clothes hadn't suffered for the brief nap. She saw the dangerous glint in his blue eyes as he drew closer. He was angry. And making no attempt to control it.

"How disappointed you must have been to see me standing outside your door last night. Upsetting the balance of your perfect little life," he said in a mocking tone. "Working day and night, sequestered away in this ivory tower, going home alone every night, to that lovely, sterile apartment of yours. And don't tell me about your busy social life, because I've been keeping my eye on you and I know you don't have one."

With the last of his words, he leaned over her desk, his face a mere six inches away. She could see the dark stubble on his chin, the sheen of perspiration on his upper lip. When her gaze reached the blue fire of his eyes, she looked away quickly, scorched by the contact.

"Are you happy, Trista? Is this—" he waved one arm to indicate her office "—what you wanted?" And when she didn't answer right away, he pounded his fist on the desktop. "Answer me, dammit! Are you happy? Is it enough?"

She wheeled back in her chair, putting some distance between them. It was an effort to stay calm, to keep her cool. She stared at the wall, just beyond him, and struggled to keep her own emotions out of bounds where they belonged. "This is the life I've chosen, Morgan, and I don't want to talk about it."

He straightened himself and shook his head bitterly. "Of course not. You don't want to talk about anything, do you? Nothing that matters, anyway." He looked away for a few minutes, drew in a long breath.

"Well, I've got bad news for you, lady. You're going to have to continue talking with me. Until I solve this case, or we both go crazy with the effort."

Chapter Four

Wednesday was Trista's evening to volunteer at Suni Choopra's campaign office. The small one-room headquarters was located just east of the Humber River, in Bloor West Village, amid the small delicatessens, cafés and boutiques that gave the area its charm. Trista rode the subway one stop beyond her own, to Runnymede, then ran up the concrete steps to the sidewalk. Flowers and tubs of fresh vegetables stood outside the small grocery shop beside the campaign office, and Trista stopped to pick up a potted mum for the front desk.

Campaign posters covered the glass front of Suni's office. Her beautiful East Indian face, with its classical proportions and unusually pale complexion—inherited, along with her height, from her Nordic mother—was arresting in itself. Then you saw her record and you were really impressed. That was why Trista was here. Suni was going to change things, and Trista wanted to help.

When she opened the door, a cacophony of noise greeted her. The headquarters was usually a madhouse in late afternoon, and now, at least a dozen other volunteers were scattered in the modest, five-hundred-square-foot space. Trista placed the mums on the reception desk and smiled her hellos. Suni was at the back of the room, talking intently with her campaign manager.

"Everything okay?" Trista asked one of the other volunteers.

"Couldn't be better," was the cheerful reply. "Early poll results were in this morning. Suni's holding on to her ten-point lead."

Then why did she look so tense? Maybe they would have a chance to talk later. Trista began folding the flyers that she and other volunteers would be delivering door-to-door later in the campaign.

At the back of the room, Suni was now standing alone. For a moment Trista thought Suni was looking at her, but then she realized the older woman was staring into space, one delicately boned hand held up to the side of her face. Her expression was one Trista recognized. She'd seen it often enough in her own mirror. What in the world was the matter? She didn't get a chance to ask until hours later, when the other volunteers had left for the night.

"You look tired," Trista observed quietly, stacking the finished pamphlets into a mailbag as Suni went about the business of closing down the office.

"It's been a long day." Suni's smile was an obvious effort.

Trista was concerned, but she wasn't going to pry. She slipped on her jacket and stepped outside, pulling her collar around the base of her neck as protection from the cool nip of the spring evening. As she waited for Suni to lock the front door, Trista's eyes scanned the street casually, stopping at the sight of a familiar car parked across from the office.

The tempo of her heartbeat picked up and she frantically tried to gather her defenses. She wasn't surprised that Morgan had found her here—he seemed to know so much about her—but she was very surprised that he would want to talk to her again so soon after that scene in her office.

As she watched, the car's engine started and its lights flickered on. At a lull in the traffic he pulled a U-turn, stopping just feet from where she and Suni stood. He got out of the car, and even with the vehicle between them, she couldn't meet his gaze.

"I have some more questions, Trista."

Of course he did. Trista glanced nervously at Suni, who was watching the scene with avid interest. "Can't they wait until tomorrow?"

"If they could, I wouldn't be here." The blunt meaning of his words was only too clear. He didn't want to be around her any more than he had to.

"Where are we going to talk? In your car?" The thought of being confined with him in such close quarters panicked her.

"Why not over dinner? The café down the street is good. They make a mean borscht."

Suni nodded. "Good cabbage rolls, too."

Morgan's glance flicked over to the politician then back to Trista. "I'll park my car and meet you there."

Trista watched as he drove off, wishing she had the nerve to ignore him.

"What was that all about?" Suni asked, her eyes also on the departing taillights. "Who's the dark handsome stranger?"

Since Morgan's car was unmarked, Trista realized that Suni had no idea Morgan was a cop. In their two years of friendship, Trista had resisted several of Suni's gentle efforts at matchmaking, and so she couldn't really blame her friend for being curious about a man suddenly showing up on the scene. Forcing herself to rise above her own reticence, Trista fought down the wall of coldness that she worked so hard to maintain. Suni was a good friend. She deserved an answer.

For a minute she contemplated telling Suni about the break-in and its possible connection to Jerry Walker's murder. Then she decided against it, opting for the more painful truth.

"He's Morgan Forester. My ex-husband."

THE RESTAURANT WAS cafeteria style, with a clean European atmosphere and mouthwatering aromas. A counter lined with stools ran along the windows, and plain wooden tables and chairs filled the rest of the space. There were racks with newspapers available to the customers, and a small counter in the center of the room with a jug of ice water and glasses.

Trista picked up a tray and joined Morgan in the lineup. She came here often and wondered if he did too. He seemed familiar with the place. What if they'd met here by chance one Saturday afternoon, what would that have been like?

It would have been preferable to meeting over a homicide investigation. But the end result would have been the same. Disaster.

"The bread here is fantastic," Morgan said. He stood back to let her go ahead of him in the line, and she felt self-conscious as she chose a fat slice of rye and a bowl of soup. They found a table near the back of the restaurant, which was busy despite the late hour.

Focusing on the food in front of her, she could feel her stomach tightening with anxiety. "So what was it you forgot to ask me?" she asked, unnerved by Morgan's silence. There was no place in their relationship for idle chitchat. Other ex-spouses might become friends, might find it possible to join each other for a casual dinner. But not her and Morgan. The only safe topic of conversation for them was the investigation that had brought them together in the first place.

"Nothing like getting right down to business."

She forced down a mouthful of soup, aware that he was watching her every move.

"Okay then." He sighed, setting down his fork. "I need to know certain things so I can get the timetable down right. When did you normally see the Walkers?"

"Tuesday afternoons." She wondered what he was getting at, why this would matter.

"So, if the last time Nan Walker was in your office was last Tuesday, she couldn't have stolen the spare key, since Brenda claims it wasn't missing this Monday."

"I guess that's right. But I thought Nan was off the suspect list already. Didn't you say she has an alibi?"

"Yes, she does. I'm in the process of checking it out, and so far, it's like she says. She went out for lunch from one to one-thirty. The clerk at the café remembers her ordering her sandwich. One of the hardware-store cashiers can verify the time Nan returned because he asked her a question about a malfunctioning cash register."

"That sounds pretty airtight."

"Call me cynical, but it seems almost *too* airtight to me."

"How can an alibi be *too* airtight?"

"Seems planned, that's all. What if she was working with a partner?"

"This is Nan Walker we're talking about, right? I don't know, Morgan. There has to be some other possibility. Do you have any other suspects?"

"I'd love to get a lead on the identity of the lady in

the trench coat. I have to admit, I was hoping you'd come up with something. There are other angles to work on though. Like Lorne Thackray. He's likely to take over as manager of the entire hardware chain now. And he has no alibi for that afternoon. He went out for lunch at one and didn't return until almost three. He claims he ate alone, then went to check prices at some of his competitors in the neighborhood. Did his name come up in any of your sessions with the Walkers?''

"No. We focused on the relationship between Nan and Jerry. The only other person they sometimes talked about was their son.''

"Okay, tell me more about that secretary of yours.''

"Again? She's wonderful. Very organized and dependable. That's why, if she says the keys were there on Monday, I believe her. And if she says she locked up every day, then I'm certain of that, too.''

"You're very trusting. I assume you checked her references before you hired her?''

Trista narrowed her eyes. Was he implying that she was wrong to trust Brenda as much as she did? If so, was it only because he never took anyone at face value, or was there something more concrete behind his question?

"She had all the qualifications for the job, and then some. Plus she had an excellent letter of reference from her previous job.''

"Did you phone her employer to confirm the information?''

"No, I didn't,'' Trista said defensively.

"I see.''

Trista sighed with exasperation. "Why do you ask? Do you know something about her that I don't?''

"I just wondered if you checked her references. It's a fairly common business practice, after all."

Trista flushed under the implied criticism. She felt worse, knowing that he was right. But in this case it hardly mattered, did it? After all, Brenda had worked out perfectly. "Why are you so interested in Brenda? You can't think she's responsible for any of this?"

He didn't answer, just picked up his fork and started eating. She tried to concentrate on her food, but it was impossible to keep her eyes off Morgan for very long. She noticed little things, details she hadn't thought about since she'd left him. The way he held his utensils, as if they were too small for his strong, capable hands. The way he slouched back in his chair slightly as he ate. The way his strong shoulder muscles bulged beneath the thin knit of his navy shirt. Morgan had always looked good in dark colors.

If he was aware of her covert glances, Morgan gave no sign. For once, his penetrating blue eyes were not focused on her. As he ate he glanced around the café casually, but Trista knew that weeks later he would be able to give a precise and accurate description of the restaurant and the people in it—including approximate ages, and educated guesses about what each of them did for a living.

"There was another reason I wanted to talk to you tonight," Morgan admitted when his plate was empty.

"Oh?" She wasn't sure she wanted to hear this.

"To apologize. For getting offtrack at your office. I appreciate that you're trying to cooperate on this case, and I realize that the only way it's going to work is if we avoid personal topics."

"That sounds reasonable." Trista sipped her water, marveling at how cool and calm they were being all of a sudden. What had happened to Morgan's all-consuming anger? She decided she didn't want to know.

"So what do you do at Suni Choopra's campaign headquarters?" Apology over, he now steered the subject matter to neutral ground.

"I'm a volunteer there." She didn't bother to ask how he'd known where she was tonight. With all the information he had on her, she didn't need to.

"Really?" Morgan shot her a puzzled glance. "I don't remember you being interested in politics."

"Things change." Wasn't that an understatement? "I met Suni two years ago. She was knocking on every door in my apartment building, asking how we felt about certain government policies."

Morgan was right. She'd never had much interest in politics. But Suni had struck her as different. Within minutes of meeting, they were sharing a cup of coffee and talking like old friends.

The bond, she'd realized, was loneliness.

Most people would find it impossible to believe someone with a life like Suni's could be lonely. She spent her days and most evenings surrounded by people. Her social calendar was full and her workdays long and varied. Yet Trista had soon realized that Suni had sacrificed many things for her political ambition, including a normal family life, with a husband and children.

"Didn't you say that you met the Walkers at one of Choopra's fund-raising parties?" Morgan asked.

Trista nodded.

"And you started your practice what—two years ago?"

"Yes." Her business was small, compared to the family-counseling practice in Yorkville, a trendy area of Toronto, where she'd worked when she and Morgan were still together. When they were a *family.* But at least it was hers, and it seemed to be successful.

"Kind of ironic, isn't it?"

"What?"

"What you do. Dispensing advice to couples, when your own marriage ended in divorce."

He sounded calm, but she knew there was hostility behind the words. "I agree. Frankly, I prefer individual counseling, but it's not always possible to separate the two. Besides, couples seem to benefit from seeing me. Most of the clients I've seen are still together."

"Really?" He leaned forward, his interest intense. "And what do you tell them? What works for them that didn't work for us?"

Why was he torturing her like this? Asking questions when he knew the answers already? She ought to leave, she knew she should. But maybe, just once, the words needed to be said out loud. "I try to help them talk to each other."

It was more complicated than that, of course. But wasn't noncommunication the crux of the problem? It certainly had been with Morgan and her.

Now he was looking bitter. "I tried, Trista. God knows, I tried."

"I know." Their divorce had been official for almost two years, but still, looking back on that time was more than she could take. "I have to go, Morgan. Talking about this isn't doing either of us any good."

His hand shot out, to grasp her by the arm. "But didn't you just say that's what people need to do? Talk?"

She pulled away from him, grabbing her jacket and her purse. "My advice is for *couples,* Morgan. It's too late for us, and you know it."

Chapter Five

Later that night, as Trista settled into bed, she went over her conversation with Morgan. She remembered everything, down to the smallest detail. Every word he'd spoken, every small look and insignificant gesture. The apology and the way he'd said they'd have to avoid personal topics if they were going to cooperate on the Walker case.

His intentions had been good, but only minutes later he'd blamed her for the breakup of their marriage.

The fact that he was right wasn't the point.

They couldn't work together on this investigation without dredging up the past. The mind couldn't be controlled so easily. A tidal wave of memories threatened to overwhelm her every time she saw his face, heard his voice. And she guessed it was the same for him.

Despite the passing of years, their healing was not complete. The pain was not fresh, but it was persistent, lying in wait beneath the surface, capable of engulfing her if she let down her defenses.

Trista drew the covers up to her neck as if she could block out her memories as effectively as she could the cool night air. Not just the bad ones, but the good ones too. Because happy memories only reminded her of all she'd lost. It was more than any woman could bear. Or any mother.

Trista clenched her hands and stared, wide-eyed, at the bedroom ceiling, thinking of the day when it had all finally ended. Or so she'd thought.

Divorce had seemed the only avenue of escape from her guilt. Regardless of what her therapist had said, she knew her responsibility for the accident would always stand between Morgan and her. So she'd driven to her lawyer's office to sign the papers, wearing a black dress that used to be a favorite, but which she'd never worn since. The beauty of the fresh autumn day had irritated her, and her stomach had almost heaved on the elevator ride to the twenty-sixth floor.

Her lawyer hadn't kept her waiting. She'd been ushered right into his expensively appointed office where the papers had been ready. Morgan had already signed them, and she could still picture the dark upright script of his name against the white background of the legal document. There was a note that Morgan had written, sealed in a separate envelope, but she hadn't read it.

In her cold, dark bedroom Trista felt tears running down her face, and she let them fall unchecked, thinking of all the times she should have cried but couldn't. The day she'd walked out of their house with only her purse and a jacket. The times she'd refused to talk to him when he came to her, alternately pleading and demanding that she come home. The unread letters, the phone messages she'd erased. Each one deserved at least a tear.

Trista Anne Forester. The sight of her name at the bottom of their divorce papers.

Trista's tears turned to sobs and soon her body was shaking with the force of her pent-up grief. For lost innocence. For her lost marriage.

And for the biggest loss of all. Their child.

TELLING HIMSELF he was the world's biggest fool, Morgan sat in his car across from Trista's apartment and kept his eyes on the two rectangles of light on the second floor of the building, until finally they blinked and vanished into darkness.

What was he doing here?

He thought of the moment in the restaurant that night when the bill had come and she'd insisted on paying half. She hadn't looked him in the eye from that point onward. Closing him out. As if she'd ever opened up to him in the first place. Morgan gripped both sides of the steering wheel as if they were the handlebars of a bike, squeezing and twisting with all his might. Sometimes the strength of his impotent fury frightened him. Tonight he was getting a little weary of it. When was it all going to end?

They were divorced. It was time to get on with his own life. She'd walked out on him, not the other way around. Apparently, without their child, she'd found no need to keep their family together.

Andrew. Four years he'd been gone, but he was never far from Morgan's thoughts. Morgan had only to close his eyes to picture his son asleep in his crib, his favorite flannel blanket tucked up under his round baby cheek. If he held out his finger, he could remember the fierce grip of Andrew's small hand only one day after he was born. The sound of a child crying could still turn his head.

He'd died just months after learning to say *cop*. He'd point out every police car on the road and say, "Cop, cop, daddy, cop." There was nothing he'd enjoyed more than riding with Morgan, although the sound of the siren had scared him. After the accident, Morgan had caught himself glancing over his shoulder, at the middle of the back seat where he'd anchored in a strap for Andrew's car seat. It was always a shock to see that vacant space. Almost as hard as facing the empty crib each morning.

He'd sold the crib after Trista left. He'd sold everything.

But that didn't make the emptiness go away. Special days were the worst. Andrew's birthday, Christmas, the first day of school.

Did Trista, like him, sit alone in the dark, imagining what Andrew would have been like, what he'd have been doing, if he were alive? And did she ever wish she had someone to share those thoughts with?

He had no idea. She'd blocked him out completely after the accident. And when she'd moved out, and he'd thought he would go crazy with losing first his son, then his wife, she'd refused to even see him, let alone listen to a word he had to say.

So why did he still feel this need to protect her? It hadn't started with the break-in at her office. Even before then, he'd made a point of knowing where she lived and worked and spent her free time. He'd watched over her. As much as he could. For three years now, ever since she first left him.

But it was time to stop, because it *was* making him crazy. There was no turning back the clock. The old Trista he'd fallen in love with and married was gone. He was a man, a cop, but he hadn't been able to protect his son, and he hadn't been able to help Trista either. For one long year, every time he'd looked in his wife's eyes, all he'd seen was emptiness.

Now she was no longer his wife, and he wasn't sure what he saw in those hazel eyes that had once bewitched him.

In fact, it seemed impossible that the willowy auburn

beauty had ever been his wife. Had she ever said she
loved him, and cradled him in her arms? Lured him into
a bathtub foaming with scented oils? Encouraged him to
talk when his job got him down, cried with him when a
case was particularly heartbreaking? Him, the tough guy
who'd never needed anyone. Until Trista came along.

He thought about her staunch defense of her secretary,
of her loyalty to her friend Suni. So like Trista. Once,
she'd been that way about him, defending him to her
friends who saw him as cold and detached. He may have
appeared that way to them, but with Trista he could never
hold himself back. It was as if she'd found a part of him
that had been missing all his life.

God knows, he'd never found that warmth in the sterile
environment his parents had created. His mother had had
him late in life, and never lost an opportunity to remind
him he hadn't been planned. As soon as he was old
enough, he'd moved out. Shortly thereafter, his parents
had sold the house and retired down south.

They had come back for his wedding. And briefly, for
Andrew's funeral.

Morgan shifted uncomfortably in his seat and glanced
at the digital clock on the dashboard. Eleven o'clock. It
was late and he ought to be getting home. But he thought
about the empty rooms, the empty bed, and changed his
mind, taking a left instead of a right and heading for the
office. He hadn't checked in since this afternoon. Maybe
there'd been some new developments. Sleep seemed all
too elusive, at any rate.

As he drove the few miles to police headquarters, Morgan forced himself to think about the Walker case, pushing thoughts of Trista out of his mind. So far he felt as
though he'd encountered nothing but a number of very
short dead ends. Maybe he needed to change his per-

spective—looking at things from a different angle usually helped.

Maybe he needed to consider the son more closely. It could be Jason wasn't as disinterested in inheriting the family business as his parents had thought. More likely it was the idea of being under mom and dad's thumb that had distressed him. And now, with his father gone and his mother putty in his hands, he'd be in a position of control...

Morgan parked his car and approached the Metropolitan Toronto Police headquarters through the large courtyard on College Street. Above him, the twelve-story tower rose in receding steps, cold glass and metal, with the fluttering form of the Canadian flag flying proudly at the top.

He passed the curved duty desk, then took the elevator to Homicide on the third floor. Too bad Kingston was several hours from Toronto. Otherwise it might have been possible for Jason to slip out after his ten-thirty class, and be back in time to make economics in the afternoon... Morgan shook his head. That he was even considering such a ridiculous theory told him how desperate he was becoming.

He'd intended to stop briefly, just checking for any new reports, but Inspector Zarowin stopped him in the corridor. A chronic insomniac, like him, Zarowin grasped his elbow.

"Let me get you a coffee."

Coffee was not what either of them needed at this hour of the night, but Morgan followed him, settling into a chair as Zarowin poured a foul-smelling brew into two big mugs.

"Pulling a double shift again, Zed?" he asked as Zarowin added sugar and cream to his own mug. "I hope you don't plan on booking any overtime for this."

Zarowin snorted at the comment, then sat down in the chair next to Morgan's. He was about fifteen years older than Morgan's 33 and about as good as they came, in Morgan's opinion. He drove people hard, but he was fair, and intelligent, to boot. "At least I show up every now and then so that people still know I work here."

"Hey, you don't solve crimes sitting on your butt in headquarters," Morgan reminded him.

"You learned that lesson all too well, didn't you? I'm lucky to have caught sight of you at all."

The way he leaned back and settled into his chair, it was clear Zarowin wanted to talk. Morgan felt his jaw clenching, even as he took a taste of the well-aged brew in his mug. Zarowin wasn't the sort to interfere in an investigation. Unless there were special circumstances. And Morgan had a pretty good idea what those circumstances were in this case.

"That was good work on the Blair case you wrapped up on Monday," Zarowin began.

Oh, God. Morgan sank farther into his chair. *He's buttering me up first. It's going to be bad.*

"So how's the Walker case progressing?"

"Slowly. You must have seen the reports."

"I've seen them," Zarowin admitted. "That's what I want to talk about—"

Here it comes!

"I noticed your ex-wife was the Walkers' marriage counselor."

Very sharp. I should have known that her using her maiden name wouldn't have fooled you. "Right."

"Trista. That's her first name, isn't it?"

Morgan felt the sharp eyes of the inspector on him,

and knew Zarowin was gauging his reaction to her name. He tried to remain impassive. "It is."

Zarowin's eyes bore into him for several seconds before he sighed. "You're a good cop, Forester. And I know you wouldn't let personal feelings get in the way of an investigation, but what exactly is Trista's involvement in this case?"

"I don't see her as a suspect, if that's what you're driving at."

"Are you sure about that?"

Morgan drew in his breath. "At the moment there's absolutely no evidence to suggest that she's involved—"

"Forget evidence," Zarowin interrupted. "In cases like this, you have to bend over backward to appear impartial. If you see the secretary as a possible suspect, why not the counselor?"

"But that's ludicrous. What motive would Trista have for killing her own client? Trying to reduce the size of her practice?"

"Cool down, Forester. I hate to suggest this, but what if Trista is the lover we're trying to identify? Unethical, of course, but it's been known to happen…"

Morgan didn't want to listen, but he knew he had to. He had briefly recognized that he was letting his own personal feelings for Trista discount her as a possible suspect. Hearing Zarowin speak, he knew that he was guilty as charged. Still, he knew Trista, and he knew her standards. Never, not in a million years, would she sleep with her own client.

"As I see it," Zarowin gave his ultimatum, "your safest bet is to step down from this case and let me assign another detective."

Morgan hesitated. He knew Zarowin had a point. And being on this case was opening a lot of painful memories.

Not just for him, but for Trista, too. It would be easier on both of them if he were to back off and let them go on trying to rebuild their separate lives.

It was the smart thing to do. Hell, it was the right thing to do, and Morgan opened his mouth to tell Zed it was what he was *going* to do. But the words wouldn't come.

When he started something, he liked to finish it. And besides, if he was off the case, how could he be certain Trista was safe?

It was *not* the smart thing to do. It was probably the *wrong* thing to do, but Morgan knew he had no choice.

"I hear what you're saying, Zed, but I want this case. I *need* this case."

When Zarowin sighed and glanced down at his hands, Morgan knew he'd be given his chance. He couldn't screw up now.

IN HER DREAM she was watching herself, as if the day's events had been videotaped and she was now at home, curled up on the sofa, watching a detective show on television. She saw herself pack a gym bag with sunglasses, hat, gloves and trench coat. Oh, and the gun, of course. Mustn't forget the gun.

She took a taxi downtown. Once there, she went into a major department store. She strolled around for about ten minutes before heading for the bathroom. A few minutes later she emerged, dressed in the trench coat, hat and sunglasses, and left the store, the gym bag safely ensconced in a coin-operated locker. She took another taxi to the motel. You couldn't be too careful.

So far so good. She stood in front of the motel office for a few minutes, gathering her nerve. She had to be cool. She had to be casual. Then she went in.

"Hello. I've locked myself out of my room. My husband and I are registered in room 124. Do you think…"

No problem. The man behind the counter held out the key in front of him. She hadn't liked the look in his eyes. As she reached for it, he deliberately brushed his fingers over hers. Then he licked his lips. She almost panicked at that point. Not because of his obscene gesture, but because she remembered she'd forgotten to put on the gloves. For a second she was tempted to back out. But it was too late for that.

She ignored his leering stare and walked out the door, turning left, following the sidewalk toward the back of the building, counting as she walked. One hundred one, one hundred two, one hundred three… Her low heels scratched against the concrete beneath them. And then, there it was. The four was a little crooked, but it was definitely room 124. Her heart really began to pound then. Her palms were sweaty as she carefully pulled on her gloves before inserting the key, ever so softly, into the lock.

The door opened effortlessly. A radio was playing. She could hear the sound of running water coming from the bathroom. Her hand reached into her pocket and curled into the gun. Squeezing the handle tightly, she slipped into the room, closing the door firmly behind her. She felt a fleeting moment of relief when she saw that the room was empty. Then she spotted the clothing. A pair of trousers. A flannel shirt. Both folded neatly on the dresser by the bed. Her eyes moved to the bathroom door. It was closed.

Slowly, cautiously, she moved across the room. The gun was out of her pocket now. How had that happened? Her hand was on the bathroom-door handle. Channel

*your energy. Remember your mission. In one quick mo-
tion she swung open the door and raised the gun.*

*She couldn't see him clearly. He was in a Jacuzzi tub
that was filled with fluffy white bubbles. The room was
steamy, very steamy, and she had difficulty focusing. She
only barely remembered the five words. She spoke them
quickly and saw the terror in his eyes as she fired the
gun. He was scrambling now, trying to get out of the
slippery tub, and she realized that she hadn't hit him, or
else she'd only wounded him. She fired again. And again.
But her shots couldn't stop him. He kept coming toward
her. Why wouldn't he die?*

Chapter Six

A loud thud woke Trista out of a fitful slumber. She sat up in her bed, heart pounding. Normally she wasn't one to worry about strange nighttime noises, but given all that had happened lately, she couldn't help but feel anxious.

She sat still for several minutes, trying to convince herself that either she'd imagined the sound, or it had been something innocent, like a neighbor's cat pouncing on the balcony that ran out front of her one-bedroom apartment.

But the thud had been loud. Cats didn't come that heavy. Another thing—pets weren't permitted in this building.

After seconds of silence she heard footsteps. Someone was out there. Someone with two feet, not four paws.

Trembling, she reached for the bedside phone and Morgan's card, which lay beside it. In the dim glow from the alarm clock she could make out the seven-digit number in the bottom right-hand corner. She punched in the numbers and almost sobbed with relief when Morgan answered on the first ring.

"It's me, Trista," she whispered into the receiver. "I think I hear someone on my balcony. What should I do?"

"Get out right now." He spoke in short, clipped words. "Go to a neighbor's."

"But I don't know any—"

"Get out, Trista," he repeated. "I'll be there in about ten minutes. I'm on my way now."

The phone was still to her ear when he hung up. She looked at the digital display of the clock and saw that it was past midnight. The sounds had stopped, but she couldn't quell the fear that churned in her stomach.

Easy for Morgan to tell her to get out of the apartment, but where should she go? She shared this floor with three other neighbors but they were all elderly. Should she wake them? Maybe if she just went down to the lobby, she could wait for him there.

Her mind made up, she slipped out of bed. She didn't dare turn on the light, so she stumbled awkwardly to the dresser. Yanking open a drawer, she searched by feel and located a thick cotton sweatshirt. She pulled, ignoring the tumble of clothing cascading out with it. Slipping it over the delicate silk teddy she'd worn to bed, she cast about for her jeans, then remembered belatedly that they were sitting folded in a pile of laundry on the dining-room table.

She went into the dark hall, stretching her hands to either side, feeling her way along the walls until she came to the living area of her apartment. It was lighter here, thanks to the sheer curtains that only partially obscured the glow of the streetlights outside. Heart pounding, she made her way to the table, slinking along the wall, not wanting to be seen by anyone lurking outside.

As she stretched a hand toward the laundry, she shot an anxious look outside, just in time to see a dark shape run past the glass door, grip the wooden railing and vault out into space.

"*Oh my God!*" The reality of the situation hit her then. Her body began to tremble and she had to grip the edge of the table so as not to fall down. Logic told her the intruder was gone now, but her emotions were still focused on the fact that only a pane of glass and about fifteen feet had stood between her and the potential danger. Her shaking increased as she thought about it, and she sank onto the carpet, hugging her arms around her knees. The break-in at her office had at least been free of human form. She could handle an open drawer much better than a human shape out on her balcony.

"Trista?" It was minutes later, and she was still squatting at the same spot on the floor, when she heard a voice and the sound of loud knocking against the steel front door.

"Trista?"

Recognizing Morgan's voice, she worked her way to a standing position, her legs numb from lack of circulation. She went to the door and, with shaky fingers, unbolted the lock, then felt the door pull open without any effort from herself.

"Are you all right? Why didn't you leave?" Morgan breezed past her into the room, poised for action with his right hand holding a very serious-looking black pistol. After a quick glance around the room, he turned back to her, the questions in his eyes fading as he registered her obvious distress.

"You're pale as a ghost. And shivering." Some of his tension, the readiness for action, dissipated.

"What happened?" He tucked the gun out of sight, then placed a hand on her shoulder.

"He left." The words seemed to wobble as they left her mouth. "I saw him jump over the balcony shortly after I called you."

Gently, Morgan led her to the sofa and eased her into it, before moving toward the window. Finding the outdoor electrical switch behind the full-length drapes, he turned it on, flooding the exterior with light. "These locks are pathetic," was his only comment as he opened the door that led out to the balcony. Trista watched him pace the length of it, leaning over the railing to look below. When he came back, he was shaking his head.

"Who ever it was has managed to make a pretty clean getaway. Did you get much of a look?"

Trista shook her head. "Not really. All I saw was a dark human shape."

"Could you tell if it was male or female?"

"Not really. I guess I assumed it was male. He looked pretty large to me, maybe that was why." Trista pulled her legs up and rested her chin on them, tensing her muscles, trying to stop the trembling. She felt Morgan rest his hand on her shoulder again and instinctively she closed her eyes, trying to will away an unaccountable desire to weep.

"It's okay, Trista. You're safe now."

His words were so gentle, his touch so comforting, it made her want to cry all the more. She bit the inside of her cheek. Hard. And took a deep breath.

"Thanks for coming so quickly."

"No problem. I was in my car when you called, on my way home."

She took another breath. It was a little less shaky this time. What she needed was a drink.

As if privy to her inner thoughts, he asked, "Could I get you something?"

She nodded and started to get up. "A brandy. I'll—"

"No. Stay put." He applied firm pressure to her shoulder. "Tell me where to look."

"Same place. In the cupboard over the fridge." Her words hung in the quiet night air, along with the implications of familiarity, of common history. She saw the light come on in the kitchen, heard the cupboard door open, then bang closed. A few more doors were opened, and less than a minute passed before he returned with two snifters of their favorite orange brandy.

He handed her one of them, then stood in front of her, eyes narrowed, watching as she took her first sip. She felt her hand tremble as she removed the crystal goblet from her lips and cursed herself for shaking like a schoolgirl at her first piano recital. Maybe Morgan would put it down to delayed shock. But her fear was already dissipating and she knew it was having him so close, in such an intimate setting, that made her nervous. It was still dark in the room—they hadn't turned on any of the lights, except for the one in the kitchen. But her eyes were beginning to adjust and she could see him quite clearly now.

The pale light from the windows threw stark shadows across his face, emphasizing the sharp angle of his cheekbones, the straight line of his nose, the determined set of his jaw. He looked tired, but that was often when she found him at his most attractive—*had* found him, she meant. Coming home from a late shift, dark stubble on his chin, the stamp of danger from the street still clinging to him. So often he'd woken her, needing the sanctuary she offered, and she loved those dark passionate nights most of all.

Had. Trista repeated the word to herself, emphasizing the past tense, drawing a halt to the senseless reminiscing. This is what she had been afraid would happen if she saw too much of him. She would remember...she *was* remembering. Suddenly she became aware of her own disheveled appearance. Hair tangled and tousled. Not a trace of makeup. This old rag of a sweatshirt. And no jeans. Lord, she'd forgotten.

Morgan was standing by the entertainment unit now. He probably hadn't noticed.

Fat chance. Morgan noticed everything.

"Could you toss me my jeans? They're on the table."

He glanced at her then, his gaze sliding slowly down the length of her legs.

Awkwardly she shifted in her seat, tugging the sweatshirt around her bottom. A moment later, he tossed the folded denim jeans onto her lap. The cushion beside her caved in as Morgan sat down beside her, close enough that she could feel the heat of his body. She took another sip of brandy, closing her eyes to savor the warmth as it flowed into her still-weak limbs.

"You were out late," she said. She had this crazy urge to snuggle in close and lean her head on his shoulder. Dangerous thoughts. Morgan was the last place she had any right to look for comfort.

"Hazard of the trade." He leaned forward, supporting his forearms on his thighs, so that she couldn't see his expression. Instead, she concentrated on the muscles in his arm, the way each individual one was clearly outlined beneath his darkly tanned skin. He'd obviously kept up his sessions at the gym. She looked at the thigh muscles straining at the cotton of his trousers. Maybe even increased them.

"Do you think he was after the Walker file again?"

"No doubt." He swirled the amber liquid in his glass. "When he couldn't find it at the office, he must have thought you were keeping it close to you."

"But why does he want it so badly? I tell you, there's nothing there—"

"But there must be, Trista. You'll have to look again." Oh God. When would this ever be over?

"I called the office on my way over. The I-dent guys should be here shortly. If we're lucky, maybe we'll pick up a print on the railing." From his glum expression, Trista thought he didn't think it was likely.

"Frustrating, isn't it?"

He turned to look at her then. "Yeah," he agreed, his eyes lowering to her legs. "Frustrating."

Trista swallowed. She'd have to stand to pull on her jeans, and already she felt utterly exposed beneath his gaze. Intimacy hung in the air, cloaked in darkness and smelling like brandy. She knew Morgan still felt anger and resentment toward her, but that wasn't what she saw in his eyes right now.

She became mesmerized by his finger as it stroked the lip of his brandy goblet. He'd turned his head away from her again, and was back to examining the contents of his glass, but she still felt a trace of fire burning the trail of his glance down her legs. The warmth burned through her body, and had nothing to do with the brandy she'd been drinking. It had been a long, long time since she'd felt this way. She took another sip of her drink. And another.

"Drinking doesn't make it go away." Morgan's voice

was deep and low beside her. He was practically whispering in her ear. "I've tried that already." He touched her half-empty glass with his empty one before setting it down on the coffee table.

Trista's heart thumped at his words. How had he guessed what she was feeling? Once he'd been able to tune in to her emotions easily. But after what had happened, after all these years, she couldn't believe the link between them was still there.

He was looking at her again, his eyes like a caress over her face, her hair, the length of her body, and back to her legs. She could feel the sensual power of his gaze sending out the message of his desire, a message her body interpreted and responded to with ease.

She felt an inner power that she could still arouse desire in him. An amazement that the attraction that had always worked between them was so resilient. Her skin tingled, as if he touched her, but he only looked, and she trembled with a passion she'd thought she'd never feel again.

"What's under your sweatshirt, Trista?"

His words were more erotic than any touch could ever be. And his eyes burned as brightly as if he could already see the silk teddy she was wearing underneath. It was impossible not to imagine how he would burn if she pulled up the cotton covering. Her body throbbed at the thought of his eyes on her breasts, barely covered by the lace bodice, or the upper portion of her thighs, revealed by the French cut of the legs.

She knew what would happen then. She would be giving him permission for something that every inch of her body was eagerly and desperately wanting.

"Take it off, Trista." His voice was a groan, and her

insides stirred in response. But she didn't answer. She was too busy fighting the urge to lift the hem and pull the shirt over her head. Her fingers wrapped around the cotton band, twisting into the fabric, as she tried desperately to find reason in this night of insanity. Beside her she felt Morgan's heat rising. Beneath the cotton of his shirt his shoulder and arm muscles tensed and released.

He was close enough she could smell the brandy richness of his breath. If she moved forward, her lips would press against the rough skin of his cheek…

She felt his hand wrap around her own, gasped at the sensual feel of his fingers on hers.

"You're spilling," he said, gently easing the goblet out of her hand and setting it down beside his.

"Oh." He was even closer now. His lips just millimeters from her own. She pressed hers together, dampened them with her tongue, parted them slightly. Waiting. Waiting.

"Show me what you're wearing," he said again, reaching for the hand she had woven into her sweatshirt hem. He squeezed it gently, pulled her other hand down to join it.

He was still asking her permission, and the knowledge both warmed her heart and ignited her passion. Her fingers tightened their hold in the fabric, she felt them go numb from the pressure. Closing her eyes, she heard a low moan escape her lips, before she clamped them shut, astounded at the depth of her own desire.

"I can't." The admission escaped from her, and she felt the letdown deep within her as every nerve cell protested the decision.

Morgan closed his eyes briefly and took a deep, ragged breath. "God, Trista." The words came from somewhere deep in his throat. Slowly he pulled away from her and she saw that his passion was being churned into fury. "Can't? Or won't?"

She swallowed, looking away from his anger. She couldn't blame him. She'd created this situation as much as he had. Maybe more. "I didn't do this intentionally, Morgan."

"Didn't do what intentionally?" He stood up, putting distance between them. "Turn me on? Or get turned on by me? Or are you going to pretend you don't want me?"

She shook her head soundlessly, knowing that nothing she said would do any good now. Of all the ways to deal with their past disappointments, having a sexual encounter now would definitely be the worst. It didn't matter how much they wanted each other. With daylight would come regret and the same anger and guilt that kept them apart.

Her therapist had suggested she set a meeting with her ex-husband, to discuss their past issues. She knew she might have suggested the same thing to a client herself.

How easy to prescribe the right treatment for someone else!

But she'd known there was no remedying the hurts between them. Morgan's chances for happiness would be better with someone new.

Of course, she hadn't counted on a murder investigation bringing them together again.

A knock on the door signaled the arrival of the men who would examine her apartment for any evidence of the intruder. Trista scurried into the bedroom to put on her jeans while Morgan answered the door and explained the situation. When she came out, he was ready to leave.

"They won't be long," he told her. "Then you can go back to bed."

Trista despised herself for feeling afraid, but she was. "What if he comes back?" she asked quietly.

Morgan paused on the threshold, his head bowed. After a few moments he swung around, reluctantly, to face her.

"Is there someplace you could stay tonight? Maybe one of your neighbors would let you use their couch?"

"That isn't an option."

"Okay." He was quiet for a few moments, considering the alternatives. "I guess you'd better come with me, then."

"But where will we go?"

"I'll book you into a hotel for the night."

She nodded. "Okay. Just give me a minute."

Morgan turned abruptly away. "I'll wait in the hall."

Trista grabbed her purse and keys. Morgan waited while she locked the door, then kept several strides ahead of her as they left the building and headed for his car. Neither of them spoke as he unlocked the passenger door, then walked round to the other side. Trista sank into her seat, fastening the seat belt and scrunching herself as close to the door as possible.

They'd decided to try the Westin downtown when Morgan's pager beeped. Quickly he pulled out his cell phone and called in.

"Detective Forester here." He listened intently for a few moments. Then, "Not another one."

The words, the despair in his voice as he said them, made Trista's heart plummet. Please, no, not another homicide.

"Where was he killed?"

Oh, God.

"The Moondust Motel? Yeah, I know. It's over on Eglinton and the Don Valley. Sure.'' Morgan ended the conversation and shot an impatient glance her way. Trista knew what he was thinking. Driving downtown and checking her into a hotel was going to delay him twenty to thirty minutes.

"Why don't you go straight there?'' she suggested. "I'm not ready to sleep yet, anyway. There's a Holiday Inn in that part of town. I can call for a cab to take me there.''

Morgan thumped his hand against the steering wheel before turning back to her, obviously torn between his need to get rid of her and his need to get to the scene of the crime as soon as possible. "Sure you don't mind?''

"Not at all.''

WHOEVER'S KILLING these men sure has an incredible sense of timing, Morgan thought as he walked toward the latest homicide victim, carefully avoiding the shards of broken glass that littered the rose-colored carpet. He was in the bathroom of room 124 at the Moondust Motel. He'd left Trista in the car, waiting for the cab he'd called for her.

The room was large, with a step-up hot tub as well as the standard shower, sink and toilet one would expect. The homicide victim—another middle-aged man—was sprawled face first in the large hot tub. The bathwater had turned a dark pink color from the blood. Unlike the last victim, this one had taken several shots before he'd finally succumbed. From the man's position, Morgan guessed that he'd been trying to scramble out of the tub when the last, fatal shot had found him.

Beside the tub on one of the steps was a bottle of wine,

sitting in a container of what had once been ice but was now a pool of water. One wineglass rested on its side. The other had been broken, and now littered the bathroom floor.

There was a faint scum on the edge of the tub. Morgan scanned the counter and stopped at an opened container of bubble bath. The bottle was almost empty.

"The man's upper body was probably covered in bubbles," Morgan speculated, speaking aloud to nobody in particular. "That might explain why it took so many shots to kill him."

"Good thinking." Kendal, the same I-dent officer who'd been on duty for the Walker homicide gave Morgan an impressed look.

"Have we identified the victim yet?"

"They're examining his clothing now, I think," Kendal replied. "We only got here five minutes before you did. Seems the door was left ajar and a dog from room 123 nosed his way in here. His owner came running when he heard the dog barking."

Great. Now they would have doggy prints to contend with, along with everything else. Morgan left the bathroom, with its large hot tub, mirrored ceiling and plush carpet, and returned to the bedroom, which was dominated by a large king-size bed. Above the bed was yet another mirrored ceiling. The sheets had been turned down, presumably by the motel staff, so Morgan could see they were red satin. Room 124 at this motel was obviously intended for one purpose and one purpose only. And that wasn't a good night's sleep.

"What's this, the honeymoon suite?" Morgan asked the man who was meticulously unfolding the dead man's clothing.

"Some honeymoon." The man snorted. "According to the desk clerk, this room sees more action in the afternoons than in the evenings. Does that answer your question?"

"I guess it does."

And it was another one of the similarities between this situation and the Walker case that made it impossible to conclude they weren't related.

Two middle-class, middle-aged men shot dead in a motel room in a compromising situation—well, it was kind of obvious. But all those shots bothered him. Walker had been killed very precisely, with one bullet. Of course, the bubbles might explain the sloppiness of this murder. And the room had probably been steamy...

A movement by the door caught his eye, and Morgan looked up to see Trista step into the room. He frowned, and gestured at her to go back to the car, but she ignored him.

"Is he in there?" she asked, pointing toward the open door of the bathroom, her eyes wide and frightened.

He nodded curtly, aware that the other officer in the room was watching her curiously. "Come on, Trista. Get back in the car. You don't want anything to do with this."

"That's true," she said, suddenly standing taller. "But you're the one who told me I didn't have any choice in the matter. You said I was involved no matter how much I wished I wasn't."

"Nice to see you're recovering from your shock," Morgan muttered under his breath. In a way, he was glad to see the fear and vulnerability gone from her eyes. It meant she didn't pull his protector strings quite so strongly. Although she'd managed to pull a few other strings earlier. He felt the old anger boiling inside as he thought of how easily he'd let her get to him. After all that had happened, you'd think he'd have known better. He *ought* to have known better.

"Do you think there's any connection with Jerry's murder?" Trista asked from her position at the door.

"Probably," Morgan said bluntly before asking the officer. "Have you ID'd him yet?"

The man glanced down at the driver's license he held in his gloved hand. "Daniel Hawthorne, forty-eight years old, brown hair, brown eyes."

"Daniel Hawthorne?" Trista echoed, her expression stricken.

"What's the matter, Trista?"

She leaned against the door frame for support. "I knew him, Morgan. He and his wife, Sylvia, were also clients of mine."

Chapter Seven

The homicides were related all right. Morgan collapsed into his chair and looked with bleary eyes at the reports that were already flooding his desk. Mentally he tallied the similarities. Both men had been at a motel in the early afternoon, signed in under false names, and according to the respective desk clerks, both men had been there before. The description of the woman they'd come to meet was also identical: trench coat, hat, sunglasses...

To clinch matters, both men had been shot by a Smith & Wesson .38, and Morgan had no doubt that ballistics testing would confirm that the same revolver was used in each crime. In fact, the only difference seemed to be the number of shots taken to kill the second victim, and the bubbles and steam in the bathroom probably accounted for that discrepancy.

Most damning of all, both men had been clients of Trista's. And he was just too bloody tired to figure out the implications of that right now.

Instead, Morgan thought about the scenarios surrounding each homicide. Walker had been cooking a spaghetti dinner, had set a romantic table and opened a nice bottle of red wine. Hawthorne had run a bubble bath in a huge tub and had obviously been expecting company to share his bottle of wine. Same vintage, and year, as the one at the Walker homicide scene.

Both situations suggested that there was a romantic as well as a sexual aspect to the relationship with the unknown lover. The question was, had both men been seeing the same woman? It seemed likely, given the wine and the similar descriptions of the woman, yet it was not necessarily so. Morgan was always careful not to jump to conclusions. Maybe, he hoped, something would turn up in their investigation of this latest killing that would help identify the mystery woman.

Which brought his thoughts back to Trista. This added link to her office would put her even higher on the suspect list. Her and that secretary of hers—Brenda Malachowski.

Zarowin's warning rang in the back of his mind and he wondered how Trista would react if she knew she was a suspect.

She'd ended up sending the cabby away last night, and he hadn't been able to drop her off at the Holiday Inn until about four in the morning. She was probably exhausted today, but he was willing to bet she'd taken a cab to work and arrived at her usual time, nonetheless.

He thought again about what had happened earlier in her apartment, or what had *almost* happened. He knew he hadn't imagined her desire. It had been as strong as his own, or pretty damn close. Yet she'd managed to tame it, deny it, the way you might twist a key in the ignition of a car, killing the engine. Knowing Trista, he wasn't surprised she had the strength to do this. But it made him hate her, just a little bit more, all the same.

TRISTA OPENED the file on her desk, but all she could think about was Daniel Hawthorne's murder. How was

Sylvia going to react when she heard the news about her husband? Sylvia was domineering and manipulative, but Trista knew that she loved her husband intensely—almost obsessively. Would his death be enough to put her over the edge?

Added to the trauma of losing her husband would be the pain of having confirmed her own suspicion that Daniel had been having an affair. Trista shuddered, thinking about the effect such a double shock could have.

She stared at the page in front of her, seeing nothing but a long body covered with a white sheet. Even sitting in the car, she'd seen enough to give her nightmares for a month. She'd watched them carry out the body, the bag containing all his belongings…images she'd probably carry with her for the rest of her life. She'd listened through the open window to all the speculations and estimates, including the coroner's best guess at time of death. He'd put it at some time early in the afternoon, which meant that she could have been talking to Sylvia the very second Daniel was being shot!

And to think how casually she'd counseled his wife to wait and talk to him later that night.

Exhausted, Trista laid her head down on her desk. There would be no more talks between Sylvia and her husband now. Just as her eyes began to drift closed, the significance of what she'd just been thinking suddenly struck her, and she sat upright again.

She had to call Morgan to let him know she'd been talking to Sylvia. How ironic if it turned out that she would be the alibi in this case. Trista dialed quickly. A recorded message came on after two rings. Frustrated, she left a message for him to call her back.

She hung up once again, and gave in to despair. What was she going to do? First Jerry Walker. Now Daniel

Hawthorne. She'd done her best to pass off the break-in at her office as coincidence, but this was too much. There had to be a connection, and it frustrated and scared her that she had no idea what that connection could be. She remembered Morgan's questions about Brenda, how funny he'd been about her not checking Brenda's references properly. Was she the missing link? It seemed too crazy to be true.

But if it wasn't Brenda, then who was it? And more important, did Daniel's murder mark the end of it, or were more people on the death list? Trista's heart hammered in her chest.

Surely not. But so many strange things had been happening. Maybe it would be safer if she closed her office for a while. Until she had some idea what was going on here, and why. Besides, she wasn't in the proper condition to work these days. It wasn't just being worried sick about the murders, but having to deal with Morgan, too. The combination was exacting a toll on her own mental health.

She walked out to reception and explained her decision to close the office to Brenda. She asked her to cancel all their appointments for the next few days and take a paid holiday.

"Would you also drop a copy of that list you made for Detective Forester on my desk on your way out?" She wanted to see exactly which people might have had the opportunity to steal the key to their office. Now that her own apartment seemed to be a target, she was ready to take this much more seriously.

Before they finished, Brenda commented, "By the way, those men still haven't showed up to change our locks. Do you want me to phone security about it?"

"Don't bother. I'll look into it," Trista decided. First

thing Wednesday morning she'd asked Joe to have the locks to her office changed. She'd expected the work to be completed by now, but Joe had probably put down the entire episode to squirrels and hadn't taken her request seriously.

After a pointed telephone discussion with the security man on duty, Trista hung up the phone dissatisfied. Tomorrow was the soonest they could get the locks changed, and as far as she was concerned that just wasn't good enough. Now she was doubly glad she'd decided to close the office for the next few days.

Ten minutes later, when Brenda brought her the list, Trista was surprised to see that Sylvia Hawthorne was included. She placed the tip of her index finger next to the name.

"Are you sure about Sylvia? I saw her Wednesday, not Tuesday."

"She was here Tuesday, too," Brenda insisted. "She didn't have an appointment, she just barged in. I would have been out at lunch, but I had some phone calls to make."

"What did she want?"

"She said to talk to you, although she wasn't willing to wait half an hour until you were finished with your client."

Trista folded the list and placed it in her purse. Funny that Sylvia hadn't mentioned anything about the earlier visit when she'd been in on Wednesday. Another thing Trista would have to remember to tell Morgan.

THE HAWTHORNES' HOME was located in the prestigious central Toronto area of Forest Hill. Stately maple and oak trees graced the streets. The homes—mansions, more like—were set back on the lots, giving the impression of country estates.

As Morgan pulled into the Hawthornes' circular driveway, he thought about the information they'd compiled on them so far. Daniel had been a university professor. Sylvia didn't work. There was no way they could have afforded this address on salary alone. Sylvia had inherited the house, as well as a substantial amount of money, when her father died about five years ago. Up until that time they'd lived in a modest bungalow in Leaside, another Toronto neighborhood.

Morgan got out of his car and headed up the walkway to the arched oak doors at the front of the house. He had a vague impression of curtains moving from the front window as he walked past. A deep breath steadied him before he rang the bell.

No one liked this part of the job. He could've easily assigned someone else to do it for him. But he'd never believed in avoiding the dirty work. And anyway, there was an important reason for him to be here. He wanted to see Daniel's wife's reaction when he told her about the murder.

Sylvia Hawthorne answered the door dressed in a fashionable sweat suit in various shades of purple. From the sheen, the fabric looked like silk. She was not overweight, but she was a large woman with a stocky build and no discernible waistline. Her hair was black, and her eyes, which registered a polite curiosity, were also black. Uncannily black.

"I'm sorry to bother you, Mrs. Hawthorne. My name is Morgan Forester. I'm a detective with the metro police department. I'm afraid I have some bad news for you."

"Bad news?" Sylvia Hawthorne stepped aside, her

skin suddenly pale in the light of the foyer. "Let's go to the den, if you don't mind."

"Fine." He rubbed his shoes against the bristles of the front mat and stepped inside. Sylvia led him to a dark room of leather and wood that looked like the setting for *Masterpiece Theater.*

"I assume this has something to do with my husband? He didn't come home last night. The first time in twenty-six years of marriage. I called all the hospitals last night, so I know he didn't have an accident. Have you found him? Is he all right?"

She gestured for Morgan to sit down in the chair next to hers. Her eyes were bright and focused on him intently, but dark circles suggested she'd been up all night. He cleared his throat. There was no easy way to say what he had to say.

"No, he's not. We found him late last night at the Moondust Motel."

Sylvia flinched.

"He'd been shot, Mrs. Hawthorne. He didn't suffer very long. I'm sorry." Morgan watched Sylvia close her eyes and clench her jaw tightly. He was trained to pick up on the smallest sign that she already knew her husband was dead, however, her reaction was giving nothing away. If indeed she had anything to give away. When she finally opened her eyes, her expression was full of pain and grief, and Morgan felt his own heart constrict with the knowledge that his words had brought another person the sort of agony he knew only too well.

"Some lunatic?" Sylvia spoke in a low voice, controlling her tears.

Morgan shook his head. "We don't think so. We suspect it was someone he knew."

Sylvia swallowed. "That's ridiculous. If you knew my

husband you would know that he had no enemies. Unless…''

''Yes?''

Sylvia turned away from him, staring unseeingly out the window to the street beyond. ''About six months ago I found out my husband was having an affair. He agreed to stop seeing her, we went to counseling…

''Just this week I suspected he might have started seeing her again. Yesterday he canceled our lunch because of an unscheduled faculty meeting. Yet, when I called the university, I was told there was no meeting.'' She looked back at Morgan. ''You found him at a motel?''

Once again Morgan nodded.

She closed her eyes briefly, pain convoluting the features of her face. ''Do you know who the woman was?''

''No.'' Morgan paused before continuing. ''Do you?''

Sylvia's ebony eyes seemed to burn for a second before she lowered them to her clasped hands. ''I have no idea.''

''You said you were seeing a marriage counselor…''

Sylvia inclined her head, acknowledging the unspoken insinuation. ''That was months ago. I thought things were better.''

''You and Mr. Hawthorne didn't have children?''

Sylvia's lips drew down. ''No. We couldn't.''

''I'm sorry.''

''Yes. So am I. So was Daniel. He had a low sperm count, you see.'' A trace of bitterness crept into Sylvia's voice. ''I could have had children with someone else. But I loved Daniel. I stuck by him. And how does he repay me?''

Morgan sat back and waited. Some people wound themselves up. All you had to do was listen.

''I could've had affairs, too, Detective. I've had my

opportunities, believe me. But I didn't. And do you know why? Because I loved my husband.''

Her voice broke, and she stood. Slowly she walked over to the desk at the corner of the room and rested her hands on it, lowering her head so that he couldn't see her face. Morgan couldn't help feeling her grief was genuine, but still there was something about Sylvia that set his instincts on alert.

As he left, Morgan told her to be sure and call if she thought of anything else that might be relevant. In his car, a bag he'd picked up from Walker's Hardware that morning reminded him of the next job on his list. Now that the interview with Sylvia Hawthorne was out of the way, he might as well get at it. He knew he wouldn't relax until it was taken care of.

On the way, he checked his messages. As soon as he heard Trista's voice, he dialed her number. At her office he got a recording: *"Trista Emerson's office will be closed until further notice. If you'd like to leave a message—"*

Impatiently, Morgan hung up and tried her home number. When he got her answering machine there he hung up. Where the hell was she? And what was this information she had that she thought was so important?

THE MINUTE TRISTA OPENED her apartment door, she sensed something was wrong. Pausing, her hand still on the door handle, she listened. There it was again, a strange tapping sound. Coming from her bedroom.

Oh, no. Not again. She was just about to make a quiet retreat when she heard her name.

''Trista, is that you?''

Morgan. The tension drained from her body and she felt a moment of relief. Then she wondered what in the world he was doing here. Was he checking up on her? Or worse, snooping behind her back?

"Yes, it's me," she called back. "The person who *lives* here." As she spoke, she shut the door behind her and followed the sound of his voice.

"About time you showed up. I got your message, but couldn't reach you at the office or at home. So I decided I'd better come over here and check things out for myself."

"I had lunch with Suni, then ran a few errands." She paused at the bedroom door. She'd been expecting a return message from Morgan on her machine when she got home—not his physical presence.

"What on earth are you doing?"

He was leaning out of the window, screwdriver in hand. His sport coat was strewn across the cream cotton of her bedspread, and the sleeves of his black shirt were rolled up to his elbows.

Morgan spared her a quick, impatient glance. "Installing window locks. What does it look like? You already know how easy it is for someone to climb up to your balcony. And these windows of yours are so simple to break into, even a kid could do it. I've already taken care of your patio door. This is the last. It would be much easier if you'd hold this damn window open for me, though. It keeps crashing down on my head."

Reluctantly Trista stepped forward. "You didn't need to do this."

He ignored her protestation, instead guiding her hands to the bottom of the heavy wooden window. "That's right. Hold it up as high as you can while I attach this mechanism to the bottom of the frame."

She tried to avoid touching him, but it was impossible. His back pressed against her side as he fussed with aligning the screws. Despite the layers of clothing separating them, it was impossible not to feel the straining of his muscles, the seductive warmth of his body heat.

Against her will her body responded. Her breathing became shallow and fast. Her heart raced. Her body throbbed and tingled much as it had last night, no matter how hard she tried to deny it. Morgan shifted his position. Now the arm that had pressed against her shoulder brushed gently against the side of her breast, and Trista pulled away as suddenly as if she'd been scalded by hot water.

"Watch it!" Morgan grabbed at the frame a split second before it landed on the back of his skull.

"Sorry." She repositioned herself and took a fresh grip on the window, turning her head away from him so she couldn't watch him work. She stared at the dresser on the wall in front of her, her gaze traveling up the large oval mirror, stopping suddenly as she caught his look in the reflection. For a second he paused and she read in his expression a hint of the smoldering passion she'd seen there last night. So he felt it, too.

In the space of a second his expression changed, turning cold and hard. He looked at her the way she imagined a murderer might look at his victim before he squeezed the trigger. It wasn't just anger. He despised her. Maybe even hated her. She felt her insides turn to ice, shocked and frightened by the intensity of his emotion. She looked away from the mirror, turning her glance even higher, concentrating on the patterns in the stippled ceiling.

"Will you please tell me why you're doing this? You're not my husband anymore. It's not up to you to look after me."

"Thanks for pointing that out." He twisted the screwdriver one more time, then threw it on the bed. "You can let go now."

Trista rubbed the circulation back into her arms as he showed her how the new lock worked.

"Thanks," she said hesitantly, turning her back as he reached for his jacket. After a few seconds of silence she glanced over her shoulder and found him standing, arms crossed over his chest.

"How do you do it?" he asked, his voice bitter. "You really couldn't care less, could you? About me, or our marriage…"

"Always so quick to pass judgment, aren't you, Morgan? You have no idea how I feel—"

"Oh don't I? Didn't I lose a child, too?"

Chapter Eight

Trista stared at Morgan, stricken. He put a hand to his forehead.

"I don't know why I said that. I'm sorry, Trista."

Why should he apologize? It was true. She wasn't the only one who'd lost a child. What Morgan didn't seem to realize was that she'd never forgotten that he'd lost his son because of *her*.

"Let's go sit in the kitchen." Morgan placed a tentative hand on her shoulder. "We need to talk."

He was trying to make peace, to call a truce between them. She followed him dully, and sat at the counter as he perused the fridge.

"How about a glass of juice?"

"Sure."

He poured two glasses.

Trista took a sip, then a deep breath. "How did you get in?"

"Through the window," He gave her a half-sheepish, half-roguish grin that reminded her painfully of the man he'd been when they'd first met. It had been passion that first drew them together, and she knew that passion was still under the surface between them. A danger, but only one of many. She looked away, trying to harden her heart against him.

"Isn't that against the law?"

"Aren't you the one who used to tell me things aren't always black and white?"

That reminded her of their university days again. He'd dropped out of law school for that very reason. Morgan wasn't keen on the color gray.

"Don't worry," he said. "I won't be able to do it again now that you have proper locks on your windows."

Trista rolled her eyes. "And I thought you had important police business to do this morning."

"I did." Morgan downed his juice in one swallow, then set down the glass. "I went to talk to Daniel Hawthorne's widow right after I called you."

"And—?"

"Well, it's never easy, as you know. If she had a hand in his murder, she wasn't giving anything away. Despite the affair, she said she really loved her husband, and I couldn't help but believe her."

Trista nodded. "She loved her husband almost to the point of obsession. If he wasn't where he was supposed to be when he was supposed to be, she would lose her grip on reality. And yet, despite her strong feelings, she was continually critical of him."

"Do you think she could have killed him?"

"I don't know how to answer that. I guess I could see her killing someone more than I could see Nan doing it. But it doesn't really matter, because she *couldn't* have. That was what I was phoning to tell you. Sylvia was in my office yesterday between one and one-thirty. She and her husband had stopped seeing me about three months ago and this was the first time I'd seen her since then."

"Between one and one-thirty," Morgan mused. "That

could well provide her with an alibi for her husband's murder. But if she and her husband were no longer clients, what was she doing in your office?''

"It is strange," Trista agreed. "She was upset because Daniel canceled their lunch engagement on account of an unexpected faculty meeting. She phoned the university and discovered there was no meeting.''

"He canceled his class to meet our mystery lover at the Moondust Motel," Morgan confirmed.

"Obviously her suspicion about him resuming his affair was true. I have another curious piece of information for you. Brenda told me Sylvia was also at our office on Tuesday around one. Supposedly she wanted to talk with me, but when I saw Sylvia on Wednesday she didn't mention a word about it…''

Morgan pulled out his pad and made a note. "So she could have taken the key. By the way, where was Brenda when Sylvia came to your office on Wednesday?''

Trista frowned, not wanting to give him the answer. The fact that Brenda happened to be on lunch break at the times of the two murders was a coincidence. But she knew better than to expect Morgan to believe that.

"Well?'' he pressed.

"Another long lunch break. But so what? Brenda often takes a two-hour lunch when she's meeting someone. Other days she brings her lunch and doesn't take a break at all.''

"It's not the length of her workday that I'm worried about.''

"You can't seriously suspect Brenda?'' She made the objection out of a sense of loyalty to her secretary, not admitting to Morgan that she herself had considered whether or not Brenda might be the connection between the two murdered men.

"Well, when I asked her for an alibi for Monday afternoon she said she didn't have one. If she was meeting someone for lunch, don't you think she would have told me about it?"

"It doesn't sound good, I admit, but there has to be some explanation."

"Any chance Brenda could be the mystery lover we're looking for?"

She gave him a disbelieving look, all the while wondering if the idea was as preposterous as it seemed. Her instincts told her Brenda was far too professional—but, even so, there *was* something secretive in the way Brenda kept to herself.

"I'm glad you decided to close your office."

"It was a difficult decision. But after last night... seeing Daniel's body coming out of that motel room on a stretcher..." How could she have carried on with business as usual? Especially if there was a chance she could be putting more of her clients at risk.

Was Brenda responsible? She still couldn't believe it, but in her heart she knew that possibility was the main reason she'd felt they had to close.

From the grim look on Morgan's face, she suspected he was thinking along the same lines.

"There must be some way of finding out who the mystery lover was."

"Undoubtedly. The scope has narrowed now that we have the two murders. It seems quite likely these men were seeing the same woman, so we have to find a link between Walker and Hawthorne. They worked in different circles, lived in completely different areas of the city. Unfortunately, your office is the only link we've discovered so far."

Her office. Trista tugged a hand through her hair. Did that mean *she* was on the suspect list?

"I'm still searching for more connections," Morgan said, possibly in an attempt to be reassuring. "I was planning to stop by the university this afternoon, to see if Hawthorne's colleagues have any insights."

He slid off his stool and Trista followed him to the front door.

"I'm not sure if this will help, but Sylvia did bring up the name of a female assistant professor regularly in our sessions. Sylvia was obviously jealous of the woman, although Daniel swore they were only friends."

"Who was it?"

"I'm not sure I should tell you her name." She could see Morgan becoming angry. "I'm not trying to be obstructive. Believe me, I want to help you find the mystery lover, more than you could believe." Wasn't it, after all, the only way she could clear Brenda, and herself, from the suspect list? "Maybe if I came along, I could try to make sure you talk to her, without actually having to identify her."

"Pardon me? Did you just say *come along?* Since when did you turn detective?"

"These are my clients that are dying, Morgan. I'm not going to stand around and watch it happen."

"When I asked for your cooperation, I didn't expect you to take this on as a full-time job."

Meaning he didn't want her hanging around him any more than she had to. She could understand that, she felt the same way. But this was something she had to do. "I may be of some use," she said. "After all, I knew the Hawthornes and you didn't."

Morgan frowned. She could see he wanted to tell her

to forget it. But he didn't. Instead, he just shook his head and walked out the door. She followed.

THE UNIVERSITY OF TORONTO was the largest university in Canada, with several campuses located in the larger Toronto area. Daniel had taught in the central St. George Campus, which sprawled from the Parliament buildings on University Avenue to the fabric district on Spadina Avenue.

Morgan parked off of St. George Street, and from there he and Trista cut across tended landscaping to the Ramsay Wright Zoological Building. It was a large, modern building of dull brown brick, not one of Morgan's favorites. He preferred the older architecture of the residence buildings across the street. He preceded Trista up the steps of the entrance on the north side, then held the door for her.

It was strange, to be on this campus again with Trista by his side. Passing a group of summer school students, he was struck by how young they looked. He remembered feeling so mature at that age, yet really, their lives were just beginning. With luck, theirs would turn out better than his had.

Who could have guessed, when he'd first met Trista, what tragedy would lie in the future? All he'd cared about at the time had been getting her attention. It had taken him weeks of maneuvering to convince her to go out with him.

"I can't believe we were in their place little more than ten years ago," Trista said as they waited for an elevator. He looked up from his notepad in time to catch a wistful expression on her face as she watched the students receding from the building.

"A lot has happened since those days." He put out a

hand to hold the elevator door for her and thought about the crowd they'd hung out with when they'd gone to university. Most he hadn't seen in years, which was just as well since he remembered the common opinion on his and Trista's relationship had been that it wouldn't last. He'd hate for those people to know they'd been right.

They had to ask directions to find Hawthorne's office. It was a small, windowless room, tidy even though most of the floor space was taken up with a desk and three chairs, and a huge pine bookshelf crammed with books. The drawers of the metal file cabinet were carefully labeled, and the papers on his desk were organized into stacks, weighed down with various rock samples.

No, fossils, Morgan realized as he picked one up and saw the delicate pattern of a fern etched into it.

Morgan remembered how neatly the man's clothes had been folded on the dresser at the motel. An organized, methodical man.

Interestingly, there was nothing personal in the room. No pictures of family members. No knickknacks. Even the coffee mug on the corner of the desk was impersonal—a plain, utilitarian white. Trista set off in search of a water fountain, leaving him to explore in peace.

Lonely. The impression lodged in Morgan's brain, and wouldn't go away. He looked over the shelves of books, opened drawer after drawer, and saw nothing that didn't appear to belong in the office of a biology professor. Finally he examined the top drawer of the desk, and in there he found Daniel's appointment book.

Morgan flipped back to last fall. For a period of about two months, every Wednesday was circled, but there was no mention of a place, a time or a person. He swallowed his disappointment. Of course he hadn't expected to find the mystery lover's identity as easily as this. But it would have been nice.

Morgan flipped forward to the current week, where, once again, Wednesday was circled in red ink. Had the affair been about to resume as Sylvia presumed? Thinking of the scene he'd found at the Moondust Motel, it seemed likely.

As he closed the appointment book and slipped it back in the drawer, he sensed someone at the door behind him. Someone who wasn't Trista.

"Yes?" He turned to see an attractive woman of about forty, with long dark hair and exotic toffee-colored eyes set in an olive-toned face.

"I was just wondering what you were doing in Daniel Hawthorne's office, but now that I see you, I realize you must be with the police." She smiled, displaying an intriguing mixture of confidence and curiosity.

"That's right," Morgan replied. He didn't like being pegged so easily, but at least it suggested the woman was intuitive. Perhaps here he would find some answers.

"So sad about poor Daniel," she said, sitting in a chair beside him. She had long, slender legs, which she crossed to show to their advantage.

Morgan glanced from her legs to her face, and saw from her satisfied expression that he'd been meant to enjoy the view.

"Did you know Daniel well?" he asked. He chose to remain standing, leaning against the desk and looking down at the extraordinary woman before him. He was confident that this was the person Trista had been referring to when she'd spoken of the colleague Sylvia had been so jealous of.

She nodded. "I'm Maxine Pellicci. I have the office next door. I probably knew Daniel as well, if not better, than any of his colleagues. No,'' she continued, noting his raised eyebrows. "I did not have an affair with him." She emphasized the *him* as if to say there had been others.

"Not your type?"

Maxine looked away before answering. "I was his friend. Believe me, if ever a man needed a friend, it was Daniel."

"I've been getting that impression, too. Do you know what the problem was?"

"Not what. Who." Maxine smoldered. "His wife made that poor man's life hell, and you don't have to take my word for it. Ask anyone, especially the secretaries who had to put up with her incessant calls. She was always checking up on him. I tell you, when he finally started having an affair, the only question in my mind was why he had waited so long."

"So you knew about the affair."

She laughed.

"Who was it with?"

"Ah…" She stopped laughing and looked at him consideringly. "That *is* the question, isn't it?"

Morgan sensed that she was annoyed. Was it because Daniel hadn't told her who he was seeing? Or because he'd chosen the wrong woman for his affair? "So you don't know who this woman was?"

Maxine glanced away. "Daniel wanted to tell me. But he said this other person had too much to lose if her identity were to become known."

"Did you ever wonder why Daniel didn't leave his wife?"

"I think he wanted to. But he felt tied to her because they didn't have children. Strange, isn't it? Most unhappy couples stay together for the children. In their case, it was the opposite. He felt he couldn't leave because she needed him so much, and he'd never been able to give her what she claimed to want most—a child.

"I think it was all a hoax, though. Sylvia as a mother? She never could have shared the spotlight. The really unfortunate thing was that she never found herself a career. Why bother when daddy had all that money? If she'd had her own ambitions, she might not have pushed Daniel so hard in his."

"She pushed him?"

"You're darn right she pushed him. She wanted him to be dean. It could never happen, of course. Daniel just isn't—I mean wasn't—that sort of a man. He really enjoyed teaching—something you can't say about most members of this faculty, myself included—and that was all he wanted to do."

Morgan sighed. Maxine was giving him a motive for Daniel to kill Sylvia, but what he needed was the reverse. It was hard not to feel discouraged. Especially since he'd found no evidence in the small office that would help identify Daniel's mysterious lover.

Unless it *was* Maxine. His eyes dropped to her legs again. One of her high-heeled pumps was dangling from her toe, and she swung her foot provocatively. He looked up and saw the same smile on her face that she'd had when they first met.

"Sorry I haven't been more help," she said, eyeing him boldly. "But perhaps I could make it up to you by buying you dinner?"

Morgan shook his head, softening his rejection with a smile. "Thanks, but I'm going to be working tonight. If you think of anything that might help the investigation, though, please give me a call." He handed her a card.

Maxine unfolded her legs and rose gracefully from her

chair before accepting it. She now stood so close to him that their bodies were practically touching. Morgan would have stepped back, but he was right against the desk. Instead, he waited, until a rush of air from the doorway made them both turn. Trista stood outside in the hall, her expression carefully neutral.

Maxine shrugged and stepped away. "Nice to have met you, Detective," she said in a soft, husky voice before leaving the room, brushing past Trista without a word.

"Maxine Pellicci?" Trista asked as she stepped into the office. When he nodded, she said, "Wonder what she'd look like in a trench coat and hat?"

Morgan grinned. "I was wondering the same thing myself, only, believe it or not, I think she might have been one of the few real friends Daniel had."

"Oh, really? Women like that don't have men *friends,* Morgan."

He was caught off guard by the intensity of her statement, as well as the words. It wasn't like Trista to prejudge. *Women like that.* She turned away from him to inspect a title on the bookshelf, but not before he saw the flush on her cheeks.

Morgan felt like laughing for the first time in at least a week. Trista Emerson jealous. Over him. It hardly seemed possible.

Chapter Nine

Morgan dropped Trista off at her apartment, walking her
to the door and checking the locks to make sure nothing
had been disturbed.

"What will you do now?" she asked, strangely reluctant to see him go.

"I should check in at the office. They like me to do
that every now and then."

"You don't solve crimes sitting on your butt in headquarters," she said automatically.

He looked at her strangely. "Right."

Trista turned her back to the closed door once he was
gone, wishing she had a busy schedule, enough work to
leave her no time for thinking. But since she'd closed
shop, the rest of the day and the evening stretched cav-
ernously before her. She paced the apartment, feeling like
a prisoner in her own home. The monotones of her dec-
orating scheme—the off-whites, creams and beiges—had
seemed at one time relaxing and comforting. Now they
struck her as cold, almost sterile. She sat on her leather
sofa, pulled the wool afghan around herself and tried to
watch television, but it was no use. Nothing interested
her. Or maybe the problem was, she couldn't concentrate.

She stood, allowing the afghan to pool to the floor, and

began pacing from the patio door and back. The new lock Morgan had installed kept drawing her eyes, reminding her that he'd been here with her only hours ago.

Trista ran a hand down the side of a curtain, the sheer fabric sliding lightly through her fingers. Hard to believe it was less than a week since he'd come back into her life. Did he have any idea how he'd shot her personal peace to hell? He kept accusing her of being so cool—did he really not know how much it hurt her to be around him?

She thought of his gibes about the two of them needing to talk. Four years ago—yes, it was what they had needed. Now, too much time had passed. She and Morgan were divorced, had been for two years. They'd suffered so much, there was no way she could ever atone for all they'd been through. All he'd been through.

Even to entertain the possibility was irresponsible. What if they did try, and it didn't work out? She didn't think she could stand the pain.

Trista made a cup of instant soup for dinner, but couldn't sit still to drink it. Instead, she paced her apartment with the mug in her hand and tried not to think about the happier days, when she and Morgan had been carefree and in love. Had he thought about those days as they'd walked briskly along the campus grounds? The solid oaks and homey maples were just budding with new leaves, the grass was fresh and inviting. She'd tried not to let it get to her, but it was difficult not to yearn for those simpler, easier, happier days.

Somehow the soup was gone. She didn't remember drinking it. Trista set the empty mug in the dishwasher, then sat on the sofa. Leaning back, she closed her eyes, and a picture came immediately to mind. Morgan, on the cushion beside her, looking at her intently and whispering into her ear, *Take it off, Trista.*

She had *wanted* to pull that old sweatshirt over her head. Oh, how badly she had wanted it. Trista gritted her teeth and stood up. Madness. That was what she was toying with here. She had to get out, had to keep busy…

Suni's office. Trista hopped on the subway, hoping she could make herself useful. But when she arrived at the Runnymede address, it was after six. The place was deserted, except for Suni who was sitting at her desk at the back of the room.

"You again? I'm starting to wonder if you're looking for permanent employment."

"Perhaps I should." Trista pretended to consider the offer. "I've closed my office for a few days and I'm bored stiff already."

"Why did you do that?"

Trista glanced at a clipping from an editorial that was pinned on the bulletin board. In a section of the article, highlighted in bright yellow ink, was an approving mention of Suni's reputation for standing up for her constituents' rights. "It's a long story. And not a very nice one."

"I've got nothing but time." Suni patted the chair next to hers. "Come on, sit down and fill me in."

Trista was touched by her friend's kindness. No matter how busy she was, Suni always made room for other people. "Thanks for the offer, but I'd hardly know where to begin."

"Your ex-husband wouldn't have anything to do with this, would he?"

Ex-husband. Trista's thumb slid round the bare spot on her finger, where her wedding band used to be. "He's working on a homicide investigation right now. It sounds horrible, but it involves some of my clients.''

''*Your* clients?''

Trista nodded. ''It wouldn't be appropriate for me to go into the details—''

Suni looked at her thoughtfully. ''Detective Forester is investigating the murder of Jerry Walker, isn't he? I read it in the papers.'' She gave a short laugh. ''Don't tell me Jerry was a client of yours?''

Trista remained silent.

''Oh, God, he was.'' Suni looked away for a moment, toward the windows that fronted Bloor Street. ''And that's why you've closed your office?''

''It's actually worse than that.'' Trista thought of the second murder, which hadn't made the morning paper.

Suni's thin eyebrows rose questioningly.

Trista sank into the chair beside her friend, and let out a long breath. ''There's been a second murder.''

Horror registered in Suni's expression. Horror and something else—morbid curiosity? Surely not, not Suni. ''Another one of your clients?'' she asked.

''Yes. Daniel Hawthorne.'' As soon as the name passed her lips, Trista worried she was not being as circumspect as she ought to be. But this information would be in tomorrow's newspaper. She glanced back at her friend, and was worried to see that Suni was turning pale, withdrawing.

And then it hit her. Would Suni want someone working on her campaign who was involved in a homicide investigation? No matter how peripherally? And how peripheral was her involvement, after all? If Brenda could be a suspect, why not her?

Suni raised a hand to her forehead. Trista recognized the gesture—Suni often suffered from migraines.

"Maybe I should cool it here until the investigation is wrapped up," she suggested in a quiet voice.

Suni shook her head. "Don't be silly."

But her forehead remained lined, and Trista could see in the narrowing of her eyes a building pain. At the moment, Suni wasn't capable of thinking clearly.

"You should get home and take care of that headache before it gets out of control."

Suni nodded her head slightly. "It's been coming on since lunch. I took a couple of painkillers hoping I could head it off. I should have known better."

Trista could almost feel the sharp shooting pains as Suni's eyes flinched and her forehead wrinkled tighter. "Let me see you home."

"No need. Really. I'll grab a cab. You know they always hang out at the pizza place on the corner." Suni was pulling on her jacket as she spoke.

"But—" Trista tried to argue with her, but Suni had already grabbed her purse and headed for the door.

"The spare key is filed under E—for emergency." Suni gave a weak smile. "Could you lock up on the way out, please? And make sure the windows are shut tight, too. The police warned us after the break-in last month that we have to be more careful."

Trista didn't have time to answer as Suni practically slammed the door behind her. She didn't mind locking up, but she wished Suni hadn't insisted on leaving alone. She'd never seen one of her headaches come on so quickly before.

AS MORGAN DROVE AWAY from Trista's apartment toward headquarters, he tried to focus his thoughts on the homicide investigation and the work he had yet to accomplish. But images of Trista kept popping into his mind.

He remembered going to see her when she'd first left him. He'd pulled a lot of strings to find her holed up in a cheap furnished apartment off of Bathurst. Even though he'd practically banged the door down, she'd refused to open it. So he'd waited until she went out, and cornered her a block away from the local grocery store.

"Trista, you can't just walk out on me—on us. Please come home. I know we can work this out, if you'll only *talk* to me."

He'd seen the tears run down her cheeks from behind her dark sunglasses. "I can't, Morgan," was all she'd said. Was all she *ever* said.

Did she blame herself for the accident? He'd told her over and over it wasn't her fault.

Did she blame him for not being there when Andrew was sick? He'd apologized for that a million times too.

He'd tried to see her, called and written so many times those first few months, never getting any response. When she'd phoned Zed, to talk about a restraining order, he'd finally given up. She'd left him, and now he hated her for that. He *needed* to hate her for it.

But it was getting harder. Despite the barriers Trista had put up between them, there were moments her defenses let down, moments when he could catch a glimpse of the old Trista. On those times, the look in her eyes— a yearning sadness—hit him like a punch to the gut. And on those few occasions when she'd smiled, turning naturally toward him, he'd felt a sudden joy that he hadn't experienced in years.

As soon as it happened, though, the moment would pass. It was as if a brick wall had risen up between them. It reminded Morgan of how he'd felt when their divorce had been finalized. Until the papers had been signed, he hadn't been able to believe she would really end their marriage.

Until that day he'd hoped. Hoped and prayed that time would heal the wounds. Hoped and trusted that her heart would open to him again. But he'd learned the hard way that there were some wounds not even time could heal. Not for her. And not for him.

Morgan pulled into his parking stall and leaned his head against the steering wheel, giving in to a sudden attack of lethargy. This case had come up at the worst possible moment for both him and Trista. Just when he'd begun to accept that their time was over. Just when she'd started to pull her life together. What happened? Two of Trista's clients were murdered and they were drawn together by circumstances beyond their control.

It wasn't fair. It just wasn't fair. Like so many other things...

A honk from a car pulling in beside him drew him out of his reverie. He looked up and recognized the crown prosecutor behind the wheel. Groaning to himself, he got out of the car and waited for her to join him. Sydney was the one woman he'd been involved with since Trista, and he always felt uncomfortable on the occasions when their paths happened to cross.

She was in her early thirties, like him, with honey-colored hair and thin, elegant features. Her physique was small and delicate, belying her robust nature.

"I hear you're on a new case." Her expression was curious, interested, and she fell into step beside him, matching his brisk pace despite the eight-inch advantage he had in height.

"Sure am, but it's going slow. Won't affect your work-load in the foreseeable future, I'm afraid."

"I've heard you say that before. Then, just when I've got my holiday booked—*wham!* You hand over the culprit." She smiled.

"I wish I shared your confidence." Morgan held the door open, then followed her to the Homicide Department. She stopped in front of a meeting room, where she obviously had an appointment, and in his mind they'd already said goodbye when she laid a hand on his arm.

"I know it's none of my business but I heard that Trista is involved in this case." She looked up at him with an expression that seemed to be all solicitude, but Morgan had learned to question Sydney's motives. "I can imagine how painful—"

"Thanks for your concern, Sydney," he said, forcing his lips to stretch into a nonchalant smile. "But it's no big deal. Good luck in your meeting." He took a couple of steps backward, to get beyond her reach, then waited for her to say goodbye before he turned and headed with relief toward his desk.

There were several things waiting for him, and the brief episode with Sydney vanished from his mind. Preliminary lab reports on Daniel Hawthorne's death, interviews from the few motel occupants who'd been in their rooms at the estimated time of the homicide, the results of the fingerprint tests taken in Trista's office the night her files were tampered with, and last, but not least, a brown manila folder that he'd requested a few days ago.

Saving the folder for last, Morgan flipped through the lab reports. The initial estimate was that Daniel had died early Wednesday afternoon between one and two, making Sylvia's alibi pretty well conclusive since she'd been with Trista from one to one-thirty. Also providing Trista with an alibi. Morgan made a mental note to include that fact in his report.

Morgan moved on to the interviews of the motel occupants. As he'd expected, not many people had been in their rooms at one in the afternoon and those that were were none too pleased to be dragged into a police investigation. Morgan sifted through the brief statements, discouraged. He'd hoped that someone would have caught a glimpse of the mystery lover, maybe seen her remove her sunglasses or her hat. No such luck.

Next, Morgan picked up the fingerprint results from Trista's office. Only Trista's and Brenda's fingerprints had been found on the desk drawer and the metal box where the spare key was kept. The same results were found on the file drawer that Trista thought had been disturbed.

Disappointing. But he hadn't really expected anything else. Finally he turned to the folder that he had saved for last. The folder with the neatly typed label, "Malachowski, Brenda," on the right-hand corner.

Morgan skimmed the information quickly. He'd thought there was something not quite on the level with Trista's secretary. His instincts had warned him that she was hiding something. Now he saw that he'd been right.

Chapter Ten

The Hawthorne file. Trista didn't know why she'd hadn't thought of it earlier. Ever since the night her office had been broken into, Morgan had been keeping the Walker file locked in his home safe.

But what about the Hawthorne file? Assuming the murderer was interested in the one, wouldn't he want the other, too? Trista knew it was still in the gray cabinet, filed under H where it belonged, because she'd added a note about Sylvia's visit late Wednesday afternoon.

The thought came to her while she was locking up the campaign office after Suni's abrupt departure, and she went back into the office to make a quick phone call to Morgan.

Once again she had to leave a message.

Back in the subway, traveling east on Bloor, Trista fumed as her body swayed from side to side with the movement of the train. The car was almost full with people of all ages, all nationalities. Beside her, a Jamaican girl popped gum in time to the music playing on her portable disc-player. An Asian woman held the hands of two preschool children seated on either side of her. And standing at the door, his arm firmly grasping a metal pole for support, an old man muttered impatiently in Italian.

What if it was hours before Morgan checked his messages? The office locks were scheduled to be changed tomorrow. That meant the file would be vulnerable all night long.

She couldn't wait for Morgan. She had to get that file.

At the back of her mind was the thought that Morgan would be furious if he knew what she was up to. But that didn't stop her. At the Spadina subway stop she grabbed a streetcar, which bumped and ground all the way to King Street.

She would just run into her office and get the file. It would take less than a minute.

By the time she reached her office, it was after seven, and the lobby was deserted except for the security guard manning his post by the entrance. She signed her name in the register and asked Joe how things were going.

"Fine, Ms. Emerson. Say, I'm sorry about the mix-up with your locks being changed. I thought we'd decided that no one had broken into your office so I told them not to bother."

Trista waved aside the apology. Since it was too late to change anything now, there was no point in getting angry with Joe. "I'm going up to the office to get some papers I need. I'll just be a minute."

"No problem."

Trista was used to being in the building after hours, but this time when she stepped into the elevator she felt as exposed as an animal in a cage. What could she do to protect herself if when the elevator stopped, the doors opened to reveal an intruder? There was nowhere to run in an elevator. Nothing to hide behind. No one would even hear her screams...

The bell sounded arrival at the top floor and Trista gave a small jump. Now she *was* being ridiculous. See?

Off the elevator, and no bogeyman waiting to gun her down. The doors made a funny creaking noise as they closed. Heart pounding, she pulled her office keys out of her purse. The key slid into the lock easily, but met with no resistance when she gave it a twist. The door wasn't locked.

Trista's nervous system fired up again. She knew she'd locked the door behind her when she'd left the empty office earlier that afternoon. So who had unlocked it? Not Joe, certainly. And Brenda had said she was leaving the city for a few days.

An intruder. Shakily, Trista withdrew her key. What if he was still there?

Slowly and quietly, Trista returned to the elevators. She pressed the down button, frowning when she saw both had returned to the main level. If there was someone in her office, he could come out any second. She didn't want to be standing here if that happened. She decided to take the stairs.

Walking around behind the elevator bank, she pushed at the heavy, fireproof door that led to the stairwell. It gave way with a dull creak, and suddenly she placed the sound she'd heard when she'd stepped off the elevator. But the insight came too late.

A numbing pain at the back of her head, along with a brief sensation of inevitability, was all she felt before she collapsed forward onto the concrete landing. Then there was nothing.

MORGAN STEPPED out of the elevator on Trista's floor and listened intently. For a split second he'd thought he'd heard a thud, but now there was only silence. According to Joe, Trista had said she'd only be a minute or two. Why wasn't she on her way down yet?

Morgan figured he'd listened to her message about the Hawthorne file about half an hour after she'd sent it. He should have known she wouldn't simply sit and wait for him.

Why couldn't the woman get it through her thick skull that she was in danger? What could have possessed her to come back to her office, alone, after closing hours? Morgan looked at the door in front of him, the brass plaque with black lettering: Emerson Counseling. His sixth sense told him that something was wrong here. Noiselessly he reached for his gun before trying the door. It wasn't locked.

He didn't think Trista would have left the door unlocked behind her. Surely even she wasn't that foolhardy. Fighting an ominous sense of foreboding, he cautiously eased the door open. The lights were off and the rooms were dull in the early dusk.

Well, she wouldn't be in here with the lights off. But if she wasn't here, then where was she? Joe would have seen her if she'd come back down the elevators. Could she have been going down while he was coming up? That was probably it, but while he was here, he figured he'd look things over.

After turning on the lights, he searched the three-room office but saw nothing out of the ordinary. No sign of any struggle. And no sign of Trista. For a moment he paused in front of the file cabinets. Since Trista was gone, undoubtedly she had the file already. But on impulse he pulled open the drawer and searched under the H's.

There it was. *Hawthorne, Daniel and Sylvia.* Morgan pulled it out and stared at the cover, adrenaline buzzing through his veins. Where the hell was Trista?

He returned to the hallway and stood silently for several minutes. And then, on a hunch, he headed for the stairwell. But he couldn't open the door. Something heavy was blocking the entrance. Heart pounding, he ran back to the elevators and pounded the button. When the door opened, he jumped inside and pressed the button for one floor down. As soon as it made its jerky stop, he flew out and raced to the stairs.

He ran up the first half flight, and as he turned the corner, he saw, dimly in the darkness, why he'd been unable to get through.

Sprawled on the concrete landing was the outline of a human body. In the faint light from the door's window, dull gold shimmered in the hair of the victim.

It was Trista.

He sprinted up the last few stairs and knelt beside her, pain knifing through his chest as he spotted traces of blood on the floor beside her. *Please let her be all right!*

Quickly he checked for a pulse, and swallowed a sob when he found it. Kneeling closer, he placed his face next to hers and reveled in the soft warmth of her breath against his cheek. Giving in to impulse, he pressed his cheek closer, right next to hers, and breathed a short prayer of relief.

Then he pulled himself up short. There was work to do here. He'd have to call the office and have someone come down to investigate. But first, and foremost, he had to get Trista to the hospital.

TRISTA MOANED as she began the journey back to consciousness. Images and sounds came to her in disjointed sequences. She was aware of colors. Red. Blue. A flash of yellow. She heard the occasional word. Something was pressing her down. She felt overwhelmed by the sensations, unable to put them in any sort of context.

Then she became aware of her own body. Her head

throbbed with pain. She realized that she was lying down but she had no idea where. She tried to think what had happened to her, where she'd been, but she couldn't remember anything. Instinctively she opened her eyes and tried to make sense of the blur of shadow and light.

It was a ceiling. She struggled to bring the line where the wall met the ceiling into focus. Three lines merged to two and finally to one. There.

She turned her head. The movement caused a spasm of pain to shoot through her head, starting at the back and moving, with excruciating slowness, forward to her temples. She winced, then opened her eyes again. Now she saw a pale beige curtain pulled back to the wall, not quite hiding the narrow bed just a few feet away, and beyond that, a door into a brightly lit corridor.

Of a hospital. Her thoughts began to swirl in her mind, moving faster, faster, funneling into a tornado of anxiety. And fear.

She gripped the metal railing of her bed convulsively. There was something wrong. Now she remembered. Something terrible, horrible, uglier than her worst nightmare. "No!" She fought against the memory, against consciousness. *Give me back the darkness, please. I can't take this, I can't!*

He's dead. He's dead. A voice sounded in her ear. She tried not to listen. She knew it belonged to Morgan.

"No! It's not true! It's not true!" She saw the truck coming at them from the corner of her eye. The metal grillwork filled the passenger windows on the right-hand side of her car. Andrew's car seat was back there. She threw her hands up around her head to block the sounds—crunching metal, squealing breaks, smashing glass, a baby's cry abruptly silenced.

Forever.

"It's okay, Trista. You're going to be all right." The voice confused her. Where was it coming from? How could she be okay? This had to be some kind of cruel joke.

"Trista, Trista," the voice continued. She felt someone stroking her hand.

Oh, God, she prayed. *This can't be true. Andrew can't be dead. Let me rock him once more, just for a few minutes. He'll come around. Let me hold him. He's mine. He needs me.* She tried to get up, to go and find him, but she felt herself being pressed back. She looked wildly around her. Something was wrong here. It didn't make sense.

"Lie down, Trista. Please, please, calm yourself."

That voice again. The words didn't fit. She opened her eyes and concentrated, really concentrated. It was Morgan beside her, but he was different. She forced herself to keep looking, to figure out what was wrong. He was older. That was it. A piece of the fog lifted from her mind and she realized this was a different time. Suddenly exhausted, she fell back limp onto her bed, turning on her side, away from Morgan.

She felt his hand on her back, gently stroking her. She wanted to tell him to stop, but the truth was it felt so good, and suddenly she could think of no reason to object to his touch. She took in a long breath. It was shaky, like the drawn sob of a child who'd been crying a long, long time.

She knew now that the accident had happened years ago, but she felt the pain, as raw as if it had been only hours. Against her will the scene replayed in her mind. All the little details that she'd fought so hard to suppress.

Don't hold back, Trista. She could hear the voice of her therapist. *You have to come to terms with this.*

She was a counselor, herself. She knew what he said was right. But how could she come to terms with the death of her own child, knowing that she *could* have prevented it?

She remembered her fear that cold winter night as Andrew's cough got worse and worse. Morgan was working and couldn't be reached. She'd turned the hot water on in the bathroom and created a room of steam. Held him in there for half an hour. But it didn't help. He was having trouble breathing. She didn't think he was getting enough oxygen. In desperation, she'd decided to take him to emergency. She would never forget the last time she had held her baby alive, when she placed him in his car seat. He had been so miserable. Sick and scared. And she had hated to put him by himself back there, but she'd done it for his safety.

His safety. The bile rose in her throat. It turned out to have been the most unsafe place she could have put him.

Trista began to sob. She could see, as if he was right here beside her, the soft blond hair, the small dot of his nose, the pink curve of his mouth. She remembered the fear she'd felt for him that night, the desperate kiss she had planted on his soft, plump cheek, before closing the door and running to the driver's seat.

The last time she had kissed her darling baby boy. She had driven like someone possessed, headed for the nearest hospital. She would never forget the sound of Andrew's hoarse heavings from the back seat as she rushed to get him medical aid. If only Morgan was here, she remembered thinking. He could get us a police escort or something. Every stop sign, every red light was agony as she felt her lungs burn with her child's need for oxygen.

And then she reached the corner of Mount Pleasant and Eglinton. The light turned yellow just as she neared the intersection. After a split-second hesitation she put her foot down heavily on the gas pedal. And then, from her right, came the truck. She had only the briefest awareness, a desperate thought of her baby in the center of the back seat, until the world had turned to darkness.

If only it had stayed that way.

"Trista. Oh Trista. I'm so sorry." Morgan put his arms gently around the woman who had once been his wife and rocked her gently. "I'm so sorry."

She turned to face him then, accepting the refuge his arms offered. He was crying too, she realized, wondering why she should be surprised by that, then remembering that he hadn't the first time, when he'd told her about Andrew.

"Shh." She felt the warmth of his breath mingling with the coolness of his fresh tears against her ear. "It's okay, Trista. You've had a knock to the head."

"I have?" Her voice came out sounding like a couple of croaks.

"At your office," he elaborated, and then she remembered. The unlocked door, the murders, the break-in, the divorce, the emptiness. Her mind rewound the events from today leading back to the day of the accident over four years ago.

"I remember." She closed her eyes, suddenly aware of nothing but pounding pain.

I SHOULDN'T HAVE BROUGHT her to the hospital, Morgan berated himself even though he knew he'd had no choice. It hadn't occurred to him that she might react like this. It was, after all, a different hospital. *But similar enough.* When she'd had the car accident, she'd been in a room not unlike this one, with a bad concussion and the possibility of internal damage. Then, as now, at the moment she regained consciousness, he'd been by her side.

With the worst news that either of them could have had. It had been the hardest moment of his life, but he'd tried to be strong for her. Not that his supposed strength had done anybody any good. There was nothing he could do to save his baby, and nothing he could do or say to provide any comfort to his wife.

He'd lost more than his son in that terrible accident four years ago. He'd lost his wife too, although mercifully he hadn't realized that at first. It was only thoughts of Trista that had helped him get through those first few days and weeks. She would need him. He had to be strong for her. That was what he'd told himself.

But she hadn't needed him. Not from the moment he told her that Andrew had died in the accident. She hadn't cried then, like she was now. Her eyes had grown blank, her face, expressionless. She'd turned away from him without a single word. It was as if she had died, too. In everything except body.

In the weeks and months that passed, he kept waiting for her—the real Trista—to come back from whatever hell she was visiting and inhabit the body of his still-beautiful wife, but she never did. Her face kept that look, that blank expression where her eyes never really seemed to be in focus.

They lived in polite silences, pretending to sleep during long, dark nights, and avoiding each other when they were awake. Moving about in the same house, sharing meals and a bed, but not talking or touching. If he so much as placed a hand on her shoulder, she would wince, as if in pain.

And she never did cry. At least, not when he was in the house. He remembered many nights when, unable to sleep and unable to share his thoughts with his wife, he'd gone into his son's bedroom. He would touch the crib, the blankets, the stuffed toys. He'd open the books he'd once read for hours: *I do not like green eggs and ham. I do not like them Sam-I-am.*

And then *he* would cry. Quietly. So as not to disturb Trista. Muffling his sobs with the flannel blanket they had wrapped around Andrew after he was born and they took him home from the hospital.

This time they hadn't been able to take him home from the hospital.

Trista's sobs were losing their intensity and he lowered her body back down on the pillows. All that crying couldn't have done her injury any good, and he wished the doctor would come in and examine her.

"How's your head?"

Trista twisted her mouth into a small smile. Her eyes were almost swollen shut from sobbing, her skin was blotchy and her lips were swollen. He thought she'd never looked so precious to him.

"It hurts," she admitted.

"I should say so." The doctor's loud voice startled them both as he walked briskly into the room from the hallway. "You've had quite a bump there, Ms. Emerson. What happened?"

"Trista was in the wrong place at the wrong time, Doctor," Morgan replied, pulling his badge out of his pocket and showing it to the doctor. "She interrupted an attempted burglary."

The doctor looked Morgan up and down and then turned his eyes back to his patient. "You've been crying. Is this man upsetting you?"

"Not at all," Trista replied hastily. "It's a long story, Doctor. I don't think we need to get into it."

"If you say so. But extended periods of crying aren't going to do your head injury any good. Now, if I could have a moment to examine my patient." He looked expectantly toward Morgan.

"Of course." Morgan gave Trista's shoulder a soft squeeze before he slipped out of the room.

"So what did he say?" Morgan wanted to know after the doctor had left.

"They want to keep me in overnight. For observation." Trista grimaced. The last place she wanted to spend the night was in this godforsaken hospital. But the doctor had made it clear she had no alternative.

"Good."

Of course he was glad. He'd probably have her under complete police protection, all the time, if he was able. For once, his protectiveness didn't bother her. She was remembering the tears he'd cried beside her, only minutes ago.

She hadn't even realized that that was what she'd been waiting for until now.

He hadn't had any four years ago. Not on the day of the accident, or later at the funeral, or even at home. She knew that he crept away some nights, to go to Andrew's room. Sometimes she heard the anguish of his sobs coming from behind the closed door. He thought she was asleep, but back then she almost never slept.

So that had become the rule. He would cry, but never in front of her. And she'd never cried in front of him. And that, she thought, had been the second nail driven into the coffin of their marriage.

Chapter Eleven

The first nail in the coffin of her marriage was her guilt.
She'd thought over the accident a thousand times, and
was convinced she could have stopped in time, if only
she'd stepped on the brake instead of the accelerator. A
split-second decision that had robbed Andrew of life, and
Morgan of a son.

Of course, Morgan had never blamed her. He
wouldn't.

"I'd like to stay with you tonight. If that's okay."

His suggestion startled her, and she was dismayed at
how badly she wanted to accept. But it wasn't fair to
Morgan. "It's not necessary. Besides, you look exhausted, you need some rest…"

"I'll get more sleep in a chair beside you than I will
in a bed worrying about you."

Trista sighed. "Always willing to sacrifice yourself.
Sometimes I think nothing's changed about you in the
past four years. Just go home and sleep, Morgan. I can't
stand to have you being so *nice* all the time."

"Nice?" Morgan looked as if she'd landed him with
the biggest insult going. He turned as if to leave, then
marched back to her bedside. "Nice? Well, what's so
wrong with that?"

Trista averted her eyes. Now she'd started something, and why? Where was it going to get either of them? It must be the medication the doctor had given her, making her dopey. "I'm sorry, I don't know what I meant by that. My brain is still a little fuzzy."

"No, tell me what you were thinking," he insisted. "Why shouldn't I have been nice to you?"

Trista shook her head, wondering why he had to be so insistent. He was leaning over her bed, his eyes narrowed and glinting, like when he was hot on a clue in one of his cases. She knew he wasn't going to let this drop. Suddenly the tears started again, and she tucked her face into the sheets.

"Trista, Trista." He sounded worried now. "Please, honey. Talk to me."

She clenched her jaw and gritted her teeth, trying to ignore him. Talk? She couldn't talk. It would hurt, hurt, hurt…

"Trista, please."

She felt his arms gently grasp her shoulders.

"Look at me. Don't turn all cold again. Don't shut me out. Tell me what you're thinking. You want to tell me, don't you? You know you can trust me."

She *did* trust him. He was right about that. But why talk now, when it was too late to solve anything? She took a gulp of air, and tried to clear the constricted feeling in her chest. Morgan squeezed her shoulder, and she dared a quick look.

There were tears running down his cheeks again. Her heart ached for his pain, and almost against her will, the words started flowing.

"I could have stopped in time, I know I could have. I saw the light turn yellow and I had a split second to decide. And I gunned it, Morgan. I gunned it, and if only I'd stopped, Andrew would still be here…"

"Trista." Morgan pulled her to his chest. "Stop. Please don't blame yourself. I saw the accident report myself—"

"I don't care about the accident report. I could have prevented it."

"The truck driver ran a red light. He was exceeding the speed limit."

Why couldn't Morgan understand this was about more than legal liability? She just shook her head against his shoulder.

"No woman with a sick child in her car would have tried to stop for that light," he persisted. "You have to know that."

Trista swallowed. "That's what my therapist said, and I know it's true. But it's also true that if I *had* stopped, Andrew would still be alive."

Morgan's hold on her hands tightened. "What you're saying is wrong. It's just another version of the deadly 'if only' game. Don't you think I've played that one myself? If only I'd been at home to help you take him to the hospital. If only I hadn't kept him out late the night before, maybe he never would have gotten sick…"

"Oh, Morgan." She pulled back from his embrace, and seeing the pain in his eyes, had to reach out, to caress the side of his face. She'd been so self-obsessed. "You were such an excellent father."

How had things gotten so tangled and twisted between them? Trista felt the tears that dampened his face, and wished she could kiss them away. If only they could have talked this way four years ago. Supported each other through their crisis. If Morgan had cried, and she had talked…

Pain slashed behind her forehead, and she leaned back on her pillow, wincing.

"You need to rest," Morgan said.

She closed her eyes, barely managing a slight nod.

This time Morgan didn't object to her request to be left alone. She sensed his presence by her bed a few minutes longer, then felt his lips brush her forehead gently. She was listening to the sound of his footsteps fading down the corridor, when the comfort of sleep finally descended over her.

"HI THERE."

Morgan's voice the next morning startled Trista. She looked up from the hospital bed and smiled uncertainly. She was fully clothed and ready to go. She just needed the final okay from the doctor.

"How are you feeling?"

"Not bad. My head was pretty sore this morning, but the pain relievers are helping. They have the unfortunate side effect of making me groggy, though." Trista avoided his eyes as she answered. She'd spent most of the morning thinking about the things they'd talked about last night, and the truth was, she didn't have a clue where they should go from here. The homicide investigation wasn't over—not by a long shot—so they would still be seeing each other. But was that where their relationship ended?

She was no longer sure how she felt about it, and she was even less sure what Morgan would think. After last night, they couldn't keep up the same barriers. But where did that leave them?

There was still caring, she knew, and physical attraction. God knows they had history. But wasn't too much of that history negative? Wouldn't it be easier for both of them to start fresh with someone new? A clean slate.

"Maybe that's a good thing," he said, "About the grogginess. You could probably use some extra rest. How did you sleep last night?"

"Not bad, considering someone kept waking me up every couple of hours, asking me my name, what year it was, stuff like that."

"I always hated surprise quizzes myself." Morgan grinned at her sympathetically.

"What about you?" she asked. "You don't look like you had much sleep."

He shrugged off her question. "By the way, I got the Hawthorne file when I was at your office, before I—found you."

"It was still there?"

"Apparently."

"Don't you think that's strange? Or did I interrupt him before he had a chance to get what he was after?"

"Possibly." Morgan ran a hand over his chin. "We haven't come up with much in the way of evidence at the scene. Did you get a look at the guy? Are you sure it's a 'he'?"

"No. Whoever it was came up from behind. It happened so quickly…"

Morgan's expression darkened, and he didn't have to speak for her to know what he was thinking.

"I suppose this is where you blast me for being stupid enough to go back to my office last night."

Morgan shook his head. "I'm hoping that bump on your head is going to be more persuasive than my warnings were. From now on—"

"Don't worry." Trista held up her hand to stop him.

"I'm going to be more careful, believe me." She fingered the tender spot on the back of her head carefully.

Just then a nurse came into the room. "The doctor says you may leave," she told Trista. "He recommends bed rest for the next couple of days."

Morgan raised his eyebrows and gave her a stern look, as if already suspecting she had no intention of following doctor's orders. She just gave them both a noncommittal smile and got up to leave. Her head protested in pain at the sudden movement and she was glad to have Morgan's arm around her, his solid support at her side.

IN HER APARTMENT, Morgan did a quick check, making sure all the windows were locked and that his phone number was beside each phone. "A police car should be cruising by about every half hour," he told her. "If you hear or see anything suspicious, call this number immediately. Okay?"

"Okay." Trista glanced at the new card he'd placed beside the telephone. She wished she could ask him to stay, but she knew that was impossible, for many reasons. If only she wasn't trapped in this apartment. There would be nothing for her to do but think, and she was tired of thinking. "I wish you would leave the Hawthorne file with me. I need something to do to occupy my time."

Morgan lifted her chin so that their eyes met. "You can look it over when you're feeling better. Please stay in bed, like the doctor ordered." He ran a gentle hand down her cheek.

The feel of his hand on her skin didn't have the soothing effect he'd probably intended. Instead, the gentle caress brought Trista an instant of intense longing. It took all her willpower to resist the urge to lean into his touch, to lift her lips to his, to press her body next to his.

Disturbing impulses. She and Morgan were divorced now. They'd traveled far down the path toward healing. What had happened between them last night could only help in the long run. Why confuse things now by opening new issues?

"I'd better get back to work." Morgan spoke stiffly, removing his hand abruptly. Had he sensed how his touch had disturbed her? "I'll try and come back later to make sure you're all right. Don't forget to lock the dead bolt and chain behind me when I leave."

Once he was gone, her apartment was accusingly lonely and she had nothing to distract her from the throbbing pain in her head. She crawled into bed, the expanse of cream-colored linen reminding her how alone she was. Her family had always been small, just her and her sister, raised by a grandmother who was now dead.

Then Virginia, who was older than her by only eighteen months, had died at the impossibly young age of twenty-nine. A brain aneurysm, they'd said. Supposedly the weak blood vessel had exploded while she was jogging along the river in Calgary where she'd moved to be close to her engineer boyfriend.

It was only a short year later that Trista had the accident and lost Andrew. Followed by the divorce from Morgan. They were gone, all of them, and while she knew in her mind that it wasn't her fault—at least not all of it—a part of her still felt bruised.

Why did she keep losing the people she loved?

Trista reached over to the night table, opened the top drawer and pulled out a hand-carved wooden box. It was the only keepsake she'd taken with her when she'd left Morgan. She'd put her wedding ring and a picture of Andrew in the small box and slipped it inside her purse on her way out the door. The box was the first gift Morgan had given her, on the first Christmas after they'd started going out.

Trista opened the box carefully. The letter Morgan had attached to the divorce papers was sitting there. She'd tucked it away without reading it, knowing that nothing he said would change her mind. Now she unfolded the white sheet.

Dear Trista,
I'm signing these papers because I know it's what you want. I hope you find some peace in your new life. But this divorce—it isn't right. I wish you could see that.

There was no signature, no final goodbye.

Trista read the short sentences over and over. *It isn't right.* No. It hadn't been. She'd been a trained therapist, and still she hadn't found the wisdom to solve her own problems. Looking back, Trista couldn't explain why it had taken the sight of Morgan's tears to release her own emotions.

But who knew if the same trigger would have worked three years ago? She set the note aside and reached into the box for the picture of Andrew. It was her favorite. He was sitting in the bathtub, surrounded by bubbles, smiling with delight into the camera. Trista devoured every detail of his appearance. His cheery smile—showing off those first small baby teeth—the sparkle in his round blue eyes that were so like his father's, the downy softness of his baby-fine hair.

Trista pressed the photograph against her heart and felt the tears gather in her eyes. God help her, it seemed all she could do these days was cry.

MORGAN PULLED his car into the parking lot of the Moondust Motel. Much as he'd hated to leave Trista on her own, he thought it was good for both of them to have a little time apart. They'd been through an emotional wringer last night and he suspected that they both needed some recovery time. He didn't know what to expect from her anymore. Somehow, it had been easier when he'd been able to hate her.

Or *tell* himself he hated her. Because he knew he'd never stopped loving her. He'd wanted so badly to comfort her after the accident. Why had it taken until last night for her to finally open up to him?

For months after the accident he'd given her compassion and kindness. When it became clear that she wasn't responding, he'd tried giving her the space she seemed to need. Maybe if they'd had more family it would have helped. But Trista had none, and his... Well, he'd never expected much emotional support from his parents, and so far they'd never let him down. They'd flown up from their winter hideaway in Florida for the funeral, but they hadn't stayed more than a few days.

A year after the accident, Trista had left him, and he'd changed his tactics once again. This time he'd tried arguing and demanding, but she shut him out at every opportunity.

Until last night. What had been so different about last night? Remembering the way she'd touched his tears, he came to a realization.

Maybe what she'd really needed was for him to talk about how he was feeling.

Something he'd never been good at doing.

Morgan set his jaw at a stubborn angle, and thought about something he *was* good at. His job. It had been five days since Jerry Walker's murder. Three since Daniel

Hawthorne's. The trail would soon be getting cold. With every day that passed, their chances of catching the murderer grew smaller. But it was still early enough that he could feel confidence. The renewed attempt to break into Trista's office told him that someone was getting desperate to cover his tracks. And if the murderer had made more than one mistake along the way, well then, his job would be so much the easier.

"Ted Sanders?" Morgan asked as he stepped from the concrete sidewalk onto the thick red shag rug of the motel's main entrance. A tall, chunky man, in his mid-thirties, nodded from behind the counter.

"That's me. You the detective that called?"

Morgan held out his badge. The walls were painted a deep purple color and the window coverings were a dusty—in the physical sense of the word—pink velvet. On the wall hung framed photographs of some of the choice rooms. Water beds, hot tubs and mirrored ceilings figured prominently in all the pictures.

Lewd and *tacky* were the words that came to Morgan's mind. His gaze shifted back to Sanders. "I need to check a few facts with you."

"No problem at all, Detective." Ted Sanders's small brown eyes glistened with interest. "What can I do for you?"

"Well, the report says that about six months ago Hawthorne was coming here every week."

"That's right." Sanders winked, and gave Morgan a knowing smile. "I recognized him as soon as he walked in the door. Wondered to myself if he'd found a new one, or what."

Morgan ignored the man's salacious grin. "Back when Hawthorne was coming regularly, can you tell me what day of the week it was? Was it always the same or did it vary?''

''I can check for you.'' Ted went into a back room for a few minutes and then emerged with his news. ''Wednesday afternoon, between twelve-thirty and two-thirty. The same every week.''

Wednesdays. The days that were circled in Hawthorne's calendar. So that much made sense, anyway. By now Morgan was certain that it was no coincidence that both victims had regularly met their lovers on the same day.

''Another thing the report isn't clear on,'' Morgan continued, ''is whether the woman who picked up the key from you this Wednesday was the same one Hawthorne had been meeting previously.''

Ted shrugged. ''I assumed she was, but I couldn't say for sure. I only ever saw her from a distance—until this time, that is. The guy usually checked in while the woman showed up in a taxi a few minutes later. She always went straight to their room. Except this time.''

''About this last time. The report has your description of a woman probably in her forties, wearing a hat, sunglasses and a large tan trench coat.''

''That's right. The trench coat seemed like it was too big for her. I remember wondering if that was because she didn't have any clothes on underneath.''

Morgan raised his eyebrows. ''We hadn't thought of that one. In past months, could you tell if the woman normally wore an oversize trench coat?''

''Not from the distance I usually saw her.''

Morgan bit back his frustration. ''Could you identify *any* differences between the woman Hawthorne normally met and the woman who picked up the key on Wednesday?''

"Hard to say. Could be the same woman. Or she could be different." Ted Sanders shrugged his shoulders again. "The clothes were the same."

"What about the way she was acting? Anything strike you as odd?"

"Well, she seemed kind of nervous."

That figured. She'd been about to kill someone, after all. "If you remember anything else, give me a call." Morgan passed the man his card.

"I will. You better believe it. This is the most interesting thing that's happened since last month when some woman's old man followed her here and kicked the shit out of the man she was sleeping with."

"Sounds like an exciting place."

"You don't know the half of it, Detective."

IT WAS SEVEN O'CLOCK in the evening and Trista thought she was about to go crazy. She'd slept for most of the afternoon after indulging in her crying bout, and had made herself a light snack when she'd awakened. Her headache had abated and she judged herself to be pretty well recovered from the attack—physically, if not mentally.

She decided to give Suni a call, and caught her on the car phone, between appointments. She gave her a mild version of last night's events, then made plans to meet for lunch the next day. She'd just hung up the phone when she heard a knock at the door. A glance through the peephole confirmed it was Morgan—who else could it have been? She tried to tell herself that the small jump of joy she felt at recognizing him had to do more with her need for distraction than for the man himself.

Her smile felt tentative as she let him in. She was relieved to see him looking relaxed. He'd changed and was dressed entirely in black—black jeans, black shirt and a black cashmere jacket. She wondered if he remembered how sexy she found him in that color.

He had her briefcase with him, which he set by the door. "You can look at the files later, if you feel up to it." He gave her a slow, assessing look that told her he noticed every curve that was revealed in her tight-fitting blue jeans and soft turquoise sweater. "You certainly look like you're feeling better. Did you stay in bed like you were supposed to?"

"I was resting all day. Honest. Would you like some coffee?"

"Sounds good," he agreed, kicking off his shoes at the door and following her to the kitchen. He swung a leg over the stool and leaned on the counter, watching while she carefully measured ground beans and water.

"Any new developments?" she asked.

"I spent most of the afternoon at the Moondust Motel. The desk clerk's information ties in with the entries I found in Daniel's appointment book."

"Curious, isn't it? Why, after six months, would they suddenly get together again?"

"Good question. Especially since she'd just started an affair with Walker."

"Assuming they were seeing the same woman," Trista said as she placed one cup of black coffee in front of Morgan and added some milk to another mug for herself.

"Yes, but for now we're going on that assumption. Too many coincidences otherwise. Like meeting on the same day of the week and the disguise the woman wore."

Trista sat down on the stool next to Morgan's and stared into her coffee cup. "Have you found any other links between the two men? Besides my office, I mean?"

"No."

Well, he certainly wasn't pulling his punches. Trista took a sip of coffee, then tried to keep her voice light as she asked, "Shouldn't you be asking me if *I* have an alibi for the afternoons of the murders?"

"I already know you have an alibi. For Hawthorne's murder, anyway."

"I do?"

"And you told me about it. At the time, you thought you were clearing Sylvia. But you were really clearing both of you."

Trista laughed wryly, remembering how anxious she'd been to tell him about Sylvia showing up at her office the same time her husband had been killed. "Well, thank goodness for that. I suppose you'd like an alibi for the Walker murder, too?"

She'd expected him to laugh it off, and was a little shocked when his expression grew serious.

"Do you have one?" he asked.

Chapter Twelve

Swallowing down a gulp of coffee, Trista went to get her appointment book from her briefcase. Flipping back the pages, she came to Monday. "I had a client session from twelve-thirty to one-thirty. Then a thirty-minute break, followed by another hour-long session. Will that do?"

He jotted down the information in his notepad, then flipped to a clean page and tore it out.

"Here." He set it on the counter between them and drew a quick matrix, with Brenda's name in the first of the top columns. "We know she took a long lunch on both Monday and Wednesday, so she had opportunity to commit both murders."

"Theoretically."

Next he wrote Nan Walker's name. "She was working at the time of her husband's death, but was out for lunch when Daniel was killed. Her son was in Kingston when Walker died, but was back home when Daniel was killed. Lorne Thackray had no alibi for either."

Trista looked down at the chart. Nan Walker—cross, checkmark. Jason Walker—cross, checkmark. Lorne Thackray—checkmark, checkmark.

"What about Sylvia?" She got up to refill their coffee then sat down again.

"Sylvia." Morgan made a checkmark, then a cross. "She told me she was shopping Monday, but I haven't found anyone who remembers seeing her. Wednesday, however, she was at your office."

"Why are Lorne Thackray and Jason Walker on your list? I thought you were pretty sure Jerry and Daniel were killed by their lover?"

"Their lover, or someone impersonating their lover. The descriptions we got from both clerks were of a woman wearing a hat and a large trench coat. Don't you think it might be possible for a man—if he wasn't too large—to impersonate a woman in that getup? Jason is a slender young man, and Lorne Thackray has a high-pitched voice." Morgan ran his hands through his hair, a sure sign that he was tired. Trista picked up on it right away.

"You need to go home and get a decent night's sleep."

"Yeah. But first I need to eat. How about you? Have you had dinner?"

"No. But I have some steaks on hand. And I could make a salad."

In the back of her mind she'd hoped he would stay. Now she took the New York strips out of the fridge and set them on the counter.

Morgan pulled the plate closer to himself. "You'd better leave the cooking of these to me. In fact, why don't you sit back and relax."

When she tried to ignore him, he pushed her into a chair. "Remember, doctor's orders…"

Trista bit back a smile, and decided to give in. This time. Despite the unfamiliar kitchen, Morgan took charge easily, putting potatoes in the oven to bake and preparing vegetables for a salad.

The evening passed simply, and for once they managed to avoid talking about either the case or their past history. But tension was still in the air. It was in the way they carefully avoided touching each other, and in the over-polite way they worded their comments and requests.

On the sofa after dinner, over brandies, they finally began to feel more comfortable. Morgan slouched down, relaxing his head against the back of the sofa and putting his sock feet up on the coffee table.

"Do you get the feeling we're walking on eggs around here? I've never heard so many thank-yous."

"We've been through a lot. The murders. That scene in the hospital…" Trista stared at the contents of her glass, sloshing the liquid along the sides, almost, but not quite, up to the rim. She played with her drink because it gave her something to do. And something to look at besides Morgan.

"I've been thinking about that," Morgan said slowly, giving the impression that each word was gingerly selected. "Trying to figure out how two normally intelligent people managed to screw things up so badly."

"Don't feel bad. At least you weren't the psychologist."

"A psychologist who is human." Morgan's gaze was gentle. "I don't know if anything could have prepared us for losing Andrew."

"No." She took another swallow of brandy. The warmth was comforting. Being with Morgan was comforting. "What did you do after I left?"

She'd always wondered, but never felt she had the right to ask.

"I stayed in the house, hoping you'd come back."

His voice, raw with emotion, rasped her conscience, and she tightened her hold on her glass.

152   *Same Place, Same Time*

"Once the divorce was finalized, I went through what I call my bar phase. I sold the house and moved to a rental. And spent whatever time I wasn't working, drinking. That lasted a few months before I realized it would be more productive to spend those spare hours in the gym so that I could fall into bed exhausted every night."

Trista swallowed, then glanced down into her drink. "And women? Has there been someone new?"

She didn't know what answer she'd expected, but she could tell from Morgan's pause that he had something to tell.

"About a year ago, I had a relationship…"

Her gaze swung toward him. He was sitting upright now, feet planted firmly on either side of him, leaning over the glass he was cupping in his hands. She waited for him to continue.

"Remember that crown attorney you always said had a thing for me?"

Trista felt as if he'd punched her in the stomach. "Sydney Jordan?"

He nodded. "We saw each other for a few months. Maybe six."

"What happened?" She leaned forward, waiting for the answer. She'd known she'd been right about that woman. And Morgan had said she was imagining things…

"She asked me to move in with her. I admit a part of me was tempted. I didn't like being on my own, and being with her deadened a lot of my pain. But I knew that wasn't fair to her. She kept saying things would change, that I'd get over…everything…and come to love her, eventually. But it just didn't feel right that way."

Trista blinked to hold back her tears. "What a terrible mess I've made of both our lives."

In a flash he was beside her, his arm over her shoulder. "Don't start blaming yourself again, Trista. It isn't that simple and you know it."

"Maybe not. But other couples manage to survive the death of a child. Why couldn't we?"

"I don't think—" Morgan's next words were cut off by the sound of the phone. They stared at each other for a few seconds. At the second ring Morgan stood and walked toward the window. "Go ahead and get it."

What had he been about to say? Could he really not blame her for the breakup of their marriage?

"Hello?" She picked up the portable phone in the kitchen and sank onto a stool. With the open layout of the apartment, she could see Morgan pace the length of the living room.

The voice at the other end of the line identified herself as one of Trista's patients. Turning her attention from Morgan, Trista forced herself to listen carefully as the woman told her about a recent crisis in her professional life. The problem was complicated and Trista wasn't aware of how much time had gone by before she finally hung up. Glancing at her watch, she was surprised to see that a full thirty minutes had passed.

She found Morgan horizontal on the couch, his eyes closed, his chest rising and falling in a slow and easy rhythm. He was sound asleep.

Knowing how little rest he'd had this past week, she didn't rouse him. Carefully, she covered him with the afghan, then turned out the light and went to bed herself.

MORGAN AWOKE the next morning, clueing in on his unusual surroundings slowly. He wasn't in his bed, or sitting in his car, or at his desk, or in any of the usual places he slept. He was on a sofa. Trista's sofa. He rubbed his eyes and then sat up, remembering that she'd gone to answer the phone. He'd obviously fallen asleep shortly after that.

Looking down at his watch, he was surprised to see that it was already seven. He hadn't had so many hours of uninterrupted sleep since this case had begun. He stood up and neatly folded the blanket that had covered him before going to the windows and pulling open the curtains. Brilliant sunshine greeted him.

He was tempted to go to work without waking Trista, but he didn't want to leave her without the dead bolt fastened, and there was no way he could do that from outside the door without a key. Tentatively he walked down the short hall to her bedroom. The door was slightly ajar. He gave it a gentle push and it slid wide open. Trista was still asleep, half under the covers and half out of them, the way he remembered.

She was sleeping on her stomach, her pillow a mass of auburn curls. A bare shoulder, its whiteness emphasized by the contrast with a thin black spaghetti strap, was visible below the curls, but her arm was tucked out of sight beneath the pillow. One long, shapely leg had worked its way out of the covers, baring a black silk-covered hipbone, and a glimpse of skin-white midriff.

Swallowing hard, Morgan took a step backward, about to beat a hasty retreat from the temptation in front of him. Trista had changed many things, like the way she decorated and the way she wore her hair, but she obviously had the same tastes in lingerie. He put his hand on the door, about to pull it closed behind him, when a hand withdrew from under the pillow, tunneled into the mop of unruly hair, and revealed one hazel eye, the straight line of her nose and the softness of her lips. Her cheek—

the one he could see—was a sleep-flushed, peachy-gold color.

"Good morning," she said in a voice one octave lower than her normal speaking voice.

Morgan cleared his throat, aware of his heart hammering in his chest, of other parts of his body responding to the arousing image she presented.

"Sorry about falling asleep on you," he apologized. "But thanks for the use of the sofa." Even while his mind was urging him to say goodbye and to remind her to close the dead bolt behind him, he heard himself say, "French toast still your favorite?"

Trista's leg beat a hasty retreat under the covers as she rolled into a half-reclined position, covers clutched protectively to her chest. "You don't need to make me breakfast."

"No. But I'm hungry," he lied. He didn't know why, but he liked the thought of cooking for her. She'd become too thin…

"In that case, go ahead. I'll be out in a minute."

Back in the kitchen, he looked inside the cupboard where he'd seen Trista keep her coffee. It felt nice to be putting two scoops of coffee into the pot instead of one.

He'd just flipped the brew switch when a sound from behind made him turn. Trista was standing at the kitchen counter, wearing an incredibly ugly pink fuzzy housecoat that looked big enough for two of her. Her hair was still a tangle of curls around her head, and she was yawning. It was all he could do not to draw her into his arms and kiss her.

"Sorry!" She laughed as another yawn overtook her. "I wanted to check that you were finding everything."

"I'm doing fine," he assured her. "Why don't you go

ahead and have a shower and get dressed while I shake up some food here.''

Nodding, she turned and left the room, and Morgan returned his attention to the kitchen. As he puttered about the unfamiliar room, trying to locate the frying pan, a bowl, the vanilla, he listened to the sounds coming from down the hall. They were wonderfully familiar and comforting. The drumming of water in the shower, followed by the blast of a hair dryer. Then a door opened and he could hear a closet door running along its track, the sound of metal hangers scraping against each other.

For a moment there was silence, and he imagined the pink robe falling to Trista's feet. First she would slip into a pair of delicate silk panties, then she would put on a little lacy bra, hardly more than a strip of sheer fabric...

Morgan whipped the eggs furiously. After all that had happened these past few days, he had no idea where things stood between the two of them. There was only one thing he knew for sure, and that was that he was still attracted to her. He couldn't look at her without wanting her.

Now wasn't the time to do anything about it, though. He wasn't sure if there'd ever be a time. They'd started to talk, that was good. But did Trista still love him the way he loved her? Somehow he doubted it.

Ten minutes later Trista was ready, dressed casually in jeans and a matching denim shirt. The clothes hugged her long, lean body, and Morgan thought keeping his distance was going to be easier said than done.

''Delicious as always,'' Trista said after her first mouthful of the toasted, egg-dipped bread.

''Good. Eat up.'' Morgan kept an eye on her as he ate his own breakfast. Every time she finished a slice, he gave her another. After her third helping, he finally felt satisfied. "Well, you must be feeling better. That's the most food I've seen you eat all week."

Trista pushed her plate aside and reached for her coffee with a sigh of satisfaction. "I told you I was fully recovered."

"If you feel this great now, just think how wonderful you're going to feel after another day of rest and relaxation," Morgan said as he cleared the table.

Trista brought her coffee mug down on the table with a definitive thud. "Who said anything about another day of rest and relaxation?"

"I believe it was that guy in the white coat—" Morgan snapped his fingers "—ah, yes, the doctor, wasn't he?"

Trista shook her head. "He was just trying to avoid a malpractice suit. I'm fine. I don't need any more rest. In fact, if I have to spend another day alone in this apartment you'll have to cart me off to an entirely different sort of hospital in the morning."

"Come on, it won't be that bad," Morgan cajoled. "What if I was to come over later and make you a killer dinner?"

She only hesitated a second before saying, "That would be good. But at least let me look over the files you brought with you. It should be safe for you to leave them here now that you've changed the locks."

MORGAN HAD RELUCTANTLY agreed to leave the files, but in the end, he might as well not have bothered. Trista couldn't find anything more relevant to the homicide case in the Hawthornes' file than she had in the Walkers'. It was so frustrating. If someone was willing to break and enter to get them, there had to be *something* there.

By midmorning Trista was ready to go for a stroll in

High Park, but Sylvia called just as she was about to walk out the door.

"My in-laws are driving me crazy," she said. "Especially my mother-in-law. All she can do is whine and complain about all she's lost. What about me? They've been here since Friday morning, and I don't know how much more of this I can take."

"Maybe you should try and get away for a while. Do you have a friend's house you could spend a few quiet hours at?"

"Actually I called your office yesterday hoping I could get in to see you. But you're closed. Is this because of Daniel's death?"

Trust Sylvia to be perfectly blunt. "In part," Trista hedged.

"According to this morning's paper, the police think Daniel's murder might be connected to Jerry Walker's. Which is so strange, because I'm sure my husband didn't know Jerry. Although we did meet the Walkers, briefly once, at a fund-raiser for Suni Choopra. Of course you know, because you were there. That's how we met you."

Trista's heart pounded. Suni Choopra. The politician, her friend, was another link between the two men. She should have thought of it herself, since she had met both the Walkers and the Hawthornes through her. Of course, she met a lot of her clients that way.

"Sylvia, if you need to talk to me, I could meet you at a restaurant for an hour or so."

"Really? I'd appreciate that. But how about my house? The in-laws have gone out to visit Daniel's godparents. Could you be here in half-an-hour?"

Trista agreed and hung up, feeling she'd been manipulated somehow.

MORGAN LEFT Walker's Hardware, amazed that the store was as profitable as it was. Located just west of Bathurst Avenue, it was definitely not in the trendy area of Queen Street. While the store itself was relatively neat, with a tidy exterior, across the street garbage was piled up in front of a secondhand appliance store, and colored neon lights blazed in the window of a decrepit-looking tattoo studio.

Morgan got into his car and thought of the interesting meetings he'd just had with Thackray, Jason and Nan. His timing had been perfect, interrupting a territorial battle between Jason and Thackray, proving that both men wanted control of the stores much more desperately than either one of them, or Nan, had let on. Jason's emotional words about carrying on for his father's sake hadn't fooled Morgan for one minute.

As for Thackray, he'd noticed Nan seemed almost as protective of him as she did of her son. Was it possible that Jerry hadn't been the only one cheating in that marriage? Boy, wouldn't that make things interesting. He made a note to get some follow-up work done in that direction.

One disappointment was that he hadn't found any connection to Daniel Hawthorne. Thackray swore he'd never heard of the man, and Morgan was tempted to believe him.

Morgan turned left onto Spadina Avenue, tires bumping as they passed over the streetcar tracks. Crowds of shoppers, determined not to pay retail, were thrumming along the sidewalks, moving from one discount outlet to the next. He remembered weekends when he and Trista had been among them. They'd shop for an hour, which was usually all he could stand, before going to one of the trendy bistros further east on Queen Street.

He drove past the gray stone towers of Casa Loma, leaving the buzzing downtown, and his memories, behind him. He headed for Forest Hill, and the Hawthorne address. A message from Sylvia had come while he was at the hardware store. It had been vague, mentioning that she'd found something and he'd better come over as soon as possible. He turned onto the broad, tree-lined street where she lived and pulled up in front of the house. Sylvia answered the door before he had time to knock.

"Good morning, Detective." She sounded slightly out of breath, as if she'd raced to the door.

Morgan nodded, stepping forward. "I got your message. I understand you found something?"

"Yes." Sylvia stepped aside to allow him to enter. "My counselor, Trista Emerson, is here, as well."

Trista? Morgan paused, then frowned when he noticed Sylvia watching him curiously. What the hell was Trista doing here? Once inside, he saw her standing by the window. Her cheeks flushed as she saw him. Obviously Sylvia hadn't mentioned she was expecting him.

"Hello, Trista." He hated how formal the words sounded in this elegant, yet uninviting room.

"You two know each other?"

"Yes." Trista spoke quietly. "Actually, we used to be married."

"Really?" Sylvia crossed her arms over her barrel chest and glanced back and forth between them.

"Did you have something to show me?" Morgan repeated impatiently.

"Yes. It was a note, included in Daniel's personal papers." Sylvia pulled a folded sheet of paper out from a side pocket in her black sheath dress.

Morgan unfolded the paper, not surprised to see the same rose border that had graced Jerry Walker's note.

Typed below—by the same manual typewriter that Walker's note had been typed on, he was willing to bet—was a brief message. *I need to see you this week. Same place, same time. xoxo.*

He felt the familiar quickening of his pulse at finding another piece of the puzzle. These notes had to prove, beyond a doubt, that the two men were killed by the same woman.

He looked up to find Sylvia's eyes, dark and intense, focused on him.

"Find her, Detective. Find her and make her pay."

Morgan glanced over at Trista. Her face was unnaturally white, and she was propping herself against the wall. Was her head bothering her? Or was it something else? She was staring at the paper in his hand with the oddest expression.

Chapter Thirteen

Trista stared at the note in Morgan's hand. It was on Suni Choopra's stationery. Trista was almost certain. Hadn't Suni sent her a thank-you note about a month ago on paper just like it? Or maybe it was only similar. Trista stepped closer for a better look.

It did look familiar—but that had to be coincidence. And yet, the typescript on the note was uneven, as if it had been printed by typewriter, not computer, and the image of Suni's portable on the side table by her desk burned in Trista's mind. Suni labeled herself technologically illiterate, and refused to use the office's computerized word processing system.

What did it mean? If Suni wrote those notes, then she must have been the mystery lover.

Was it possible? Could Suni have had an affair first with Daniel Hawthorne, then several months later, Jerry Walker? But why would Suni do something like that? If the press found out, the publicity could wreck her entire career.

In the midst of all these unanswered questions, Trista knew only one thing. She wasn't going to tell Morgan that she thought she recognized the stationery, or that both the Walkers and the Hawthornes had known Suni, until after she had a chance to talk to her friend. There had to be an explanation. Maybe Suni's stationery was only similar to the one used on these notes. Or maybe it was a readily available pattern, more common than one might expect.

"Are you okay?" Behind the question, she could sense Morgan's curiosity. He'd noted her strange reaction. Keeping this information to herself was not going to be easy.

"I'm fine," she insisted.

"Well, if there's nothing else, Mrs. Hawthorne, I'd better be going." Morgan put the note away and took his leave.

After Morgan was gone, it took a few minutes for Trista to wind up her earlier conversation with Sylvia. As she left, she said, "You'll call me if you need to talk again?"

"I sure will, Trista. Thanks for coming."

Out on the street, Trista was dismayed to see Morgan waiting by his car.

"I'll give you a ride to the subway stop," he said.

There was no point in arguing, so she climbed past the open passenger door.

Once he'd started the engine, he turned to her. "There was something about that note that bothered you, wasn't there?"

"I don't know what to think," she answered as honestly as she could. "Was Jerry Walker's note similar?"

"Almost identical. Both were on that same flowered stationery. Both looked like they were typed on the same manual typewriter. And both used that phrase, 'same place, same time.' I don't think there can be any doubt that the notes were sent by the same woman."

"The mystery lover." Trista tried once more to imagine Suni in that role. It still didn't seem to fit.

"Yes. And the murderer."

The blunt words made Trista wince. Suni a killer? No, it was impossible.

When Morgan pulled up at the St. Clair subway stop, she tried to exit quickly, but he caught her by the shoulder and gave her an intense look.

"Are you sure there isn't something bothering you?"

Trista swallowed. Of course, he would sense she was holding something back. But, at this point, there was nothing she could say. "I want this case solved as much as you do, Morgan. If I had something I felt I could tell you, I would."

"Not good enough, Trista." He looked at her through narrowed eyes, his expression set firmly in disapproval. But he let go of her shoulder, as if accepting that he couldn't make her say any more. At least not yet.

She stood on the sidewalk and watched him drive off, with a guilty feeling knotting up her stomach. She hadn't actually lied, but that was just a technicality. When he found out that she hadn't told him about the stationery, he was going to be furious. And frankly, she wouldn't blame him.

THE SAMENESS of Oliver's, with its blue-and-white striped chairs, fashionable clientele and young attractive servers, came as a surprise to Trista. With all that had been happening lately, it seemed strange to find that some things carried on unchanged by the drama that was monopolizing her life.

She'd made a reservation and was led to a corner near the front of the restaurant where she could watch the door for Suni's appearance. She picked up the menu, opened it, then put it down without reading a word. She was nervous. What was she going to say? *Did you send notes to those two men who were murdered? Were you their lover? Did you kill them?*

Hardly. But what could she say? How was she going to get the information that would exonerate Suni, without putting her through the humiliation of a police interrogation?

A rush of fresh air announced a new arrival and Trista looked up to see Suni, dressed in a coffee-colored suit with a blouse a shade lighter, breeze into the restaurant. Trista raised her arm and Suni nodded in recognition, joining her at the small round table.

"Sorry I'm late. I was doing some door-to-door work in the neighborhood, and time got away from me, I'm afraid." Suni ran her hand through her hair, patting the thick, black strands back into place and smiling warmly, a picture-perfect smile. Her skin was smooth, her almond-shaped eyes still young-looking. No wonder the cameras loved her.

The waiter arrived to take their orders and they both chose the daily pasta special after an offhand glance at the menu. Trista waited until their drinks were in hand before she plunged.

"By the way, I really like the stationery you used for that thank-you note you sent me a few weeks ago. I keep meaning to ask you where you got it." She took a quick swallow of her wine, hoping the cool liquid would quell the color she could feel rising in her cheeks.

"The stuff with flowers on the top?"

Trista nodded, fussing with her napkin, adjusting it over her lap.

"I've had that for ages. I can't remember where I got it." Suni answered the question absentmindedly, her eyes watching out the window as if expecting someone. Trista recognized the look. When she was in public, Suni hardly ever relaxed, at least not completely. She never knew when someone might come up to shake her hand or to ask a question.

Trista's hands settled on her lap, and the tense set of her shoulders relaxed marginally. Surely Suni wouldn't have spoken so nonchalantly if she were guilty.

"You probably ordered it from the company where you buy your other office supplies, don't you think?" she prodded gently, determined to get a reasonable explanation for the coincidence that she could deliver to Morgan.

"What?" Suni looked back from the window, a frown creasing her forehead. "Oh, you mean the stationery… No, I don't think so. It just caught my eye one day when I was out shopping—I don't remember where. Seems to me I was out of the country on a business trip."

"Oh well." Trista shrugged, her heart sinking. She'd hoped the stationery was a common variety, the kind hundreds of people might own. But if it had been purchased in another country, it might not even be available in Toronto.

"I saw Steven Reid the other night."

Suni's comment caught Trista off guard. "Steven Reid?"

"He asked about you."

Then Trista remembered. He was a lawyer that she'd met at a breakfast meeting where Suni had been speaking. Attractive, in his mid-forties. They'd sat at the same table and she'd been momentarily charmed by his gentle good humor and obvious intelligence. When he'd phoned the next day asking her out to dinner, however, she'd refused.

"That's nice."

"Still not interested I see." Suni placed her hand gently on Trista's arm. "Now that I've seen your ex-husband, I think I understand a little better. You know I've never tried to push anything with the men I introduce to you. But if I were you, I'd think seriously about giving Steven a chance. He's been a widower for a couple of years now. His friends say he's ready for a real relationship."

"Good for Steven. I wish I could say the same for me. Sometimes I wonder if I'll ever be ready to take that plunge again." She thought of Morgan, and the disappointment she occasionally glimpsed in his eyes. It had been hard for him to accept the divorce. Would he ever want to remarry?

"If Steven is so great," Trista said, "why don't you date him?"

Suni slid her hand back to her side of the table and gave a short laugh. "Really, Trista, he's much too young for me."

"Come on, what's ten years in this day and age?"

"It's still quite a lot when it's the woman who's older, believe me. Anyway, I'm not the sort of woman men look for when they're ready to get serious."

"What do you mean by that?"

"Trista, the last thing a man wants is an ambitious woman. Especially a woman whose ambition includes a career in politics."

"I'm sure there are men who might find it difficult to deal with a woman who's achieved as much as you have, but Steven doesn't seem like he suffers from an inferiority complex."

"Believe me on this one." Suni laughed gently, but her eyes were not merry. "I've learned the hard way."

"INTERESTING, all right." Zarowin was holding the two notes in his gloved hands, doing a visual comparison, before Morgan sent them off for analysis. "Any new leads on her identity?"

"Not yet." Morgan was as frustrated as his superior. There had to be some link between the two men, besides Trista's office. There just *had* to be.

"You're playing your cards a little too close to the vest on this one, Forester."

"That's the way I operate. You know that."

"And usually we can cut you a little slack. But this case is different. Not one homicide, but two. This has the potential to blow into something really big—"

"No way." Morgan rose out of his chair and loomed over the broad figure of the inspector. "This isn't a serial killer on the loose. I'm sure of it."

Zarowin wasn't intimidated. He stared Morgan in the eye before replying. "You'd better be right. But first, you better find out who this mystery lover is."

Morgan turned, staring at the bookshelves where Zarowin's collection of family photos was displayed. Zarowin's three sons, dressed in soccer uniforms and posed around a black-and-white ball, smiled back at him. "I have a feeling we're almost there. I just need to follow up on a few things. I should know by tomorrow."

"Good. I hope you're right. I also hope you're not overlooking the obvious. The only connection we have between the two men is still Trista's office. Trista may have an alibi for the murders, but that doesn't mean she wasn't the one having the affairs."

Morgan shook his head. He knew that simply wasn't possible. But how could he explain as much to Zarowin?

"Just keep an open mind," was Zarowin's parting comment as Morgan reclaimed the notes.

The words barely penetrated Morgan's consciousness. He kept remembering Trista's strange behavior at Sylvia Hawthorne's. The difficulty she had meeting his gaze when he dropped her off at the subway. The more he thought about it, the more certain he was that she'd felt some shock of recognition when she saw that note.

So why not tell him? Was she protecting somebody? A client, her secretary, somebody else? Morgan felt his gut twist at the thought. If she was keeping something back, she could be putting herself in danger again. Or even worse, her involvement in this might be more than he'd ever suspected. Both of those options were bad enough, but what bothered him most about her silence was that she obviously didn't trust him enough to confide in him. Just when he'd thought the gulf between them was beginning to narrow, she had to go and wedge it a little wider again.

"WELL, THAT CURRY was great," Trista said with forced cheerfulness.

After their uncomfortable scene outside Sylvia's house that morning, she'd half expected Morgan to concoct an excuse for why he couldn't come by for dinner. In fact, she'd hoped for as much. But he'd shown up at her door at six o'clock with a bag of groceries in hand and a bottle of red wine. Then he'd proceeded to cook dinner, insisting that she sit down and relax while he worked. It would have been very enjoyable—being pampered like that—if he hadn't kept giving her these strange looks. Sort of sad, yet curious, too. Trista knew he was still suspicious about what had happened at Sylvia's, and a part of her longed to blurt out the whole story, just to clear the air between them.

But she still wasn't ready to do that. Her conversation

with Suni hadn't been as conclusive as she'd hoped. Suni hadn't seemed at all upset by the mention of the stationery. Surely that meant she was innocent. What if Morgan didn't see things that way?

Worse, Trista had begun to have her own doubts during their lunch. She thought about Suni's bitter tone as she talked about men and their inability to accept a woman who was more ambitious, more powerful, more influential than they were. They'd discussed this topic before, but she'd never imagined Suni was really serious. In her mind, Suni remained single because she was too busy for a relationship.

Could Suni's disillusionment have led her to have affairs with married men? If she had, why would she send those notes? A public figure like Suni ought to know better than to put anything private down on paper. No, it didn't make sense. Moral issues aside, Suni was too politically astute to risk ruining her career by taking such unnecessary risks.

"Have some more," Morgan offered, getting up from the table to refill her plate, despite her protests. She picked away at the second helping, her mind scurrying to find safe topics of conversation. But no matter what subject she chose, the best she could get from Morgan were monosyllabic responses. She could see anger building in his eyes and knew that he was waiting for her to confide in him.

She reached the end of the meal with a sense of relief, insisting on doing the dishes since Morgan had cooked.

"You should be resting," he argued.

"I've been resting all day," she countered, taking a plate out of his hands.

"How about your visit to Sylvia's?" he came back at her, his voice not at all pleasant.

Trista avoided his eyes as she shrugged. "Except for that, of course."

"And I should believe you, shouldn't I, Trista? After all, you would never lie to me. Would you?"

Biting her lip, Trista stacked dishes next to the sink. She could feel his anger, his disapproval. And it hurt. What did he expect from her? She was doing what she thought was right. Couldn't he trust her instincts, just this once?

He came to stand beside her, sighing heavily. With a gentle finger he wiped a tear out from the corner of her eye.

"Look, I'm sorry. I don't know what got into me."

"That's okay." She turned to the sink, inserting her hands into the sudsy water. It was the only way she could fight the sudden impulse she'd had to throw herself into his arms. He was being more patient than she had a right to expect.

She was scrubbing the final pot when she felt Morgan place his hand on her neck. He was standing behind her. Not close enough that his body was touching hers, but close enough that she could feel his warmth. Slowly he worked his thumb against the muscles at the base of her neck. The steel wool she'd been scrubbing with slipped out of her fingers.

It felt wonderful to have his hands next to her skin, to feel his presence behind her. The longing she'd felt for him the other day returned suddenly, even stronger than before. She closed her eyes and gripped the counter in front of her.

He stepped a little closer. Now she could feel the firmness of his chest and his thighs against her. The warmth of his breath against her hair. Still his hand stayed at her neck. She tilted her head, inviting his touch, and his hand slid up to caress her cheek, then down, sliding to her shoulder, underneath her sweater.

They stood like that for a long time. The only sound she could hear was the beating of a heart, fast and loud. She didn't know if it was his or hers. Or both of theirs. His hand caressed the soft skin of her neck and shoulders, and she longed for it to move lower, to where her breast was now aching to be touched. But he kept it where it was, massaging her gently, but never moving beyond the boundary of the crew-neck sweater. She gritted her teeth. Pleasure became frustration.

With a low moan she turned to face him and his lips crushed against hers so fast she knew that this was what he'd been waiting for. Her wet, soapy fingers dug into his shoulders as he engulfed her in his arms. She gave herself totally to his kisses, a part of her recognizing the familiar smells and textures of his skin, while another part of her felt as if she was experiencing this for the first time. This hard, strong man—needing *her,* wanting *her,* holding *her.*

"Trista. Oh, Trista," he whispered in her ear, his hands caressing her shoulders and then trailing down her back.

Had it always been this wonderful? Had he always known exactly where to touch her? She moved, letting his hands guide her. Now they stood only inches apart and his hands were down at her waist, slipping under the sweater. Inching upward. She caught her breath. Waiting. Finally they were there. His strong hands cupped her breasts within the lacy confines of her bra, and she let out a sigh of pleasure.

He kissed her again, pulling her body tightly into his. She knotted her fingers in his hair, holding him as if she'd never let go. Then he lowered his mouth, kissing her neck, her shoulders. He stopped when he reached the sweater.

"Come." He was half dragging her, half carrying her, toward the bedroom.

She felt too impatient to wait that long. Her fingers dealt quickly with the buttons of his shirt and her hands caressed the hard muscles of his chest, making their progress even slower. Finally Morgan gave up, lifting her and carrying her the last few feet until they reached the comfortable softness of her bed. Quickly they stripped off each other's clothes before falling to the bed wrapped in a tight embrace.

Passion had always been a strong link between them, but Trista had never before experienced such a surge of urgency. His hands couldn't touch her fast enough, his body couldn't come to hers soon enough. At the last moment, when it was much too late to stop, she heard her voice ask, "Is this a mistake?"

She didn't know why she choose that moment to speak—she wanted him so desperately nothing on earth could have stopped her from giving herself to him.

"If it is, I don't care," was Morgan's muffled response, his lips nuzzled against her breast.

If it is. Trista's body arched underneath his and she threw her head back with pleasure. She hadn't felt this good in years.

A MISTAKE. Curled next to Morgan, her head resting on his chest, the words echoed in her brain once it was over. It had been wonderful, but would the pain to come be worth the fleeting moments of pleasure? Sleeping together now was only going to make it more difficult for both of them when the time came to go their separate ways again.

"What's wrong?"

His voice was soft and low in her ear, and she fought the urge to nuzzle her face into his neck and tell him, nothing. Instead, she eased herself out of his arms and got out of bed, quickly wrapping her naked body in her pink robe.

"What's wrong?" she repeated, sitting down on the edge of the bed, across from him. Her eyes were adjusting to the low light. She could see the creases in his forehead, the straight line of his lips. "I don't even know how to begin to answer that question. I think we're both mature enough to know that what just happened between us doesn't solve any of our problems."

He lowered his eyes from her, and in that small gesture she saw his disappointment and frustration. "Nobody said making love was going to solve our problems," he said after a brief silence. "That's up to us, isn't it?"

"Are you talking about what happened at Sylvia's today?"

"That's part of it. I don't suppose you want to try and tell me you haven't been holding something back?"

Now *she* was averting her eyes.

"I thought so." He sat up, planting his feet on the carpeted floor, as if preparing to eject himself from the bed. "You don't trust me, do you?"

Trista sighed. That wasn't why she couldn't tell him about the stationery. It wasn't a question of trust, it was simple loyalty to an old friend. Or was it? Now she felt confused about her own motives. "Just give me a day or two," she pleaded.

He looked at her disbelievingly. "You don't ask for much, do you? Remember how we swore we'd never keep secrets?"

"That was when we were married." She knew it was

cruel to bring up their divorce at that moment. But didn't they both need to face reality?

"Thanks for the reminder."

"Don't look at me like that. I'm trying to be realistic." She wrapped her arms around her pink robe, around herself. "This has been a terrible mistake." She realized now that it was true. "We're supposed to be starting our lives over. Sleeping together only confuses the issue."

"That's exactly where you're wrong, Trista," he said quietly, but firmly. "We never worked to make our marriage last after the accident. You just walked away from it. Don't you think what's between us is worth a little more effort than that?"

With the tip of her index finger, she traced the outline of the quilting stitches on the bedcover. "It's not that I don't think it's worth it. It's just—" Her voice broke and she had to wait a few seconds to compose herself. "I don't know if it would be fair to either of us. Some mistakes can't be reversed, and I'm afraid we've made too many of those kind. Or at least, I have."

"Maybe you just need time."

"I've had four years," she reminded him.

Her comment hung in the air for a few minutes. Finally, with a tired sigh, Morgan stood up and she turned away from the sight of his naked body. She listened to the sounds of him dressing, unable to stop herself from imagining things happening differently. Morgan pulling her back into bed with him. A night spent in the safe cocoon of his arms. But as tempting as the thought was, she knew that to indulge in it would be irresponsible.

He dressed without speaking. She heard the zip of his pants, the slap of his belt as he cinched it tight. Listening with her eyes shut, it wasn't until she felt his hand on her shoulder that she opened them and saw him standing in front of her.

"I'm sorry, Morgan—" He put his hand over her mouth to stop the words.

"I've heard you say that more than enough times for one week. Don't get up. I'll see myself out."

She bowed her head and listened to him walk down the hall to the door. There was a pause while he put on his shoes, then she heard the dead bolt click and the door swing open. "Lock up behind me," were his parting words, punctuated by the slamming of the door.

She sat on the bed for a long time after he'd gone, her mind blank of all thought. There had been too many confrontations between them, and she was tired of trying to deal with them. Not to mention the memories. Sighing, she locked the door, then slipped her housecoat to the floor and went to take a shower.

With the water pouring over her, Trista soaped her body, thinking about what Morgan had said. He was right. She'd apologized too often. It was time she started solving her problems instead of feeling sorry about them.

Starting with Suni. If that *was* her stationery, if she *had* written those notes, then she had to tell Morgan. And if she couldn't ask Suni directly, she had to find out for herself.

That meant getting a piece of the stationery from Suni's desk and a sample of typing from her portable typewriter. As she toweled off, Trista realized how easy it would be. She still had the key to the campaign headquarters—she'd forgotten to return it the day Suni had rushed off with her migraine. It would be easy for her to slip into the office and get the sample herself.

The best time to do it would be after business was closed for the night.

Like now.

It was almost eleven. No one, not even the diehards, would be working this late. Trista pulled on a pair of black stretch pants and a cotton T-shirt. Her conscience pricked at the thought of sneaking behind her friend's back. But she was doing this for Suni's own good. If she could prove the stationery was different, if the type didn't match, then Suni would be cleared before any journalists got wind of a potential connection between the popular government member and the Motel Murders, as they were now being called in the local press.

Trista grabbed her purse and keys and called a cab to take her to the campaign office. She often took the subway late at night, never feeling nervous or afraid, but tonight she wasn't willing to take any chances. The cab would drop her off right at the headquarters' door, and what could be safer than that?

Trista's sneakers squeaked as she stepped out of the cab onto the cool concrete sidewalk. There were still a few people strolling in the neighborhood. Mostly couples, frequenting the assorted restaurants in the area.

Yet, her fingers trembled as she inserted the key. The door opened easily, and she hurriedly turned on the light for the back of the room where Suni's desk was.

It was weird being there alone. The absence of any noise was spooky, and Trista rushed to complete her mission. The sooner she got this done, the sooner she could leave. There was Suni's desk, immaculate and orderly as usual. Trista sat down in the chair, and tried to pretend she had a right to be there. She started with the top middle drawer. Pens, papers, a checkbook, paper clips...her fingers quickly searched through the mild clutter. Nothing.

There were two drawers to the left. The first contained

files. Trista flipped through them rapidly. Notes about people Suni had met, a collection of humorous anecdotes and copies of all the speeches Suni had given in the past year or so.

The last drawer contained the stationery. Trista's heart sank as she stared at the shaded pink blossoms. It *was* the same, exactly the same, as the paper Sylvia had found. She eased a sheet from the top of the pile then shut the drawer. Turning to the typewriter on a table to the left of the desk, she inserted the single sheet of stationery. Pulling back the lever to position the machine to the top left-hand corner, she adjusted the spacing. And then she typed, from memory, *I need to see you this week. Same place, same time. xoxo.*

Trista stared at the distinct black letters against the creamy white background. To her horror it looked exactly like the note that Sylvia Hawthorne had found in Daniel's papers.

Exactly.

Trista was rolling out the paper, when she heard the sound of a key scraping in the lock of the front door.

Heart pounding, she yanked the paper out of the typewriter. This couldn't be happening. Who could be coming to the office at this late hour? She reached for the phone, Morgan's number in her mind, then pulled back as the door opened.

And Suni walked into the room.

Chapter Fourteen

Trista was folding the paper into her purse, when Suni saw her.

"Trista." The voice was sharp, disapproving. "I was just stopping by to pick up my speech for tomorrow's breakfast meeting. What are you doing here?"

"Suni. Thank God it's you. I thought…"

"Yes?"

"I thought you were an intruder." Trista twisted the clasp of her purse, trying not to look frightened. This was Suni, after all. Her friend.

But she'd written those notes.

"I hope you don't mind that I was using your typewriter. I needed to type a few short notes."

"Really?" Suni began walking toward her. "Why didn't you use the computer?"

"The letters were simple. I didn't want to bother turning it on, and waiting for the printer to warm up." Trista swallowed, unable to look Suni in the eyes as she lied to her. What could she tell her? *I know you sent those notes.*

That wouldn't be very smart. Not while they were alone, late at night. Trista had never thought it was possible that she could fear Suni, but now she did. Morgan was convinced that whoever had sent those notes to Jerry and Daniel had killed them, too.

If Suni would kill her lovers, why would she hesitate over a friend?

"I should be going…"

Suni was beside her now. She opened the bottom drawer of her desk, her gaze still on Trista, then pulled out a sheaf of papers. "My speech for tomorrow's breakfast meeting. I forgot it when I left today."

Trista nodded, and slowly rose out of the chair. She had to stay calm, and act naturally, but it was hard when her instinct was to bolt for the door.

Then Suni opened her purse and Trista froze. Would she bring out a gun? The same gun that had killed Jerry Walker and Daniel Hawthorne? The police still hadn't recovered the weapon.

But no. It was nothing but a tissue. Trista swallowed, but there was no moisture in her dry throat. She watched Suni's long, elegant hands dab the corners of her eyes.

"It's so cold out tonight, my eyes are watering. I'm sure the temperature has dipped below zero."

Trista felt a momentary sensation of relief. Perhaps she'd imagined the suspicious look on Suni's face. But then she remembered the note in her purse. The note that might very well link Suni to the scene of both murders.

"The worst is yet to come according to the weather report. I heard it might snow tonight. Can you imagine? Snow in May?" As she spoke, Trista walked toward the door, her alarm returning when she realized Suni was following close behind.

"Stranger things have happened," was Suni's reply, and Trista reflected that this was definitely so.

By the time she reached the door, Suni was beside her. She stepped forward, effectively blocking Trista's exit.

Trista tried to raise her chin, knowing that, if nothing else, her difficulty in looking her friend straight in the eyes must be giving her away.

"Trista?" Suni gripped her shoulder as she spoke.

"Yes?" Trista swallowed.

"Maybe you should leave the office key behind."

Trista sucked in a lungful of air. "Of course." She pulled the key out from her purse, but not before Suni caught a glimpse inside. The pale rose border on her personal stationery was clearly visible.

MORGAN PULLED HIS CAR into the parking lot behind Trista's office building the next morning, then stepped out into several inches of freshly fallen snow. He buttoned his overcoat against the chill in the air and silently cursed the fates that had delivered this freak snowstorm in the usually warm and sunny month of May. Was it a sign? he wondered. If so, how should he interpret it? Was he about to get some fresh clues? Or be snowed under?

Did he dare hope it would be the former? Certainly things were beginning to look hopeful. After he'd left Trista's last night, he'd spent hours going through Walker's and Hawthorne's canceled checks for the entire year. It had been early morning before he'd found the connection he'd been searching for.

Political contributions. Both Walker and Hawthorne had made sizable donations to Suni Choopra's political campaign. What did it mean? Morgan wasn't too sure of that yet, but at least it gave him a new angle to work on.

First, he had to see Trista. She'd phoned him early this morning from home, awakening him from his four hours of sleep. She'd sounded upset and told him she needed to talk to him as soon as possible. Although he'd pressed her to tell him then, she'd refused to discuss it on the phone, instead asking him to meet her at her office. She'd decided to reopen. She said she'd tell him why when he got there.

Morgan stamped the snow from his boots on the mat in the lobby, then made his way to the elevators. Brenda was at the front desk, dressed in a black suit and white silk blouse. She frowned when she saw him.

"Trista's on the phone. Could you wait a minute?"

She was uncomfortable with his presence and that made him curious. Was it because she was worried he would tell Trista about her past? Or did her anxiety spring from her involvement with this case?

"Thanks for the list," he said. "I suppose you've had a chance to look things over a little more thoroughly since we last spoke. Has anything turned up missing?"

"No."

"Did Trista say why she was reopening the office?" He'd thought she intended to remain closed until the case was solved.

"No."

Not exactly chatty, this Brenda. He saw her chest heave with a sigh of relief when Trista opened her office door.

"Sorry to keep you waiting, Morgan."

Trista looked more than just tired this morning. Dark circles underlined her eyes, and her expression seemed both sad and resigned. Morgan's stomach tightened as he wondered just what new blow she was planning to deliver to him this time.

"When's my first appointment, Brenda?" Even her voice sounded dispirited.

"I've been phoning people to let them know we're open again. I've got someone coming at eleven, and then another appointment for one."

"We've got lots of time then." Trista went into her office, gesturing for him to follow.

Morgan glanced back at Brenda and was interested to see the naked curiosity in her expression. Frightened of him, and yet anxious to know whatever it was he and Trista were about to discuss. The plot thickened.

Trista closed the door firmly. "Sit down, Morgan." She waved her hand toward the grouping of chairs, but ignored them herself as she strode to the window and pulled open the blinds.

"I think I'll stand, thanks." His back to the door, he watched her. Her movements were fast and nervous, increasing his own curiosity about what she had to tell him. He didn't press her for a quick answer, though. Let her go about this her own way. She stood staring at the gray choppy waters of Lake Ontario for a moment before finally turning to him.

"I have something to tell you about the note that Sylvia showed us yesterday."

Morgan took a sharp breath. She wanted to talk about the case. He'd figured that was it. But now he realized that in the back of his mind he'd been hoping she'd wanted to apologize for her abrupt turnaround last night. He still couldn't believe how quickly she'd changed from a warm, responsive lover, to the cool, withdrawn woman he was beginning to know too well.

Trista went to stand behind one of the chairs, linking her hands together and resting them on the back. "I was over at Sylvia's because she needed to talk. We'd had a cup of tea, and she told me she'd called you, but I didn't know that you were on your way over."

She put her hand to her chest, fingering the gold chain that he'd given her for Christmas once.

"When she pulled out that note, Morgan, the stationery seemed familiar to me."

He'd known there was something about that note. He waited for her to continue.

Trista took a deep breath. "I wasn't sure, though, and I wanted to check it out before I told you."

"What do you mean, 'check it out'?"

Her gaze flew back to the window. "I thought the stationery was similar to the kind used by Suni Choopra in a note I received from her once."

Suni Choopra. Lightbulbs flashed as Morgan thought about the political contributions that he'd uncovered earlier this morning. Every successful case had a moment like this, when everything seemed to fall into place. He tried to temper his sudden hopefulness with caution. Sometimes, these burning illuminations turned out to be dead ends.

"Why didn't you tell me?"

"I wanted to be sure the stationery was the same. You know she's running for reelection this month. You can imagine what the press would make of her being interviewed by the police..."

Trista's voice beseeched him to understand, but of course he couldn't. Because this was the most damn unreasonable thing he'd ever heard. "It's *my* job to check out details like that. Not yours."

"I know. But it seemed like a simple thing to do."

Oh, God. What had she done this time?

"I needed to know if the stationery was the same. So I went to the campaign office late last night and I typed this—" She pulled a folded piece of paper out of her purse and handed it to him

Morgan unfolded the paper, trying to control his fury. "You went out, alone, in the middle of the night..." He forced himself to stop. To take a deep breath. Finally he calmed down enough to go on. "Didn't it occur to you that if Suni *had* written the notes, you could be placing yourself in danger? You should have phoned me, at least. I would have come with you…" Morgan's words trailed off as he looked at the paper.

To the naked eye it appeared identical to the one Sylvia had given them yesterday. He'd have to get the lab to check it out, of course, but he was positive that both notes had been typed on this typewriter. The stationery, for sure, was a dead match. By the miserable expression on Trista's face, she thought so too.

"I wasn't afraid because I was so sure Suni couldn't have written those notes," she admitted.

"You still should have let me be the one to figure that out."

"You don't understand. If the notes *hadn't* matched, then Suni would never have had to be involved. Any connection with a homicide investigation will be the kiss of death for her reelection chances."

"Tell that to Jerry Walker and Daniel Hawthorne. I guess they've felt the 'kiss of death,' all right." He wondered if Trista had lost her mind. "Don't you think the electorate has a right to know that their member of Parliament has had affairs with married men while in office? And that she might have killed them as well?"

Now that he thought about it, Morgan realized Trista had been working against him this entire case. There was always somebody she had to be looking out for, and it was never justice, and most certainly never him. Her clients, her secretary, now it was that bloody politician.

"I *knew* you would jump to conclusions. *That's* why I didn't tell you about the similarity in the first place."

"Jump to conclusions?" He could feel his bad temper

move across his forehead, into his temples where the blood pounded furiously. "You think I'm jumping to conclusions?"

Trista began to pace. "You know how you steamroller over people once you get an idea in your head. Is it any wonder I had to check things out before I told you about it?"

"Check things out," Morgan repeated furiously. "Have you forgotten what happened the last time you decided to *check things out?*"

She ignored his outburst. "I know the notes match, but I still can't believe Suni Choopra is capable of murder."

"Is she capable of having an affair with a married man?"

Trista couldn't answer that.

"It's always a mistake to assume you know what someone is capable of. Given the right motive, more people than you might think will commit murder. You've already given me the perfect motive for Suni Choopra to have committed this crime."

"I have?"

"To protect her career. Maybe one or both of these men were threatening to go public about the affair. As you've already pointed out, that kind of publicity could have blown her electoral chances."

Trista sank into her chair. "You've already made up your mind that she's guilty, haven't you?"

She sounded so depressed, Morgan had the strangest urge to move behind her. To gently massage her tired neck and shoulders, and try to give her comfort. Why was it that even when she made him madder than a hornet, he still hated to see her distressed? He shoved his hands deep into his pockets and tried to answer her question diplomatically.

"Let's just say Suni Choopra has become my number one suspect."

"What happened to innocent until proven guilty!"

"I swear, sometimes you remember more about law school than I do!" He couldn't keep the bitter sarcasm from his voice.

"This is no joking matter, Morgan. Suni is my friend. You have no idea how much she's done for me."

"Are you saying I should ignore evidence in a homicide investigation because this woman happens to be a friend of yours?"

"Of course not! I just don't want you to jump the gun. Keep your mind open to other possibilities."

"A lot of people have been telling me that recently," Morgan muttered under his breath.

"What did you say?"

"Oh, nothing. Look, I'd better be going. I've got a ton of work to do this morning."

"I suppose you'll be wanting to talk to Suni today."

"As soon as possible."

"Well, could I at least come with you? I feel like I owe her that much."

Morgan took a few steps closer toward her. As he did, he noticed a faint amber light glowing on the intercom button of Trista's phone. "That's fine with me, but let me warn you, it's not going to be a pleasant scene." He took another couple of steps forward, then motioned Trista to be quiet, pointing to the light and raising his eyebrows questioningly.

Trista compressed her lips and pointed to the door, in the direction of Brenda's desk.

Morgan cursed softly under his breath. He should have thought to check the two-way intercom system, but it was too late now. He wondered what Trista's secretary would make of the new information she'd just overheard.

TRISTA HAD FINISHED her last appointment for the day when Morgan phoned with confirmation from the lab. The typescript on the note she'd given him had matched that of the two notes found by Walker's and Hawthorne's wives. Trista took the news calmly. It was, after all, exactly what she had already known must be true.

When she and Morgan walked into the Runnymede Street office at shortly past five o'clock, Suni didn't seem surprised to see them, although she barely glanced at Trista. A few other people were also at the office—a receptionist and two men who seemed anxious to conclude their conversation with Suni.

But she put them off. "I'll call you later this evening," she said, walking them to the door. Then she told the receptionist she could go for the day.

Trista watched her friend with great sadness, conscious that however this turned out, their relationship would never be the same. What she'd done had been out of a desire to protect Suni, but it was doubtful that the politician would see it that way.

Once they were alone, Suni spoke to Trista. "I knew last night that you suspected I'd been having an affair with Jerry, and that I'd previously had an affair with Daniel. But I couldn't figure out how you knew. I still can't."

"It was the notes," Trista told her. Although her heart ached for her friend, she was relieved at Suni's honesty. "Both Jerry's and Daniel's wives found the notes setting up their husbands' rendezvous. Those notes were written on the same stationery that you use for your personal correspondence. When you saw me last night, I'd just taken a sample from your manual typewriter. Morgan took it to the lab this morning and they've made a positive match.''

''I don't understand.'' Suni stared at her blankly. ''What notes are you talking about?''

Trista looked at Morgan uncertainly. Was Suni just pretending to be dumb? If she was willing to admit to the affairs, why lie about the notes?

Morgan took over. ''The note you sent to Jerry Walker setting up a meeting for Monday, May seventeenth. And the note you wrote to Daniel Hawthorne arranging another meeting for the following Wednesday.''

Suni's confused expression didn't change. ''I'm afraid you're mistaken. I never set up my—meetings—in writing. I always phone and I never give out my home number or allow anyone to call me at work.

''Yes, I was having an affair with Jerry. We'd started seeing each other a few weeks ago, but it was always on Wednesday, not Monday. As for Daniel, we'd stopped seeing each other at least six months ago.''

Morgan pulled a pad out of his jacket pocket and jotted something down. ''You say you *never* sent notes?''

''Do I look stupid to you, Detective? I took a lot of pains to keep my affairs private. The last thing I wanted was any physical evidence that someone could blackmail me with later. Why do you suppose I had affairs with married men?'' She shot a glance at Trista. ''That was the only way I could be certain that I wouldn't wake up one morning to find my face plastered all over the front page of the paper because some man decided to reveal the details of his affair with me. Married men have their own reasons to keep quiet.''

Trista couldn't believe Suni had such a cynical view of her sexual relationships. ''What about all those wonderful men you have escorting you to all the political functions?''

Suni laughed bitterly. ''Those wonderful men enjoy the attention of being seen with me in public, but when it comes to private, long-term relationships, they aren't interested. I'm too intimidating. Don't shake your head. It's true. There was a man once...''

She shook her head bitterly. ''No sense going into that. But I learned quickly, I always have. Men just aren't interested in women who are more successful than they are. Unless it's on the side, of course. Then, it's something completely different.''

Trista was saddened by Suni's cynicism. Whatever had happened in her friend's past, it had obviously been very disillusioning.

''I'm having trouble with this, Suni,'' she said. ''Both Jerry Walker and Daniel Hawthorne have wives. Didn't it bother you that you might be ruining their marriages by having affairs with them?''

''Believe it or not, Trista, I didn't set out to seduce these men. Daniel and I had a long conversation once during a fund-raiser. It was perfectly innocent. After that, he asked me to coffee. One thing led to another, but I didn't wreck his marriage. He was already deeply unhappy at that time. I found him very romantic and gentle and finally I agreed to become involved with him.''

''Why did you stop seeing him?'' Morgan asked.

''Why? We fell in love, that's why. He wanted to marry me, but how could I let him leave his wife for me? It would have been political suicide.'' Suni closed her eyes briefly. ''I hated to break it off, but I had no choice. I would have been labeled a home wrecker.''

Trista felt sorry for both of them. Daniel, trapped in

his unhappy marriage, and Suni, trapped by her own cynicism.

Morgan's voice, however, was cold as he continued the questions. "What about Jerry Walker? How did you meet him?"

"It was about a month ago, when I was speaking at a business luncheon. I was still so lonely after Daniel, and Jerry was obviously interested. He asked me for lunch, and so it began…" Suni put a hand to her forehead. "It was different with Jerry. Neither of us wanted anything complicated."

Trista couldn't believe Suni thought you could make love with a man and not have it become complicated. Her experience with Morgan just last night disproved that idea.

"Don't look at me that way, Trista!" Suni burst out. "Of course I felt guilty. But you don't understand the pressures of a public life."

"I guess I don't," Trista said sadly.

"So where does this leave me?" Suni asked frankly of Morgan. "I was hoping that if I was cooperative, you might be willing to keep this information confidential. I know my affairs were moral transgressions, but I've done nothing against the law. Surely there's no need to drag the press into this?"

Morgan was taken aback. "Still concerned about your political future, Ms. Choopra?"

"Well, of course I am! I've been sick ever since I heard of Jerry's murder, hoping against hope that no link to me would be found. And then when Daniel was killed, I thought I'd go crazy. Personally, of course, I was very sad. Politically, I was terrified. Surely you understand that if word of these affairs gets out my career will be finished?"

"Your political future should be the last thing on your mind right now."

"Pardon?"

"You're a hell of an actress. It must come with the territory. But you can't expect me to believe you knew nothing about the notes. Not to mention the murders."

"But—"

Morgan ignored her attempt to interject. "Surely you must realize by now that you're a suspect for murder. And I'm not going to rest until I find the evidence that will put you where you belong. And that, Ms. Choopra, is definitely not back in Parliament."

Chapter Fifteen

Brenda was unusually talkative at work the next morning. She chatted about a couple of appointment changes, then she mentioned a new restaurant she'd tried the previous evening. Finally, after a careful sideways glance at her employer, she asked what Trista had done after leaving the office yesterday.

Having listened in to her conversation with Morgan, Brenda probably had a very good idea what she had done, but Trista wasn't about to provide her secretary with the sad details. She couldn't understand why the normally reticent Brenda had suddenly turned into such a gossip.

At any rate, if Brenda wanted details, she wasn't going to get them from Trista. The scene with Suni yesterday afternoon had left her bruised and vulnerable, and she'd had another restless night. She cut off Brenda's inquisition with short answers, and escaped to her inner-office sanctuary.

Trista sank into her chair, trying to remember the last time she'd had a good night's sleep. Not since Morgan had been back in her life, that was for sure. And now that they'd made love, sleeping was even more impossible. As was everything else. How was she supposed to get on with her life when the memory of Morgan's dark head lying on her pillow was so recent?

Her only hope for sanity was to get this case solved, and Morgan out of her life. But not at Suni's expense. Morgan had been so hard on her yesterday—unnecessarily hard. It was as if he'd already condemned her, even though the evidence was certainly sketchy enough. Just another thing for the two of them to disagree about.

Then there was Brenda. Her receptionist had been acting strange ever since that first office break-in. Was it just curiosity, or did the woman have something to hide? Last night when she'd realized the notes were from Suni, she'd thought it would be okay to open the office, since obviously Brenda wasn't the mystery lover.

But her secretary's continued peculiar behavior was causing her to second-guess that decision.

After checking her watch, Trista saw that there were fifteen minutes before her first appointment of the day. On impulse she went to the credenza that contained her administrative information. She opened the long drawer and ran her fingers over the blue tabs, searching for the file with Brenda's name on it. There it was: Malachowski, Brenda. It wasn't thick, and took only a few moments to review.

There was nothing that leaped out at her. Brenda's application for the job, her payroll data, the review letters that Trista wrote every year. Trista flipped back to the beginning, going through everything once more.

No, there was nothing in here of much interest. But there was something that was missing. Brenda's letter of reference from her former employer.

Trista knew it had been in this folder when she'd hired Brenda. It had been attached to her résumé, which was still here, only minus the letter of recommendation. What could have happened to it? Had it, by any chance, been the target of the office break-in? The only other possibility was that Brenda must have taken it herself. But why would she do a thing like that? It had been a glowing letter.

The tender spot at the back of her head throbbed. Trista knew she had to talk to Morgan. He'd been suspicious of Brenda from the start. He'd even asked her if she'd checked Brenda's references. Maybe he would know what to do.

She reached him on his cell phone. His tone was brisk, and he admitted he was on his way to Suni's house. With a search warrant.

"I'm calling about Brenda," she told him.

"Oh, yeah?" Morgan sounded distracted.

Trista rolled her eyes at his lack of interest. "She's been acting unusual ever since the office was broken into. And this morning, she was very curious about where I went after work yesterday. I think she was hoping I'd seen you arrest Suni. And another thing—"

"Yes?" Morgan sounded impatient.

"I just finished looking through Brenda's personnel file, and guess what? Her letter of recommendation is missing."

There was a pause. A muffled sound that might have been him talking to someone else. "Perhaps you misfiled it?"

"Misfiled it? Morgan, are you listening to me?" She should have known he wouldn't take this seriously. He'd developed a one-track mind. He had his guilty party— Suni Choopra—and he wasn't interested in gathering any evidence that didn't fit with his personal theory.

"I'm listening."

"Yeah, right. Well, where would I have misplaced it? In one of my other employee's files perhaps?"

"Have you tried asking Brenda what happened to it?"

"I thought you didn't want me conducting any more investigating on my own. Why do you think I called *you?*"

"Look, Trista, I agree it's a little odd, okay? You did good to call me, but I have to go now. You let me know if anything else unusual happens. In the meantime—" there was another pause while he spoke to someone else again "—I've got to get back to work. Why don't I drop by your office around noon? We can talk then." And the line went dead.

Trista stared at the receiver disbelievingly. Morgan hadn't listened to a word she'd said. She was certain of it.

Maybe Morgan had changed more in the past three years than she'd thought. The old Morgan cared about justice. The old Morgan kept his mind open, reviewed the facts objectively. Now it seemed he wasn't interested in any information unless it supported his theory. That Suni Choopra had murdered her lovers to protect her political career.

And that was that.

Unless someone challenged his theory. And maybe, if no one else was up to the job, that someone was going to have to be her.

MORGAN CLENCHED his teeth as he hung up the phone, glancing sideways at the officer in the passenger seat beside him, before turning his attention back to the road. Trista was ticked off at him, he knew that much, but this was hardly the time for him to explain why he wasn't concerned with Brenda's missing letter of reference. He'd suspected for a while that she'd probably forged it.

Morgan pulled up in front of Suni Choopra's house, a few blocks north of her campaign office in Bloor West Village. He'd have to explain everything to Trista later. Right now he had a job to do. He got out of the car, the officer following suit, but staying behind him as he walked briskly up the steps to the front door of the two-story brick building.

Morgan hammered on the front door. There wasn't time for niceties. The adrenaline was pounding in his veins and he had that feeling of heightened awareness that he always experienced when a case was drawing to a close.

Suni opened the door, obviously startled to see him. But she recovered quickly. She was wearing a pinkish-colored suit, with coordinating high heels and hat. Even her long fingernails had been painted to match. Did she think she'd be campaigning as usual today? Man, this woman still didn't know what she was facing.

"Good morning, Detective. How can I help you?" As she spoke, her eyes scanned the street behind him.

Looking for signs of the press, Morgan thought contemptuously. "We have a search warrant, Ms. Choopra." He held up the official document for her to see. She took it from his hands and read it carefully before stepping aside to let them enter.

"I believe I'll call my lawyer," she said quietly.

"You do that." He nodded to the junior officer behind him. "You start with the house. I'll search behind the house and in the garage."

"Just what is it you expect to find?" Suni demanded, her voice for the first time betraying a hint of fear.

"Who knows?" Morgan looked at her and felt no

compassion whatsoever. "Nothing, if you've been smart. But you've already made one mistake, haven't you? Who knows, maybe you've made another."

MORGAN LOOKED different today, Trista thought as she watched him walk toward her outside the main doors of her office building. His eyes were bright and alert, and there was an all-too-familiar spring to his step. She knew the signs. He felt he was closing in, that the case would soon be solved.

Trista's heart sank. No one wanted this case solved more than she did. But not at the expense of an innocent woman. And the more she thought about it, the more convinced she was that Suni wouldn't have committed those murders.

"Who'd have guessed we'd be wearing boots in the middle of May?" Morgan asked as he drew nearer.

The sun was shining, in the process of turning yesterday's snow into a thick pool of sludge. Trista looked at her mud-splattered boots and shrugged. It was part of life in Toronto. Snow one day, slush the next.

"At least it's warming up." Despite her words, Trista pushed her hands deep into the pockets of her trench coat and shivered. Suddenly she wished she could have postponed this talk. She didn't think she was ready for the news Morgan was about to tell her.

"Would you like to go for a walk?" Morgan asked. "I noticed a hot-dog vendor down the street a few blocks."

"Why not?" They fell in step together, arms brushing against each other occasionally. Despite the years apart, and the problems between them, Trista's natural inclination was to reach out her hand to him. But she kept both fists sunk in her pockets. This was no casual afternoon stroll, and the problems ahead of them were much more serious than whether to order hot dogs or sausages from the street vendor ahead.

"We searched Suni's home today."

Morgan's words brought home the stark reality of their most pressing problem. The investigation. That was where it had started and she supposed that was where it would end. But now she wasn't sure if she had the strength to see it through. Was it too late for her to pull back, to tell him that she really didn't want to know what he'd found during his search of Suni's house?

But would that be fair to Suni? She couldn't abandon her friend now, when her need was the greatest. "Yes?"

"We found the gun in her garage. A Smith & Wesson .38, taped to the bottom of her garbage pail."

"No!" Trista stopped in her tracks and stared at him in disbelief. What he was saying was absolutely impossible. "I don't believe it! It's just too pat. Don't you see, Morgan? This is all coming together much too neatly. Someone must have planted that gun."

Morgan scowled. "Somehow I knew you were going to say that."

"Don't you think Suni would have been smart enough to get rid of the murder weapon?"

Morgan stared at her, his eyes didn't flinch. "Not if she thought she might need it again. Guns aren't as easy to come by as you might think."

Trista shook her head, not willing to admit there was any reasoning behind what he was saying.

"We're going to arrest her, Trista. Look, I'm sorry. I know that she's your friend…"

Trista swallowed hard. It was what she had expected. But somehow, hearing Morgan say the words out loud made it so much harder to take. "You're making a mistake," she said quietly. "I'm absolutely convinced of it."

For a second she caught a glimpse of agony in Morgan's expression, but it was quickly replaced with that rock-faced certainty of his that could be so infuriating. "I'm not out to get your friend, Trista. I can't believe you'd really think I would do something like that. The gun *is* circumstantial evidence, but there're also the notes. You saw how they matched yourself. Suni's admitted to the affairs. What more is it going to take to convince you?"

"What about the office break-ins?" Trista asked. "Or do you think it was just coincidence that my office was broken into twice, and I was whacked on the back of the head?"

"I've thought about that. Did Suni know the Walkers and Hawthornes were clients of yours?"

Trista was about to say no when she remembered an earlier conversation with Suni. Oh, God. She put her hands to her face. "I did tell her. After Daniel's death and I'd closed my practice, I went to Suni's office looking for something to do. I didn't volunteer the information, but when she asked, I told her."

"If I was Suni, I would have wanted to make sure neither man had mentioned me during their marriage counseling sessions," Morgan said.

Damn. It did sound reasonable. But it hadn't happened that way. Trista just knew it.

"Doesn't this whole thing strike you as being a little too tidy?" Trista spoke desperately. "Shouldn't you at least consider the possibility that she's being framed? Couldn't someone have put that gun in her garage?"

"Possibly. But who? Who else had a motive for killing both Jerry Walker and Daniel Hawthorne?"

"You're asking me that question as if it's my job to solve this case. But it isn't. It's yours. I'm not surprised you don't have any other suspects when you ignore any evidence that doesn't support your own theory."

Morgan's chest heaved, and she thought he was finally going to blow. Then he exhaled and asked in an artificially calm voice. "I see. I suppose you think I should be arresting Brenda. Because she snitched her letter of reference."

"Very funny." Trista lifted her chin defiantly. "And do you have some logical explanation for why she would have done such a thing?"

"As a matter of fact, I think I do. Brenda took that letter because she was afraid you'd find out that it was forged." He turned away from her and resumed walking.

Trista stared at his receding back. "Forged?" For a second she stood still with the shock, then she trotted forward, grabbing Morgan by the shoulder when she caught up with him. "Why do you think Brenda forged her letter of reference?"

Morgan kept his eyes focused in front of him as he walked. "I guess she did it because she wanted the job."

"Morgan." She pulled on his arm, forcing him to stop. "You're being deliberately obtuse."

Morgan glanced up into the sky, then finally met her gaze. "Brenda's gay, Trista. She thinks she lost her former job because of it."

"Gay?" Trista sputtered out the word. "Brenda gay? It's not possible. She dates so many men…" Suddenly Trista's thoughts did a tailspin. Brenda dated a lot. But it was only Trista's assumption that she dated men. After all, Trista had never met any of them. Only heard Brenda's low voice when she was speaking on the phone. "I guess it's possible."

"It's more than possible. It's a fact." Morgan spoke crisply. "When she lost her last job with the school board, she filed a grievance with the union, but later she dropped it. I don't know why. I don't have any proof that she doctored her reference letter, I only suspected as much, based on her history. If you want to pursue it, we could call her former employers and see if they have a copy of the letter."

"No. Don't do that."

"Why not? It's only circumstantial until we get the evidence."

Trista ignored his sarcasm. She was floored by this news about Brenda. She couldn't care less about the secretary's sexual orientation. Surely Brenda would have known that. Why had she felt she had to keep it secret?

Because of the forged letter? After all, Brenda hadn't known her when she applied for the job. Perhaps her past experiences had made her legitimately cautious.

At least this accounted for her recent strange behavior. She must have known that Morgan would check into her background. She must have lived in daily fear that he would spill the beans. God, she'd probably been worried that the police would have the same prejudice against her that her former employer had.

If only Brenda had been honest, instead of stealing that reference letter. Trista could understand why Brenda might not have been willing to tell her the truth at the beginning, before she knew her. But now...

Actually, Trista realized, she shouldn't be surprised that Brenda hadn't come to her. She'd never encouraged closeness between the two of them. So why would Brenda decide to trust her with her biggest secret? Trista wrapped her arms around herself, against the damp chill of the wind off the lake.

Morgan's arm slipped around her, and for an instant she leaned into him, needing his strength and his warmth. "Poor Brenda, the agony she must have been going through."

He pulled her in closer. "Poor Trista. If I know you, you're blaming yourself again. You aren't responsible for Brenda's actions."

Trista nodded. She felt so safe and protected here in Morgan's arms. She'd missed him last night. Postponed eating until almost eight, unable to stop from hoping he'd drop by. She should have known better. After the way she'd practically thrown him out of the apartment the night they'd made love, he'd probably never come back. Which was what she'd thought she wanted at the time.

"So you haven't considered Brenda a suspect right from the beginning?" she asked Morgan.

"I didn't say that." Morgan removed his arm to place their order with the vendor. Then, hot dogs and cans of pop in hand, they headed for a small park farther up the block.

"Knowing she was gay, of course I realized she wasn't the mystery lover we were looking for. But I've never discounted her as a possible suspect for the murders. All that resentment and hatred that she's been suppressing... I figured she could have stepped over the edge. Plus, she had opportunity..."

"So when did you decide she didn't do it?"

"Today. When we found the gun."

Morgan looked directly into her eyes, but Trista had to look away. She tore the wrapper from her hot dog and took a bite. They were back to the gun again.

"Where did Suni get this weapon, anyway?"

"That's the interesting part. The gun was registered to Jerry Walker. I stopped in at Walker's Hardware to ask

Nan if she'd noticed when it had gone missing, but she wasn't there. Neither was Lorne Thackray. Guess where I found them?"

Trista caught the cocky edge to his grin, and quickly discerned the reason. "No! Not Lorne and Nan?"

"Yes, Lorne and Nan. They were at his place. And from the look on their faces and the length of time it took them to answer the door, I have little doubt what was going on. You should have seen Nan. Blushing and chewing her nails at the same time…"

"So what did Nan say about the gun?"

Morgan popped the tab off his soft drink. "Nothing very helpful. She knew Jerry had one but she didn't know it was missing. She didn't even know where he kept it."

"So how do you figure Suni got hold of it?"

"Well, she either asked for it—maybe told Jerry she was worried about her own safety, something like that— or she took it. Either one is possible."

A mother, or possibly a nanny, strolled up to the park then. She was pushing a buggy with a pink-wrapped baby inside, while a young boy, about five or six, held on to the side of the handle and walked beside her. The buggy left thin tracks in the melting snow, and the little boy's mittens hung empty from a string of yarn tucked inside the sleeves of his coat.

They headed for the tire swing at the other end of the grassy clearing. There was a wooden bench, and the woman sat on it while the little boy took running leaps at the rubber tire.

Trista was accustomed to turning away from sights such as these, but this time she felt compelled to watch. Andrew would have been about the same age as this young boy. Their coloring was about the same. This fall she would've been registering him in kindergarten.

"Give me a push," the boy demanded, but his caregiver had picked up the baby, who had started to fuss once the buggy stopped moving.

"Makes you think of Andrew, doesn't it?" Morgan said from beside her.

"Yes." The word seemed to catch in the back of her throat. "Yes, it does."

Morgan tossed his used wrapper and pop can into a nearby trash container, then ambled toward them. Trista was surprised to hear him ask the woman, "Can I help?" When she nodded, he turned to the boy, starting him off with a gentle swing.

The boy looked at him scornfully. "Harder!"

"Okay. Hang on, buddy." Morgan increased the strength of his pushes gradually, until the boy was swirling around in a big circle.

Trista prepared herself for the burning pain. The kind that started in her chest, building in intensity until it seemed as if thousands of little darts were exploding through her bloodstream. Morgan should have been pushing his own son on the swing, not this stranger. It wasn't fair.

No. It wasn't fair. But the pain in her chest felt lighter somehow. And the little boy on the swing *was* having a grand time. He was giggling now, shrieking when the tire came near, but never touched, the side poles.

After ten minutes the baby was asleep, and the woman took over. Morgan rejoined Trista and they began to walk back to her office.

Neither of them said a word about the incident on the swing, and they walked in silence for several minutes before Trista noticed they'd somehow begun holding hands.

THEY SAID their goodbyes at the corner by the parking lot, where a mature maple tree was growing in the boulevard. Trista let go of Morgan's hand, and reminded herself of her loyalty to Suni.

"I guess my suspicions about Brenda were off base, but I still think you've got the wrong woman. I think the real murderer planted the gun in Suni's garage so she would look guilty."

Morgan sighed wearily. "Any ideas on who this 'real murderer' could be?"

"As you've reminded me in the past, I'm not the detective here."

"My point exactly."

She shook her head with frustration. "Are you sure you've looked deep enough? There has to be some other connection between the two men. Besides my office and Suni. Or isn't it possible the murders are the work of a madman, like the newspapers are saying. Someone trying to rid the world of cheating spouses."

"If that's the case, it sure will wreak havoc with your practice, won't it?"

"That's not funny, Morgan."

"It is to me. If there's another connection between these men, I sure as hell haven't been able to find it. As for the madman theory, so far I haven't had to stoop to the level of the tabloids to come up with my leads."

"I don't understand you. Don't you care about justice? You're acting like all you're concerned about is wrapping up this case, never mind if you have to arrest an innocent citizen to do it. The Morgan I knew would never have stopped searching until he was certain he had the right person." Tears filling her eyes blurred her vision and she stumbled.

Morgan put a hand to her elbow, pulling her off the

sidewalk and onto the grass. "Well, maybe the Morgan you knew no longer exists. What, exactly, do you expect from me?"

Before she had a chance to answer this question, he pulled her in close. She stared at the dark stubble on his lower face, the fire in his eyes, and then she saw nothing as he pressed his mouth to hers and blocked out the present with the intense fury of his kiss.

At first Trista battled the taste of his mouth, the feel of his skin, the scent of his hair. But, even as her own anger soared, she parted her lips and wrapped her arms tightly around his back.

His response was to pull her in closer and deepen his kisses. His tongue probed and demanded, his arms tightened like steel bands. She felt as if she were being devoured, as if her very essence was being absorbed into his.

"God, Trista," she heard him groan as he picked her up and pushed her against the solid trunk of the maple tree. The bark was rough and dug into her back through her coat as he pressed his body against hers. She was pinned now, like a butterfly on display, and once more she felt the onslaught of his kisses.

"Morgan." This was not the tender lovemaking of the previous night. This was a man exacting payment for four years of pain and loneliness. She could feel his anger, taste it. It swirled around the tree, like a cyclone, lifting them higher and higher.

I'm sorry. She didn't think she'd spoken the words, but the hand she placed on his head was tender. She felt his lips, which had been hard and demanding, soften. The kisses stopped, and for one long moment there was only the warmth of his breath against her cheek.

Her lips could still feel the pressure from his mouth,

and her chin stung from the friction of his unshaven face, but she knew that sanity was returning. Trista could see the fine drops of perspiration on his forehead, hear the ragged rhythm of his breathing. His eyes were on her lips, but his jaw was clenched, as if denying what had just happened. She swallowed hard, resisting the urge to press her lips once more to his, then felt him step back, setting her feet back firmly on the ground.

"I told you not to say that anymore." Then he turned and walked away.

Chapter Sixteen

"I didn't send those notes. You have to believe me!" A frantic Suni paced back and forth in Trista's office later that day as Trista stood at the window, looking across the street at the sullen waters of Lake Ontario. "And I didn't take that gun from Jerry, either. I didn't even know he *had* a gun!"

"I'd like to believe you, Suni. But it's a little difficult right now." Trista placed a hand to her lips. They still felt tender from the onslaught of Morgan's furious kisses only a few hours ago. Where had he gone? What was he doing? Was he really convinced that Suni was the murderer? And was it possible that he was right?

"When I met you, I really thought you were different from all the other politicians." Trista couldn't help but feel disillusioned, betrayed. She turned to face the other woman, pressing her hands behind her, against the windowpane.

Suni stopped pacing and stood in front of her, holding out her hands in a vaguely entreating manner. For once, she looked every one of her forty-plus years. Lines had etched into her face overnight, making her appear worried and apprehensive, as well she might. Even her body seemed smaller, her vivacious spirit dampened, if not extinguished.

"I know it's hard for you to understand why I had those affairs. But I don't see why that makes you question my motives in politics. If I didn't believe in what I was doing, I would never have chosen this life-style, believe me. I've given up the chance to have a husband and children, to be part of a family. Am I really to blame for daring to have a sex life?"

Trista listened. She was very good at listening. After all, it was her job to hear what people were saying, to understand them, to help them understand themselves.

But Suni wasn't her client. She was her friend.

"I'm sorry, Suni, but I can't feel any sympathy for you, and I certainly can't condone what you've done. I recognize that they were your decisions to make, but despite what you might have thought, you had alternatives."

Suni bowed her head, as if accepting Trista's criticism.

"At the same time, I don't think you deserve to be arrested. And I can't believe you sent those notes."

"You have no idea what a relief it is for me to hear you say that. To know that you still believe in me."

"I wouldn't go that far."

Suni frowned. "Then what are you saying?"

"Only that sending those notes would have been a very stupid thing to do if you really were planning to kill those men. And if you *did* set up your meetings by letter, why were only those two notes found?"

"I suppose one might argue that the others had been thrown away," Suni countered reluctantly.

Trista shook her head. "Then why weren't these last notes discarded as well? No, it doesn't make sense. The only thing I can think of is that someone else wrote them, hoping to implicate you.''

''Of course that's what really happened. And now that I think of it, I know how they did it.''

''How?''

''Remember the break-in we had at the campaign office last month? Maybe the murderer was planning ahead. Maybe they stole some of my stationery and typed out those messages, which they later planted in order to incriminate me.''

Trista felt a ray of hope. ''It's possible, of course. But how can we prove it?''

''We have a police report documenting the break-in,'' Suni pointed out. ''Surely that at least raises the possibility that I might not have sent those notes.''

Trista nodded slowly. ''Yes, but it's going to take more than that to convince Morgan.''

''What else can we do?''

''We need to find another suspect. Someone with a motive for the murders even stronger than yours.''

Suni frowned. ''Why do you say, even stronger than mine? I still don't understand what my motive is supposed to be.''

Trista felt a flicker of that old enemy—doubt. It seemed that Suni was protesting a little too loudly. For the moment, however, she felt she owed her friend the benefit of the doubt. ''The police think you murdered Jerry and Daniel to protect your reputation.''

''But that doesn't make any sense. Why would Jerry or Daniel have revealed anything about our affairs? They had their marriages to protect.''

''Not the greatest marriages in the world,'' Trista pointed out. ''And if they thought they could get enough money out of you to make it worth their while…''

"I don't buy that. If Daniel wanted out of his marriage, the last route he would've picked was a messy, public divorce. And as for the blackmail angle, he didn't need money. His wife had a very comfortable inheritance from her father. And Jerry didn't need money, either. His business was very profitable, as I'm sure you know. And he would never have risked his marriage."

"Why not?" It had never struck Trista that Jerry had any particularly strong feelings for his wife.

"Jerry liked having a wife he could control, and taking his pleasure elsewhere. This wasn't the first time he'd cheated on Nan. Besides, Jerry loved that business of his. Consider that under Ontario law, he would have been required to split his assets fifty-fifty with his wife. Jerry would never have been willing to do that."

Trista had to admit that Suni had a point. The one thing that everyone invariably agreed on about Jerry Walker was his commitment to his business. "What you say makes sense," she agreed. "But it still doesn't give us any answers."

"No, but can't you at least try to talk to your ex-husband? Surely if you can see the improbability of this, you can convince him of the same?" Suni's voice was close to pleading. "They're going to arrest me, you know!"

"I *have* tried talking to Morgan. But maybe I could do a little checking around myself."

"Oh, I'd really appreciate that."

Trista put an arm around her friend. It was impossible for her to stay angry at Suni when she was in such misery. "Try not to worry too much. Morgan is a reasonable man. When he's proven wrong, he'll admit it."

The only problem was, of course, proving he was wrong. How in the world was she supposed to do that?

EXHAUSTED, Trista flopped down on the sofa in her office, kicking her tan-colored Italian shoes to the floor. She'd just finished her last session for the day, and Brenda had left only minutes ago.

She and Brenda had talked earlier, after Suni had left the office. The confrontation was initiated by Brenda, who'd walked into her office silently, handing her a piece of paper containing her resignation. Trista had been shocked initially, but when she'd had time to study the expression on Brenda's face, she'd realized that the woman had finally reached the end of her rope. The secrets had become too burdensome.

"This isn't necessary, you know." Trista had picked up the piece of paper and tried to return it.

At first Brenda had refused to look at her, staring off out the window. For a moment all Trista had seen was her profile. Jaw set. Eyes blinking.

"I know that you're gay. I know about the forged letter. I'm sorry about what happened in the past, but you've done good work for me."

Brenda had turned slowly toward her. "You don't want me to leave?"

"Of course not." Trista had pushed the letter back into her hands. "The forgery, of course, was not a good idea."

Brenda nodded again, and there was more blinking. "Well, if you're sure, I guess I'll stay."

Then she'd gone back to her desk. And that had been that.

One day they might be able to talk about it. At least, Trista hoped so. But now wasn't the time. This case had to be settled. One way or another, all of them were being affected by it.

She thought about her promise to Suni and wondered,

yet again, how she was going to keep it. Then she heard a knock at the door. Dragging herself off the couch, she slipped her feet back into shoes that now felt about half a size too small.

Morgan was standing on the other side of the door, looking tired and discouraged. What had happened to the adrenaline rush he'd had earlier in the day?

"I figured you'd still be here," he said. In his hands he held two files. Stepping forward, he tossed them on her desk. Trista didn't have to ask whose they were. Or what their return meant.

"Oh no, Morgan."

He turned to face her, half sitting on her desk, resting his hands on his thighs. "We took some things from Suni's house to the lab this afternoon. Looks like there are fibers from the motel carpet on her shoes, and ballistics testing shows the bullets were fired from the gun we found at her place."

He stood and shoved his hands into his black trousers. "We arrested her half an hour ago."

"Oh, God." Trista wrapped both hands around the back of her neck. Poor Suni must be freaking out. Had the press discovered the news yet? Trista could just imagine the mayhem that would erupt in the campaign office once that happened.

"You wanted the case solved," Morgan reminded her. "Now it's solved."

"I wish I thought that was true."

"And I wish I could understand why you're so sure we've made a mistake. How well do you know Suni Choopra, anyway? Remember when you told me she couldn't be having affairs with married men? Well, you were wrong about that. Maybe you're wrong about the murders, too."

"I'm not wrong. She's being framed. And we figured out how, too."

"We?"

"Suni and I. We were talking earlier and she reminded me that the campaign office had been broken into about a month ago. The murderer could have stolen her writing paper to type those notes."

"I know about the break-in. I've read the police report. If the notes were all we had to go on, I might be more willing to believe you. But the gun—"

"Oh, come on, Morgan! Leaving the murder weapon in her garage. You don't think that was stupid?"

"Like I told you before, guns aren't that easy to come by—"

She ignored that point. "It was stupid, Morgan. And Suni isn't stupid."

"But I am. Is that what you're saying?"

Trista clenched her hands into tight fists. "No. That is not what I'm saying."

"I can't believe this. I thought when this thing was over we'd finally have time to talk about the two of— about our future…"

Our future. There was something seductive about those words, but remembering the pain she'd felt after he'd kissed her, then walked away, Trista knew better than to kid herself. "There is no two of us, Morgan. Not anymore."

"We had a life together once. A damn good life. I know there's no turning back the clock, but there still might be some sort of future left for us."

Trista fought to control the swell of emotions rising inside her. Fear and pain. But hope and joy, too. Perhaps he was right. Perhaps there was a chance… But what if he was wrong? What if it didn't work out? Could she survive that pain again? And what about Morgan? How could she risk putting him through the ordeal of a second separation?

"I just can't do it, Morgan. It's too late for us. Don't you see?"

"No, I don't. You're making this whole thing too complicated. You forget that I like things black and white. Remember? So tell me you don't love me, Trista, because that's what it's going to take to get me to walk out of your life and never come back."

"Love? What's love, Morgan?" Trista met his blue eyes squarely. "I can admit that I'll probably always feel this connection between you and me, but—" she held up her hand to stop him from stepping forward "—you and I both know that life is much more complicated than that. Even love can't solve all our problems."

"You may know that. I'm not sure that I do. I love you, Trista. Even when I was hating you for leaving me, I was still loving you, just not able to admit it."

"You feel sorry for me," Trista said softly. "You feel like you need to protect me. That's not necessarily love."

He took a step toward her. "Don't tell me what I feel. When we made love the other night, did that seem like protectiveness to you?"

She shook her head, blood rushing to her temples at the memory.

"So answer my question. Do you love me or not? Tell me, dammit!" He closed the distance between them, lifting a hand to her chin and forcing her face toward his.

She twisted away, wrapping her hands tightly across her chest. "I don't know, Morgan." She choked out the words. "I just don't know."

Silence. She took several deep breaths, fighting to re-
gain control. Finally, when she thought she could trust
her voice to speak again, she turned around. The space
where he'd been standing was now empty. He was gone.

Chapter Seventeen

To hell with this paperwork. Morgan was at his desk and it was Saturday. He'd phoned Trista that morning to ask her to lunch. Now he wasn't sure why he'd bothered. He wasn't going to get her to change her mind about the two of them. Maybe it was time he accepted that.

"Hear you made an arrest. Good going!" A fellow officer slapped Morgan on the back as he walked by.

Good going. Morgan stared blankly at the forms in front of him. Normally he felt on top of the world after an arrest. But not today. And it wasn't just because of the way he'd botched things with Trista yesterday. He didn't have the same feeling of confidence, of justice well served, that he normally did.

And he couldn't put his finger on what was bothering him. Was Trista getting to him with her insistence that he'd arrested the wrong suspect? Was it possible that she was right, that he'd been so anxious to wrap up the case that he'd missed something important?

Normally Morgan trusted his instincts. But he was too involved in this mess to trust them this time. Solving the case meant protecting Trista—no longer could any sliver of doubt point her way.

But did he really have the right woman? The evidence

said yes. And Zarowin was pleased as punch. Yet, he was beginning to have his doubts.

It was those office break-ins. They only made sense if Suni knew that the Walkers and Hawthornes were Trista's clients. Trista'd said she told Suni shortly after Daniel's death. *But by then her office had already been broken into once, and an attempt had been made at her house.*

When the phone rang he answered gruffly, annoyed at the interruption. Hearing Sylvia Hawthorne's voice on the other end, he wished he'd let it ring.

"Detective Forester. I read in this morning's paper that you've arrested my husband's murderer." She sounded pleased.

And why not? Justice was being served. Or so the article had said. MP Shoots Ex-Lovers, had blared the headlines of the *Toronto Star.*

"There is one thing I don't understand," she continued.

"Yes?"

"Your ex-wife phoned me last night with some questions about Daniel. Why would she be doing that, do you think?"

Morgan slammed his fist onto the desk. Damn Trista, she just wouldn't give up. "What sort of questions?"

"Questions that sounded like she didn't think Suni Choopra was guilty. But of course, she and Suni are friends. She wouldn't want to believe the truth about that woman."

"Well, try not to worry about it, Mrs. Hawthorne. I'll make sure Trista doesn't bother you anymore." He'd put *Trista* behind bars, if he had to. The damn woman was so determined to free her friend, she hadn't thought about the danger to herself.

What if the real murderer found out she was playing Nancy Drew?

TRISTA WAS in the kitchen, trying to decide how to spend the hours before her lunch with Morgan when the phone rang. It was Sylvia Hawthorne.

"Oh, Trista! I'm glad I caught you at home." Sylvia spoke in a breathless rush.

"Sylvia! What's the matter?"

"Oh, it's nothing and it's everything. After I talked to you last night, my in-laws told me they want some keep-sakes of Daniel's. His father wants his fishing gear, and his mother wants a set of books they gave him when he went away to university. All that stuff is at the cottage, and as they're planning to leave tomorrow, I only have today to get it. I don't want to put it off and give them a reason to come back soon."

"Okay." Trista couldn't see what any of this had to do with her.

"The problem is, there are so many memories wrapped up in that cottage for me. I don't think it would be a good idea for me to go on my own."

Trista knew her problem of how to spend the day was now solved. "Would you like me to come with you?"

"Oh, you're so kind. Yes, that would be wonderful."

She would have to cancel her lunch with Morgan, since the Hawthornes' cottage was a two-hour drive away. But maybe that was for the best, anyway.

"I'll come by and pick you up," Sylvia said. "What's your address?"

Trista recited her street name and number mechanically, thinking that perhaps this would give her the opportunity to do a little more investigating for Suni. Although truthfully, she didn't think it would do any good.

She'd called both Nan and Sylvia last night, hoping against hope she could dig up something that would convince Morgan he'd arrested the wrong woman.

But she'd found nothing.

Trista roamed her living room restlessly after hanging up the phone. If she was fair, she had to admit that arresting Suni had been a logical move on Morgan's part. It was only because she knew Suni that she felt he was making a mistake. If she could find even one shred of hard evidence to make him reconsider his conclusion...

On impulse Trista pulled her briefcase out of the closet and retrieved the files Morgan had returned yesterday. She'd brought them home, thinking she might find something she'd missed before, but upon rereading them last night she'd been as discouraged as ever.

First she glanced through the Hawthornes' file, then the Walkers'. She'd barely got past the first page when one of Nan's comments leaped off the page at her.

It was the session when Nan had let her anger out, and Trista wondered why she hadn't focused on it earlier, when Morgan had mentioned the gun. *Sometimes I feel like taking that gun out of his night table and shooting the television! Right in the middle of* Star Trek!

Hadn't Nan told Morgan she had no idea where her husband kept his gun?

Trista was certain she remembered Morgan telling her that. If Nan knew about Jerry's gun, why would she have lied? There was only one answer that Trista could think of, and it was an answer that would set her friend free. She reached for the phone.

She got Morgan's answering service, and bit her lip in frustration as she waited for the recorded voice to stop and the beep to sound. When it did, the words came pouring out.

"Morgan, it's me. I was just looking over my notes from my sessions with the Walkers and I came across something you should know. You told me Nan said she didn't know where her husband kept his gun. Well, she was lying. In one of our sessions she said he kept it in his night table. I can go over the file with you when I get home later tonight. I'm sorry I have to cancel our lunch, but Sylvia's asked me to go with her to the Muskokas. She and Daniel had a cottage up there and Sylvia wants to bring back some of Daniel's things."

Trista hung up with a sense of satisfaction. When Morgan heard that, he'd be forced to consider other options. Like the possibility that Nan and Lorne Thackray had planned the entire thing. Maybe Nan had known about Jerry's affair. Maybe she'd asked for a divorce, and like Suni had said, Jerry had refused, giving her only one way out. Looking at it that way, Nan had a motive. And Daniel's murder had been part of the cover-up. To frame everything on Suni.

The more she thought about it, the more it made sense. True, Nan didn't seem to have the psyche for murder, but she *was* the type to be dominated by someone stronger. Someone like Lorne Thackray? Trista collected her purse and keys and headed out the door to wait for Sylvia in the lobby.

Nan Walker and Lorne Thackray were in love. That much had been proven by Morgan, who'd caught them in bed in the middle of the afternoon. Lorne wanted to run the stores—he was already doing it, so that had to be right, too. According to Suni, and Trista was inclined to agree, Jerry would never have agreed to a divorce. The perfect solution to Nan and Lorne's dilemma? Kill Jerry.

Of course, Trista mused as she walked down the stairs to the front entrance of her apartment building, Nan had an alibi for Jerry's murder. But Lorne didn't. And with Lorne's high voice, he could easily impersonate a woman if he were wearing a trench coat, sunglasses and hat.

Across the street she saw Sylvia's navy Volvo pull to a stop. She waved her hand to draw Sylvia's attention, then watched as Sylvia negotiated a tight U-turn and managed to stop her car by the front doors. Trista opened the passenger door and slipped into the soft gray leather seat.

"Hello, Sylvia."

Sylvia was looking peaked, and unnaturally agitated. Her fingers drummed rapidly against the steering wheel as she drove, and her eyes kept flashing between Trista and the road as if she couldn't settle on which was the most important.

"Thanks for coming," Sylvia said, shoulder-checking as she changed lanes. They drove along Bloor to Westen Road, where they merged onto the highway system that would take them north into cottage country.

"I'll be so glad when Daniel's parents have finally gone back to Timmins," Sylvia confided once they were settled on Highway 400 and the traffic wasn't so intense.

"I guess they feel pretty upset about losing their son," Trista murmured.

Sylvia's dark eyes glittered. "A son they saw maybe five days out of the year. Really, what is their loss compared to mine? Neither of them seem to have one ounce of appreciation for the fact that I've lost my husband."

"Well, in times of grief we don't always see things very clearly."

Wasn't that an understatement. She'd fallen apart after Andrew's death, and she'd destroyed her marriage in the process. Now her new life seemed to be crumbling around her, too. Her close friend had been arrested for murder, and her secretary had turned out to be someone she barely knew.

Trista stared out the side window, watching as they left the industrial buildings of the city behind. Ahead was Canada's Wonderland, the steel frame of the roller coaster weaving a convoluted figure eight against the hazy blue sky.

When she considered her life dispassionately, she had to admit she'd made a real mess of things. Which made her wonder why was she so adamant about refusing Morgan's offer to try again. It wasn't as if she had anything to lose.

MORGAN WALKED UP to the motel clerk at the Moondust Motel, publicity photographs of Suni Choopra in hand. He wanted peace of mind, and he was hoping this gambit of his was going to provide it. If, by some stroke of luck, the clerk could identify any similarity between the woman he'd seen last Wednesday afternoon and these pictures of Suni Choopra, he'd be able to set his conscience at ease, knowing he'd done everything possible to make sure he had the right woman. And then he'd be free to focus his energy on Trista. To convince her that they belonged together.

Ted Sanders looked eager to see him. Morgan had called earlier to make sure he was on duty.

"You found her, hey, Detective?"

"We think so. Here." He slapped the three eight-by-ten glossies he'd managed to collect, on the counter in front of Ted.

"Ring any bells?" He watched the other man carefully as he examined first the close-up picture, then the one of Suni at her desk, and finally, a distance shot of her walking across a street.

Sanders took a long time. He studied each picture in turn, then focused on the middle one—a shot of Suni sitting at her desk, one hand on the telephone in front of her, the other holding a pen poised above a pad of paper.

Sanders's forehead creased in a frown. ''I guess it could be her, but you've got to remember—her hat was low, and her sunglasses covered half of her face. It isn't exactly bright in here, either.''

Morgan put out a hand to collect the pictures.

''Wait a minute.'' Sanders examined the photo of Suni at her desk again. ''I remember when I passed her the key, her nails were a real mess. Bitten to the quick, and ragged. Not long and shiny like these.'' He pointed to the perfect ovals in Suni's publicity shot.

Morgan's gut tightened, remembering the perfect manicure he'd noticed on Suni yesterday. Could a woman grow nails like that in a little over a week? No. He knew it was impossible. Unless she had those fake ones, the kind that were glued on. He'd have to check into that, because assuming they were real, his case was in deep trouble.

''You're sure about the nails?'' he asked the clerk.

Sanders nodded again. ''I'm sure.''

The trip back to headquarters went by in a flash. He knew of only one suspect who chewed her nails, and that was Nan Walker. He remembered noticing it the first time he'd met her, when she was wearing her widow-black dress, acting the part of a bereaved spouse.

Obviously Nan was a better actress than any of them had suspected.

Apparently she was much smarter than any of them had guessed, as well. He never would have thought she could plan and carry out murders as complicated as these, plus manage to frame her husband's mistress in the bargain.

Of course she'd had help. She must have, since she'd had an alibi for her husband's murder. Lorne Thackray would have done that one. Then later, Nan had killed Daniel, in an attempt to camouflage Jerry's death, and focus attention of the mystery lover—Suni Choopra.

She and Lorne had planted a note in Hawthorne's papers. As for the gun—Nan, after all, was the one with the easiest access to the murder weapon—they'd hidden that at Suni's. Then they'd sat back and laughed, because he'd done exactly what they'd expected, and arrested the wrong woman.

The more he thought about it, the more convinced Morgan became. The fact that the murders had been committed by two people explained why one shooting had been so precise and tidy, while the other was sloppy and amateurish. It hadn't been the steamy room, the bubble bath at all. It had been the marksman. Or woman, in this case.

At headquarters Morgan jumped out of the car and loped into the building. First he would have someone check to make certain that Suni's nails were her own. Then he was going to pay a call on Nan Walker. Two hours alone with the woman and he was sure he'd have her ratting on her partner.

Ten minutes later, it was confirmed. Suni's nails were real. He dispatched some men to pick up Nan Walker and bring her in for questioning and began the paperwork that would set Suni free. Half an hour later, the former member of Parliament for Toronto West was standing by his desk.

"I owe you an apology," he began, but was interrupted by a young woman from the front desk.

"Detective Forester? You have a message."

Morgan turned impatiently. "What is it? Who's the message from?"

The young woman consulted the piece of paper in her hand. "Trista Emerson."

"Let me see that." He grabbed the note and scanned the contents briefly. The first bit of information confirmed his new theory. Nan Walker had lied about not knowing where her husband kept his gun.

The second piece of information gave him pause. Trista couldn't meet him for lunch because she'd gone to the Hawthornes' cottage with Sylvia.

"Phone call, Detective."

Morgan scowled. "I can hear, thank you." He grabbed at the phone on his desk. "Forester here."

It was one of the officers he'd asked to bring in Nan Walker. "We can't locate her, sir. We've been to her home and to the store. No one seems to know where she is."

"Have you talked to the son?"

"Yes. And the store manager, too—Lorne Thackray. He said she usually works Saturdays, but that she called to say she wouldn't be in today. She didn't give any explanation. He seemed mildly worried about that himself."

"Damn." Morgan slammed a fist onto the desk beside him. "Keep looking. Check with friends, neighbors, anyplace you can think of." He hung up, wondering if he should call in Thackray for questioning. If Nan was working with a partner, he was the most likely suspect....

But neither of them had been on Brenda's list of people who'd been in the office in the proper time frame to have stolen Trista's office key. Nan hadn't been in the office on either Monday or Tuesday. And Lorne had never been there.

Was it possible Trista had been right again? That her office break-ins were completely unrelated to the homicides?

Then a new possibility occurred to him.

Sylvia Hawthorne.

Chapter Eighteen

Morgan clasped Suni by the shoulder. He must have used more pressure than he'd thought, because she winced and pulled away.

"Do you have any idea where the Hawthornes' cottage is?"

Suni's eyes widened. "Yes, I do. Daniel and I spent a day there once. Why do you ask?"

"Because Sylvia's taking Trista there. And I have a feeling Trista's about to get more than she bargained for." As he was speaking, Morgan was preparing to leave. He pulled on his jacket and groped for his keys in both jacket pockets before he found them in his pants pocket.

"Is she in any danger?"

"I think she might be. Can you write out those directions for me?"

Suni was silent for a minute. Then she shook her head. "I was only there once. I'm not sure I could give adequate directions. But I'll remember when I get there."

"What are you talking about?"

"I'm coming with you."

Morgan patted his pocket, feeling for his gun. "This is official police business."

"Yes." She agreed. "And it's also my best friend's life. Trista's the only one who believed in me during this entire nightmare and I don't want anything to happen to her."

"Believe me, neither do I." He hesitated a moment, waiting for her to back down, then he gave up. There wasn't time for this. "Okay, fine. Let's go."

He headed for his car, and Suni followed.

TRISTA TOOK a sip of the coffee they'd stopped for at the drive-through restaurant in Barrie. The Hawthornes' cottage was on Lake Muskoka, and the closer they got to their destination, the quieter and more anxious Sylvia became. Her hands were gripping the steering wheel so tightly they'd turned white from lack of circulation. Trista could feel the tension shooting out from the other woman—it was as palpable as the coffee aroma that had settled into the luxurious sedan.

"I read in the morning paper that they've arrested Suni Choopra for my husband's murder."

"That's right." Trista shifted uneasily in the leather seat. There was a note of triumph in Sylvia's tone that made her uneasy. She could understand Sylvia wanting vengeance for Daniel's murder. But to sound so smug...

"But you don't think she's guilty, do you?"

Trista sighed deeply. "I have my doubts."

"Well, you're wrong. That woman is guilty. And she's got to pay the price."

Trista's sense of discomfort grew when Sylvia turned off the main highway onto a private access road. For some reason, the isolation made her feel uncomfortable. This early in the season, many of the cottages hadn't been reopened from the long winter hibernation. Windows were covered in blinds, water craft safely secured in boathouses. Only the odd cottage had smoke curling from its chimney, or vehicles parked out front, giving evidence of human occupation.

Trista gripped her door handle tightly as Sylvia took a sharp turn at the end of the gravel road. They were on a smaller road now, about thirty yards long and deeply sloped, toward the lake.

Between the thick foliage of pine trees and smaller bushes, Trista could see the outline of an A-frame cottage built out of pine and stained a light honey color. A screened-in veranda protected the front entrance and would provide respite during the early spring from blood-hungry mosquitoes and black flies. About fifty yards to the left, a small white boathouse sat at the base of a long pier. A rowboat rocked gently in the water.

Sylvia parked by the cottage and turned off the engine. In the sudden silence, Trista could hear the lapping waves and the carefree song of jays as they flitted from tree to tree. As she stepped out of the car, the woodland smell of pine and grass, combined with the cleansing scent of water, cleared her head. No question, it was a beautiful setting. And the rustic style of the cottage blended beautifully with its surroundings.

Trista stretched her arms back over her head, and that was when she noticed the second vehicle. It was parked behind a small shack, some sort of utility building. In front of the shack stood an old tree stump, marked with an ax that was stuck in the center. Trista knew it was only for chopping firewood, but it gave her an eerie feeling all the same.

She was letting her imagination get to her.

Sylvia walked round from the driver's side, pocketing her keys and shifting her purse from one hand to the other. "Come on inside," she said. "I'll make you some coffee."

Trista didn't want more coffee. She was jumpy enough already. And a new question had just occurred to her. If Nan and Lorne had committed the murder, how had they managed to get the key to her office? Neither one had been on Brenda's list.

But Sylvia had.

Not possible, Trista tried to reassure herself. Sylvia had been talking to *her,* Trista, when Daniel was murdered.

But not when Jerry Walker was killed. In her mind she could picture the little chart that Morgan had drawn that night at her apartment. Sylvia had an alibi for only the first murder. So she could have done it—with a partner.

And then Nan Walker came to the door of the cottage, and Trista knew exactly who that partner had been.

"YOU'VE FINALLY made it," Nan said. "I hope you don't mind, Trista. Sylvia asked me to meet you down here."

That explained the second vehicle. Trista felt Sylvia's presence behind her, propelling her forward. After she'd stepped over the threshold, she heard Sylvia twist the dead bolt behind them. Excessive security measures for an afternoon in the country. But then, this wasn't your average day in the country.

Although rustic in style, the cottage was far from primitive in design. The west-facing wall was almost completely glass, taking advantage of the splendid view of Lake Muskoka. Pine and hunter green upholstered furniture huddled around an enormous rock-faced chimney that went up the full two stories of the vaulted ceiling. A modern, efficient-looking kitchen was visible behind the granite slab counter that separated the dining table from the food-preparation area.

Trista looked at her two clients. Sylvia was watching her with an air of triumph, while Nan wouldn't meet her eyes. Striving for a tone of normalcy, she attempted conversation. "I didn't realize you two knew each other."

"Actually we've become quite good friends." The malevolence in Sylvia's voice sent shivers down Trista's spine. "After all, we have so much in common. Starting with the woman that our husbands were sleeping with."

Not necessarily the *best* basis for a relationship.

"Make us some coffee, Nan," Sylvia requested with all the charm of an army sergeant. Nan didn't seem to mind. Obediently she walked behind the counter and began to run water from the tap.

"You can't use that water, you imbecile!" Spit sputtered out of Sylvia's mouth, along with the insult. "Use the stuff in the fridge, that I've already boiled."

Nan nodded, but Trista saw the flash of anger in her soft, uncertain eyes.

"I see you haven't lit a fire. It's so cold in here." Sylvia walked over to the hearth and started laying the kindling.

Trista watched Sylvia's every move carefully. Just what was the older woman up to? That she had some sort of plan was obvious. Her body was practically giving off an iridescent glow, her nervous energy was so high. Nan was nervous too. And scared.

It looked bad, Trista thought. And unfortunately, her options were limited. She could make a run for the door. Maybe she'd get out before either Sylvia or Nan could stop her, despite the dead bolt. But what then? She'd noticed that all the neighboring cottages seemed to be vacant. And she didn't stand a chance of making it to the nearest town without a car.

Sylvia's keys were in the pocket of her slacks, and

Trista had seen no sign of Nan's. She was as trapped as she could possibly be. Unless. She eyed the black phone hanging on the wall by the kitchen counter.

"I just realized I forgot to cancel luncheon plans with a friend of mine. Do you think I could use the phone?" She moved toward the counter.

"Sorry." Sylvia smiled placidly. "We haven't had it reconnected for the summer yet." She struck a match and the crumpled newspapers she'd placed in the mouth of the fireplace flamed bright orange. Soon the small cedar chips that had been tucked around the papers were crackling, too.

Trista moved toward the warmth. It *was* cold, and the air felt damp. What she wanted was the sunlight, warm against her back, but for now the fire would do. Or at least it would have to. "Did you want to go through the photos of Daniel now?" she asked.

Sylvia just laughed.

"But—" Trista turned to remind her of their plans— she had to keep pretending things were normal. But once she saw what Sylvia had in her hands, she knew that was no longer realistic.

Sylvia was cradling an antique revolver like a baby. "Beautiful isn't it? It belonged to my grandfather, then my father, and now to me." She looked up at Trista, her dark eyes bright. "It may look old, but it still works."

"That carving looks intriguing," Trista lied. "Could I get a closer look?" She held out her hands, but Sylvia just grinned.

"You crack me up, you really do. *Can I please make a phone call? Can I please hold your gun?*" She mimicked Trista's voice with a saccharine undertone. Slowly she walked toward Trista, her hands gently stroking the weapon in her hands. "My father taught me to shoot. I have a very steady aim, you know."

"Really? I've never been that keen on guns." Trista thought about Morgan's description of the murders. The first one so precise, almost professional. The second a little more sloppy. Now she knew why. Sylvia had killed Jerry Walker. And Nan had killed Daniel Hawthorne. When she thought about it, it was ingenious, really. By killing each other's husbands, they'd each been able to establish an airtight alibi for their own husband's murder.

Then they'd framed the whole thing on the woman who had been having an affair with their husbands. Just for icing on the cake.

Morgan, Trista thought longingly. If only she could get word to him that she was in trouble. If he got the message she'd left earlier, he'd know she was at the Hawthorne cottage, but he had no reason to suspect she might be in danger.

"Yes, really," Sylvia said calmly. "Which would make it very easy to kill you right now, but that's not the way I have things planned."

Trista's throat was suddenly so dry it hurt to swallow. "You're not going to kill me, Sylvia."

"Oh yes I am." Sylvia opened the sliding glass doors to the deck that spanned the window side of the house. "But let's sit down for a minute first. I don't want the coffee to get cold."

MORGAN DROVE past the picturesque town of Bala barely noticing the river streaming through the center of town, the old stone church set in a grove of trees by the waterfall, or the quaint, tourist-attracting cafés and shops lining the highway.

"We want the Acton Island turnoff," Suni said. She

was watching the road as carefully as he was. This was not the time to make a wrong turn.

Morgan glanced at the clock. If Trista and Sylvia had started driving shortly after she left that message for him, they would have been at the cottage about half an hour ago. He didn't want to think about the possibilities that amount of time could provide. Did Trista know she was in danger? Exactly what plan had Sylvia and Nan cooked up?

If anything happened to Trista it would be his fault. True, he'd warned her to keep out of police business. But if he hadn't made the mistake about Suni, she wouldn't have felt she had to investigate on her own.

The only reason he'd stayed on this case was to protect Trista. If she was hurt, or worse, he knew he'd blame himself forever.

He wasn't ever going to stop loving Trista. She was his wife, dammit, he didn't care what the lousy divorce papers said.

And all this crap about building a new life and going their separate ways. He didn't think she really believed it. She was just hiding. For some reason, she couldn't admit what it was she really wanted from life. But he wasn't going to let her get away with that kind of hiding anymore.

Morgan cursed as he advanced on a slow-moving farm vehicle. Steady traffic from the opposite direction made it impossible for him to pass. He slapped on his siren, and within seconds the rickety half-ton truck had pulled to the shoulder and he resumed speed.

"There's the sign," Suni said, pointing ahead.

He nodded. "How much farther from here?"

"At least another ten minutes."

Ten bloody more minutes. He glanced at the clock once more. *Hang on, Trista. I'm coming.*

SHE DIDN'T WANT TO DIE. Most people don't, but for Trista the realization was a revelation. Because after Andrew's death, she'd always thought it would be the perfect solution. Now that it was facing her—in the form of a gun held by a woman who had killed, and who would kill again—she found the prospect terrifying.

Sitting at the patio table with the two women who had been her clients and who she now knew to be murderers, Trista could feel her every nerve screaming out in protest against this fate. The very beauty of their surroundings made it seem all too absurd. Yet there was the gun, gleaming in the sunlight beside Sylvia's cup and saucer. And there was the woman whose crow-black eyes promised death.

I want to live. Trista could feel the longing and the need expanding within her, soaking up positive energy the way a bag of peat moss soaks up moisture. She wanted to fling off her clothes and swim naked in the glittering blue water of the lake. She wanted to pick the berries that would soon be growing on those bushes by the rocks. And most of all she wanted the chance to tell Morgan that she loved him. The chance to make him happy. To walk hand in hand, to cuddle while watching a movie, to make love under the stars and between freshly washed sheets, and anywhere else it might occur to them.

"More coffee?" Nan asked her. She was presiding over the table like the mistress of the house. Or maybe the servant.

Trista could see that whatever her plans, Sylvia hadn't shared them with Nan. Nan looked almost as apprehensive as Trista felt, and her eyes kept pulling back to the gun in morbid fascination.

Trista shook her head to the offer of more coffee, then turned to Sylvia. "What I don't understand is, where was the satisfaction? I do see why you had to kill each other's husbands, so you could have your own alibi, but if it was revenge you were after, wouldn't it have been more fulfilling to pull the trigger and watch *Daniel* die?"

Sylvia's eyes glittered, like hard polished marbles. "The main thing was that they *knew* why they were being killed."

"And how did they know?"

"Because we told them. Say it Nan. The way I made you practice."

Staring at the table, Nan raised her hand, index finger pointing right at Trista's chest. "This is from your wife," she said, enunciating clearly, if flatly. Then she squeezed her lower three fingers tight against her palm. "Bang!"

Sylvia smiled proudly, like a mother whose child has just played the piano for company. "Enough coffee. It's time for a boat ride, don't you think?"

"I've never been that keen on boats either, Sylvia," Trista said.

"Really?" Sylvia seemed amused. She lifted the gun, not pointing it in Trista's direction, merely making its presence known. "But I'd like you to take a boat ride. And so would Nan. Right, Nan?"

Nan had begun to tremble. Still staring at the table, she said, "When is this going to stop, Sylvia? This wasn't in our plan, it wasn't part of our agreement."

"It's your mistakes that have made this necessary, not mine!" Sylvia snarled. "Who forgot to wear her gloves? Who blurted out a stupid comment about her husband's gun while she sitting in the therapist's chair? I never did manage to find that file…'' She turned to Trista. ''Is that what tipped you off?''

Trista didn't answer. Instead, she fingered the tender spot on her head that was only just beginning to heal. So it was Sylvia she had to thank for this. She might have known.

''And who couldn't wait until the trial was over before slipping between the sheets with her new boyfriend?'' Sylvia continued. ''Now get out of that chair and lead the way to the dock.''

For a moment Trista knew a brief hope as Nan hesitated. Would she stand up to Sylvia, finally take a stand? She must realize by now that the woman was seriously disturbed. Didn't Nan realize that once Trista was disposed of, *she* would be next?

If she did, she didn't appear to care. Wordlessly she got up from the table to lead them down the stairs and along the dirt path to the boathouse that Trista had noticed when she'd first arrived.

A warm wind mussed Trista's hair as they stepped away from the protection of the house. The dirt path was carpeted with needles and felt springy under her black loafers. It gave her the urge to run, to experience the joy of physical exertion and the illusion of freedom. So what if she was shot in the back? At least that way it would end quickly, and it would be a difficult scenario for Sylvia to talk her way out of.

But she didn't run.

Because there was still a chance, wasn't there?

She *couldn't* die now. She *wouldn't*. As they neared the dock, Trista knew instinctively that Nan was her best hope.

''Nan,'' she pleaded. ''You can't go along with this. You know it's wrong, don't you? You let your husband dominate you when he was alive. Now you're in an even worse situation. You have to draw the line somewhere.''

In front of her, Nan hesitated. Immediately Sylvia barked, ''Don't listen to her, Nan. We have no choice now. Our marriage counselor is going to have a little boating accident. It's my cottage. No one will ever make a connection between the two of you. I'll phone the police in a couple of hours and report that my guest went for a ride and still hasn't returned. They probably won't find the body for months. You have nothing to worry about.''

Trista shivered at the cold heartless description. The woman was clearly psychotic. But clever. Probably the worst combination that the fates could have provided.

''How can you justify killing me, Nan?'' Trista persisted. ''I can understand how you felt about Jerry. He treated you badly. He didn't love you and he was having an affair. But what have I done? I tried to help you. Is killing me something you want to have on your conscience?''

Nan stopped and slowly turned around. ''She's right, Sylvia. It would be wrong to hurt her. Let her go.''

''Are you crazy?'' Sylvia raised her gun, switching it from one woman to the other, as if she couldn't decide who to shoot first. ''You let her go and we go directly to jail. How do you think your son's going to feel when he finds out that his mother killed dear old dad? He may not have had any love to spare for the old man, but believe me, when he finds out you were behind his death…''

Trista had to give it to Sylvia. She knew how to pull Nan's strings. Nan's defiance melted like snow in warm rain. Wordlessly she continued to walk along the boarded dock, to where the boat was tied.

Trista's mind whirled as she realized that if she was going to get out of this alive, she had to do something while they were still on dry ground. With a sudden twist of her body, she flew backward into Sylvia, hoping to knock her down and somehow wrestle the gun from her grasp.

"DAMN THESE DIRT ROADS," Morgan cursed as the jostling of the car on the dried ruts forced him to lower his speed fractionally.

"We're almost there," Suni said encouragingly, leaning forward in her seat, her eyes searching out the road ahead of them. "Their cottage is at the end of this access road. We'd better not turn in, though, or we'll alert them that we're coming."

Morgan nodded, saying nothing in reply. The closer they got, the more alarm bells went off in his head. His last call to headquarters had confirmed that they still hadn't managed to locate Nan Walker. He was sure he knew why. Trista had walked right into a trap, and he himself had provided the cheese.

Morgan squinted against the glare of the midday sun. Surely that was the end of the road just up ahead?

"There it is!" Suni confirmed. "Slow down!"

Morgan reduced his speed, parking behind a group of cedars that effectively blocked the view of their vehicle from the road.

"Okay, we'll go by foot from here." Morgan hopped out of the driver's seat and Suni was right behind him as he cautiously made his way down the driveway, walking through the thick underbrush along the side of the road.

In the driveway they could see Sylvia Hawthorne's navy blue Volvo. Far off to the right, behind a shed of some sort, Morgan thought he caught a glimpse of sun-

light on metal. That would be Nan Walker's vehicle, or
he would hang up his badge and start cleaning cars for
a living.

Telling Suni to wait, he quickly sprinted toward the
shed to get a closer look. When he returned a minute
later, his expression was grim. "That's Nan Walker's
car."

"You think both women did it, don't you?" Suni
asked quietly.

Morgan nodded.

"Stay back here in the woods where they can't see
you," he said in a whisper. "I'm going to move up closer
and try to assess the situation. If any trouble breaks out,
run back to the car and drive the hell out of here. I've
called for backup, but it will be at least fifteen minutes
before they get here."

He ran ahead a few yards, then stopped and cocked
his head. The gut-wrenching fear and anxiety he'd felt in
the car had gone now. In its place was a cold determi-
nation, and the pure relief of finally being able to *do*
something. He could hear the sound of voices quite
clearly all of a sudden. Remembering the way sound trav-
els over water, he turned toward the boathouse. He had
to push forward and get out from behind some low-lying
bushes, before he could get a view of the lake.

And there they were. Three women standing on the
dock. The dark-haired one—Sylvia—was holding something in her hand. Something metal, that seemed to glow
in its reflection of the sun's rays. So there was another
gun. Just his luck.

SYLVIA FELL to one side with the impact of Trista's ma-
neuver, but she didn't lose her grip on the gun.

"Stand back!" she shouted, pointing it at Trista as she

slowly worked herself back to a standing position. "That was very stupid. Next time you try it, you'll have a bullet in the head for your trouble." She shoved the gun into the small of Trista's back and pushed her up the long length of the dock.

Trista gritted her teeth in frustration. If only she'd hit her a little harder, her ploy might have worked. Now she doubted she'd get a second chance.

"Get into the boat!" Sylvia ordered.

Trista glanced around, desperately seeking some means of escape. Just then she heard a stifled cry from Nan.

"There's someone out there!" Nan pointed to the brush behind the dock.

"Where?" Sylvia whirled, gripping Trista firmly with one hand, while she kept the gun trained on her with the other.

Trista recognized Suni immediately. From the soft gasp behind her, she realized her captors had, too. Suni's dark hair was uncharacteristically flat and unstyled, her clothing rumpled and complexion gray as she emerged from the underbrush and walked slowly but deliberately toward them.

What in the world was she doing here? She was supposed to be in jail, where at least she would have been safe. Couldn't she see Sylvia's gun? Didn't she realize that she was walking toward two women who hated her more than anyone else on earth? Yet she didn't look afraid. She acted as if she knew what she was doing.

Trista opened her mouth to yell a warning, but Sylvia's gun jabbed her in the ribs.

"Not a word—" Sylvia's whisper was harsh in her ear "—or I'll shoot both of you, I swear!"

Nan's composure was disintegrating with every step

Suni took. "It's Suni Choopra! I thought she was supposed to be in jail! I thought you said they arrested her!"

"Just stay calm, you twit," Sylvia ordered. "I'll handle this."

"What's going on?" Suni asked as she reached the dock. She looked first at Trista, then at the other two women. "Isn't it a little early in the season to go boating?"

Didn't she sense the danger? Trista couldn't understand what Suni was doing—besides making an open target of herself.

"Out on bail already, are you?" Sylvia asked. "That didn't take long."

Suni hesitated. "I didn't kill your husband."

"No? Next you'll be trying to tell me you didn't sleep with him, either."

Suni said nothing, and Sylvia laughed. "I have a great idea, Nan. Let's say Ms. Choopra shoots her good friend here while they're out on the boat. Then let's say Ms. Choopra has a little accident, and falls in while attempting to dispose of the body. That ought to tie everything up nice and tidy, don't you think?"

MORGAN SLUNK DOWN on all fours, crawling through the tall grass that bordered the lake. As he drew near to the dock, he could see that Sylvia was trying to get Trista into the boat.

Damn, what was he going to do now? If he stood up, waving his gun and shouting "Police!," Sylvia would be as likely to shoot Trista as she would be to surrender. He couldn't put Trista in that sort of jeopardy. Suddenly, out of the corner of his eye, he saw Suni walking calmly toward the trio on the dock.

What in hell! Why hadn't she stayed put as he'd told

her? Morgan watched the reaction of the women on the deck to Suni's approach and suddenly he understood what she was doing. She was providing a distraction. An opportunity for him to do something. But what?

Gritting his teeth, he hastily pulled off his shoes and threw down his jacket.

ALL AT ONCE, Trista understood why Suni had walked so calmly into danger. She was acting as a decoy. On the other side of the dock, a dark shape glided into the water. Water that had to be only just this side of freezing. Trista wrapped her arms around her body, allowing herself a ray of hope. She might make it out of this alive, yet.

"Okay, the two of you into the boat." Sylvia waved her gun at Trista and Suni as she spoke. "I'm going to get the motorboat out and tow them to the middle of the lake. You'll have to hold the gun." She motioned toward Nan, who eyed the cold hard metal uneasily.

Trista and Suni moved slowly, stalling for time. But Sylvia wasn't putting up with any more delays. She tucked the gun in closely, then reached out to give Suni's arm a tug. Suddenly two arms came up from the water behind her, took a firm grasp of her ankles and pulled.

A gunshot rang out in the air as Sylvia fell backward into the lake. Trista heard a cry of pain, but she couldn't take the time to see who'd been hurt. Instead, she reached across the boat for an oar, and before a bewildered Nan Walker could figure out what was going on, she catapulted her into the icy Muskoka waters.

"My gun, Trista!" She heard Morgan cry out from the lake behind her. He was trying to pin down Sylvia but she was giving him the struggle of her life. "It's under my jacket on shore!"

Nan Walker was splashing on the other side of the

dock, and for the first time, Trista noticed that Suni was clutching her left shoulder and moaning in pain. But she refused to be distracted. She ran down the wooden planks to where Morgan's jacket and boots lay, hidden in the tall grass beside the dock. She grabbed the gun, and the coat, and raced back toward the struggle. Sylvia's revolver was no longer in sight. Probably at the bottom of the lake by now.

"Okay, Morgan," she called out, brandishing his gun in the air. "I've got it."

Seeing the weapon safely in Trista's custody, Morgan let go of the flailing Sylvia and hauled himself up on deck. Trista's heart went out to him as he shivered with cold, and she passed him his jacket and the gun.

"Are you okay?" he asked, smoothing a wet hand gently over her cheek.

"I'm fine," she assured him. "But I think Suni was shot."

Morgan glanced over to where Suni lay huddled on the deck, her hand protectively cupping her bleeding shoulder. "I know. We'll get her to a hospital as soon as we round up these *ladies*." He held his gun steady as Nan and Sylvia hauled themselves out of the water. Both shivered uncontrollably, the skin on their faces blue-white with cold.

"Take Suni to the car," Morgan instructed Trista. "Help should be here within minutes. I'll get these two back to the cottage and wait for backup."

In the distance, Trista could already hear the wail of sirens on their way. Relief flooded her heart and she looked at the man who'd risked everything to save her.

"I love you, you know."

Morgan took his eyes off his suspects for a split second in order to reply. "You better."

Chapter Nineteen

Five minutes later two police cars and one ambulance were on the scene. Suffering from delayed shock, Trista could never remember exactly what happened next. She had a vague recollection of Sylvia and Nan being hand-cuffed and taken away in separate cars. Nan was crying, Sylvia screaming.

She remembered a quick hug from Morgan and a promise that he would call her when he could. Then she remembered crawling into the ambulance after Suni to go to the hospital in Bracebridge. This time the narrow cots and curtained rooms held no demons for her. A quick checkup verified she was fine. Suni was not so lucky. She had to have the bullet removed from her arm.

Trista waited, even though the doctor told her she'd be better off going home and straight to bed. She needed to make sure Suni would be okay. She was asleep in her chair when a nurse finally came and told her the patient was resting now and could see her for a few minutes.

"Suni?" Trista stood at the door to the private room. Suni's eyes were closed. About to turn and leave, she was stopped by her friend's words.

"Hell of a day, wasn't it?"

Trista bit back an hysterical giggle. Trust Suni. "I thought you were sleeping."

"Almost, but not quite. I wanted to talk to you. They told me you've been out there, waiting."

Trista sat down in the chair next to the bed. "If you hadn't walked out on that dock today…"

Suni squeezed her hand with her good arm. "Don't think about it, Trista. Even if I hadn't provided that distraction, Morgan would have thought of something."

"But you put your life at risk for me. Those women are crazy. For all you knew, Sylvia might have shot you as soon as she saw you."

"But it was my fault you were there. If you hadn't been so determined to convince Morgan that I was innocent, they would have left you alone. You believed in me, Trista. Don't think I'll ever forget it."

"And don't think I'll ever forget what you did for me." She was so relieved that Suni had been exonerated from any involvement in the murders. But with all the negative publicity in the past two days, there was no way she could go back to the life she had led. "What are you going to do now?"

"I thought a lot about that during my day and a half in jail," Suni said wryly. "A change in career is obviously called for."

"But you're so passionate about what you believe in."

"I've thought about that, too. The government isn't the only place where a dedicated person can have an impact, you know. I've been considering joining an environmental lobby group. I've had offers from them in the past."

Suni's eyes crinkled at the corners. "So what about that detective? You two going to work things out or what?"

Trista smiled. ''I hope so.''

''He was almost out of his mind with worry on the drive to the cottage. He really cares about you.''

''I know.''

''I'd count myself lucky if I were you.''

''I do.''

''Okay.'' Suni gave her hand a final pat. ''Let me know how it all works out. Now I think I've got to rest.''

Trista took a taxi back to Toronto. She tumbled into bed, exhausted, and slept eight solid hours. When she awoke, she felt a desperate need for Morgan, but he was still at work. He'd told her he would call. She just had to be patient.

She showered and changed, did her hair, had breakfast and read the paper. Still no word. Finally she decided to do what she always did at times of crisis. Go to the office.

AN HOUR AND A HALF LATER, the sound of her office door opening caused Trista to smile. She'd left it unlocked, knowing he would find her here eventually. She looked up to see him standing in the doorway. Dressed in blue jeans and a formfitting black crew neck, he was obviously off duty. Finally.

''Sunday office hours?'' he asked quietly. A shadow from the open door fell across his face, obscuring his expression.

''You have an appointment, I presume?''

''A standing one,'' he assured her.

Trista nodded. She was so happy to see him, but it was more difficult than she'd expected. She didn't know what to say, or how to make the first move. So she went to the window and stared out at the lake. It was a sunny day, and the water glistened with a hundred sparkling hues of blue and silver. It was a very pretty sight.

She ought to explain. "I thought I could block everything out and start a new life. A different sort of life. One where I couldn't—"

He came up behind her and put his hands on her shoulders. They were heavy and strong, and full of warmth. Slowly his fingers worked at the knot of muscles around her neck, and she closed her eyes in appreciation.

"Where you couldn't get hurt again. I know. But it didn't work out that way, did it?" He whispered the words against her ear.

"No." She tilted her neck and leaned back slightly as his hands began a circular motion along the side of her shoulders.

"Because you still cared. It wasn't possible for you to stop. For your clients, for Suni, even for Brenda—as much as you claimed to want to keep your distance. All those people mattered to you, even when you thought you'd locked your emotions away forever. You're a giving person, Trista. That's why I've always loved you, and why I always will."

Trista twisted into him, pressing her face hard against his chest. Oh, he smelled like heaven to her, and being in his arms seemed like the safest place on earth. She rubbed her skin against him like a cat, and smiled when she felt him rest his cheek against the top of her head.

"I'm still scared."

"I know, Trista. But you're stronger than you think. You survived. We both survived. Now that we're together again, it's going to be so much better. I know I've learned a lot."

Trista nodded. She believed him. Her heart felt lighter than it had in years. "I used to think having another baby would be an injustice to Andrew. But I don't think so anymore." She looked up at him, her eyes searching his for signs of pain. She saw none. A little sadness, maybe. But no pain.

"Another baby. I'd love that." He hugged her tighter. "I know we only had such a short time with him. But they were wonderful months, weren't they?"

They were. Trista couldn't say the words yet, but maybe one day she would. It was still hard enough just saying his name, *Andrew.* But behind the pain there *was* joy, and Morgan was the only person on earth she could truly share that with. Even if she hadn't loved him already, that fact alone would have been enough for her.

But she did love him. His loyalty, his strength, yes, even his protective instincts. He had always been her man. And she was just thankful that she'd realized, before it was too late, how much she wanted him to stay that way.

Amnesia…an unknown danger…
a burning desire.

With

HARLEQUIN®

I N T R I G U E®
you're just

A MEMORY AWAY

from passion, danger…and love!

**Look for all the books in this
exciting miniseries:**

**THE BABY SECRET (#546)
by Joyce Sullivan**
On sale December 1999

**A NIGHT WITHOUT END (#552)
by Susan Kearney**
On sale January 2000

**FORGOTTEN LULLABY (#556)
by Rita Herron**
On sale February 2000

A MEMORY AWAY…—where
remembering the truth becomes
a matter of life, death…and love!

Available at your favorite retail outlet.

Coming in January 2000
Classics for two of your favorite series.

SECRET VOWS

by REBECCA YORK
&
KELSEY ROBERTS

From the best of Rebecca York's

Till Death Us Do Part

Marissa Devereaux discovered that paradise wasn't all it was cracked up to be when she was abducted by extremists on the Caribbean island of Costa Verde.... But things only got worse when Jed Prentiss showed up, claiming to be her fiancé.

From the best of Kelsey Roberts's

Unlawfully Wedded

J.D. was used to getting what he wanted from people, and he swore he'd use that skill to hunt down Tory's father's killer. But J.D. wanted much more than gratitude from his sassy blond bride—and he wasn't going to clue her in. She'd find out soon enough...if she survived to hear about it.

Available January 2000 at your favorite retail outlet.

HARLEQUIN®
Makes any time special ™